TWISTED CAGE

Konstantin & Nikoletta

usa today bestselling author
beck knight

Edited By: Editing by Kimberly Dawn

Cover Design: Wildheart Graphics

Cover Image: Regina Wamba

TWISTED CAGE / Beck Knight. — 1st ed.

CONTENT WARNING

Illicit sex between godfather and goddaughter (she's 18) –
You're welcome, LOL
Graphic Violence
Threats of Rape
Situations of claustrophobia/anxiety/panic
Underground crypts
Incest/Molestation (recalled in memories – not on the
page/not in detail)
Violation of sacred spaces – Yes. Fucking. Please.
Knife and Blood Play
Dubious Consent
Forced Breeding
Captivity
Emotional Bullying
Manipulation
Degredation
A little bit of Lactophilia *shrug* – I make no apologies, I
thought it was kind of *side eye* too, until he did it and then,
welp *shrug*

JUST A LITTLE NOTE FROM BECK...

Sup? *head nod*

I make no apologies for digging a
good fucking age gap. Forbidden? Sign me all the way up.
Defacing religious anything with dirty motherfucking bump
and grindage? Oh yeah. Add virgin blood...fuck yes.
That's just the cherry on top, PUN absolutely intended.
Listen, I will fall over with my legs in the air for all that.
So, go forth and jump on Konstantin's
forbidden godfather rocket.
And fuck him back... he likes it.

Mom, look away, you didn't raise me like this and I ain't mad
about it. To my daughters, if you see this...
I'm proud of you.
And horrified.
But more proud.
By the way, you're fucking grounded.

HELLO VORACIOUS READERS...

A QUICK NOTE ABOUT KONSTANTIN AND NIKOLETTA'S ORIGIN STORY

When I wrote *Twisted Cage*, I realized to do the book justice it deserves, readers really need to read Konstantin and Nikoletta's origin story *Twisted Lust*.
And guys, I love this couple so freaking much, I really wanted to do them all the justice.

So, *Twisted Cage* starts with the novella, *Twisted Lust* which some of you might remember for the *Sacrilege* anthology of 2023. If you've already read *Twisted Lust* and want to jump right in to where it left off, hop on Konstantin's godfather rocket and ride it to chapter ten.

***Also... if you have not read the content warnings, I strongly advise you skip back and read them. Reading should be fun and only traumatizing in a good way, so practice a little self care here and stay safe!

PLAYLIST

Feeling Good • Nina Simone
Dirty Thoughts • Chloe Adams
If Lovin' You Is Wrong • Faithless
I Put A Spell On You • Annie Lennox
Find You • The Phantoms
Guardian • Æther Realm
Santuary • Welshly Arms
Older • Isabel LaRosa
Unholy • Hey Violet
Take Me To Church • Hozier
Way Down We Go • KALEO
Locked Out Of Heaven • Bruno Mars
Hoax • Taylor Swift
Lost The Game • Two Feet
The Only Time • Nine Inch Nails
Sloppy • KiNG MALA, UPSAHL
Little Girl Gone • CHINCHILLA
Mad Woman • Taylor Swift
Blood On Your Knees • Suzanne Santo

Kill Of The Night • Gin Wigmore
Private Eyes • Lenachka
Straight On • Heart
Blood In The Water • Joanna Jones as The Dame
River • Bishop Briggs
Who's Afraid Of Little Old Me? • Taylor Swift
The Man • Taylor Swift
Guys My Age • Hey Violet
Vigilante Shit • Taylor Swift
Dark Room • Michele Morrone
Play With Fire • Sam Tinnesz, Yacht Money
Closer • Nine Inch Nails
Dirtier Thoughts • Nation Haven
Animals • Architects
Cold Blooded • The Pretty Reckless
Like You Mean It • Steven Rodriguez
Hit Me Like A Man • The Pretty Reckless
Blood • In This Moment
Dark Side • Ramsey
Go To War • NOTHING MORE
I Did Something Bad • Taylor Swift
Daddy Issues • The Neighborhood
Sex on Fire • Kings of Leon
Like U • Rosenfield
Flawless • The Neighborhood
Born For This • The Score
Dark Things • ADONA
Black Magic Woman • VCTRYS
Bad Things • Nation Haven
Start A War • Clergy, Valerie Broussard
Blood In The Cut • K. Flay
Craving' • Stiletto, Kendyle Paige
White Flag • Bishop Briggs

LABOUR - the cacophony • Paris Paloma
Pretending • HIM
Join Me In Death • HIM
Don't Fear The Reaper • Blue Öyster Cult
Tainted Love • Soft Cell

PROLOGUE

Nikoletta

A ruthless man made me.

Powerful men shrouded me.

I grew up in a gilded cage inside a cruel world bathed in blood.

Shielded by my very own warrior. My godfather.

My every breath belonged to brutal gatekeepers who guarded me like the rarest spun glass. Maksim Ivanovich Romanoff's only daughter born from his forbidden paramour, I thought my father's weakness for my birth mother could sway him. The way he coveted her could make him more human, more understanding.

But I never quite understood the cold, stark truth. A man like him, a man who'd been hollowed out by his own parents and formed in a cruel world, could ultimately only cherish me for one reason... my value to his empire.

Nurtured, indulged, and refined until I could prove useful, he never intended for me to be anything more than a commodity between superpowers.

An isolated life and guarded from sins of the flesh meant to preserve my worth, with my virginity up for sale to the family offering the most advantageous combination of money and power.

However, they never considered my isolation in their cage left endless time to study everything beyond the steel bars of my confinement. The more they bound me, the more I could see.

Even men motivated by money, by the threat of death are fallible. They falter.

Leaving slivers of opportunity.

They should have clipped my wings.

Because the first time those cold bars failed to click shut —I soared.

CHAPTER

1

Nikoletta

- ONE YEAR AGO -

Goosebumps bloom on my skin as I glide the cool satin along my forearm and over my elbow. The cuff of the fitted glove settles along the bottom edge of my biceps with a firm tug. I wiggle my fingers until the seams of the fingertips settle along my long nails.

Curling my fist, I let out a calming breath and study myself. Warm lights framing the dressing room mirror bathe my dark hair in a shimmering glow, twisting and turning with every wave rolling over my shoulders and down my back.

Dancers in varied states of undress breathlessly flit back and forth behind me, snatching makeup and costume pieces from one another as they prep for their sets. Despite their flurried movements, I catch the occasional narrowed side-eye they aim my way.

Because I'm the new girl, with no experience on the pole, and I've convinced the owner to highlight me on a crucial night where he's fully booked with Manhattan's powerful elite. When I did, I put an immediate target on my back.

Secrets rumble discreetly from dangerous men over the din of ice tumbling in crystal glasses, their indistinguishable echoes weaving through tendrils of smoke in the air. Politicians, power players in secret societies, the mafia, they all converge here, at Illusions Cabaret.

Concealed in shadows, they're almost impossible to recognize. Their calculated perusal captured only by the occasional muted glow of a strategically placed sconce. Their interest will be impossible to gauge from the vantage point.

Armed with my intuition and my years of dance on much different stages, I have one shot.

One product to sell.

My virginity.

I have to make it count.

And then when it's gone, it's one less bargaining chip for my father.

"Rich bitch cunt."

The whispered barb snakes through the air over my shoulder in the wake of three dancers clustered together, sailing past me. A flash of temper streaks through my blood, lighting my veins on fire. Female or not, the Romanoff need for vengeance pumps heavily through me. Years of watching my family rule with an iron fist, instilling respect through brutal power, fear, and a promise of retribution lives deep within despite the circumstance of my gender.

There will come a day when everyone will pay. But to attain that future, I have to be smart and in control now. Like my brother Nikolaj as he builds an army in the war against our brother Vlad.

Vlad—my tormentor. The one who haunts the darkness to this day, despite being thousands of miles away.

Bile bubbles to my throat when I think about what he— no. No. If I let those memories in, I won't be able to do what I need to do.

I've convinced the owner, Silas, to give me one night to do this my way. One night to earn the price I set on my innocence.

Half a million dollars.

He laughed. Not just a chuckle. The smug bastard practically split a gut wheezing like a fucking hyena on crack.

Resolve fills the space where shame should be. I will show him. Half a million for one night, then get gone before the buyer realizes just who they have in their clutches. Success is the only option. If the buyer figures out he sullied Maksim Romanoff's Bratva princess while I'm still in his grasp, I'll never get away. Because possessing me is the ultimate in leverage with one of the biggest power players in the game.

My father.

How hard can it be in a place like this where bottle service starts at ten grand? Increments of a hundred don't exist here. Four figures and up only. The tamest of lap dances starts at two thousand. Private dances ten thousand. A room for the night with one of Silas's elite girls, be ready with twenty-five grand minimum.

And the elite menu? A night of indulgence, priced by kink or—in my case—virgin, begins at fifty thousand.

Patrons frequent this place with a private army of men in tow just to carry the cash they spend here between the price tags and the hefty damage deposit. That's right... Silas likes to protect what's his. Not that the money down does anything to shield his women. It only guarantees Silas will have an unexpected windfall to help lessen the blow to his supply while his dancer is out of commission waiting for the bruises to heal.

A shudder rocks through me. I've tried to ignore that part.

I've tried to forget that while there are powerful men out there who just want to add the claiming of one's virginity to their list of conquests, there are others for whom that's only the beginning.

Men like Vlad.

Claiming a virgin's innocence only feeds a dark power within. A frenzy is born for more power, more control, and to make sure that virgin never forgets who destroyed them.

I run my fingers over my upper thigh, missing the safety of the knife I usually keep strapped there. I'll be defenseless the minute I leave that stage and wind my way through the patrons, doing my best to sell them a high-priced fantasy.

Silas appears behind me, silent as the brilliant snake he is, slithering through his jungle. His hands settle on my shoulders, and I fight the urge to shake him off. In another time, another place, he'd pay for touching me... my Konstantin would take his hands and wear his blood as a badge of honor for protecting his goddaughter.

"You're up next, Nikoletta." His eyes look almost friendly, but then he bends down, stopping with his mouth just an inch from my ear, his serious gaze locking on mine in the mirror. His fingers bite into my shoulders with silent warning. "Do not make me regret this. Understood?"

I don't blink. Determination swells within me until a slow smile forms on my crimson lips. "I'll make the sale."

He tilts his nose into my hair and sucks in a long, deep breath. His eyes drift shut and his body shifts closer, his growing erection pressing against me. "You better." He strums my throat with his thumb, and I barely resist giving him the pleasure of feeling me swallow hard. "Because if you don't, I won't hesitate to put you on clearance."

My smile slips as his grows.

Failure is not an option.

He disappears with the same eerie silence, and I blow out a trembling breath.

A three-song mashup over the course of six minutes. That's all I have to sell my innocence. I wobble slightly on my stilettos as I make my way to my fate. Hovering in the darkness, I watch as Silas takes the microphone and addresses his treasured patrons. He schmoozes with banter designed to make every customer feel like he's talking to them, and only them.

I close my eyes and clear my mind. It's a performance. Nothing more, nothing less. The consequences—well, I'll deal with those later.

All too soon, he's wrapping up his calculated flattery and sliding into my intro.

"Tonight we have a rare treat for you... a precious gem, the single most exquisite virgin in the history of Illusions. She's cultured, educated, and a stunning masterpiece among young women. But most importantly, she's certified, and for a cool half million she can be yours... and only yours."

For one night only, you bastard.

"Without further ado... gentlemen, meet our most-prized jewel, Bee."

The spotlight bathes the stage and the single pole dead-center in a dizzying glow.

With my shoulders pulled back, I put one foot in front of the other and saunter out of the shadows and onto the empty stage, my every step in tune with the heavy sultry beat.

It's just a performance. I'm conveying a feeling, evoking emotion with the music, with my movements. It's like every other dance performance I've done. Jazz, lyrical, tap—performing is a part of me. This is no different.

Conveying innocence and shyness, I eye the pole curiously. Between the glow from the wall behind me framed with retro bulbs and the spotlight on the pole, the audience is swallowed by almost complete darkness. They're nothing more than flickering tea lights in the inky depths of the crowd.

I'm all careful movements as I sell the tantalizing image of a sheltered young woman in a risqué place, drawn to scandalous things. I use the picture of naivety to tap into their primal urges, their ego, and taste for control.

Curling my fingers around the cool metal, I tug as though I'm testing its durability in this new playground I've stumbled upon. I carefully swing in a circle, letting a discreet giggle break free when I come to a stop with my back to the crowd. My curtain of waves swish over my shoulder to settle to one side, over my breast. Peeking over my bare shoulder, I dart my tongue over my bottom lip, tug it into my mouth carefully, and let it slowly slide back out.

These women think selling sex is how much skin you show. How dirty you're willing to get. They're in your face and brash in a cutthroat world where everyone wants their due, with only so much to go around. Brazenness to the point of recklessness is a short game with high stakes.

It's not where the promise of monumental reward is found.

Whetting their appetite and tapping into their hidden desires starts with deliberate, accentuated moves. My body merging with the sultry beat until they're one. A virgin discovering her power to entice.

Someone covers their grunt with a cough and that's when I know I'm on the right track.

One finger at a time, I tug at my gloves, slash them through the air, and snap them down along my hip before letting them drop to my stilettoed feet. I let my mind slip away into another time, another life, to a forbidden fantasy—

of him. The only man who has ever evoked lustful cravings inside me.

No crushes.

No other desires.

All I wanted then, all I want now, is him.

What if this was all for him? What if it were just the two of us here and every fantasy I scrawled in my journal late at night had the chance to come to life? If I could just tell him here and now with every movement of my body?

I drop low and swing my bent knees out, leaving me wide open. I sensually roll my hips, giving the crowd a seductive glimpse of my legs as the slits of my dress give way and reveal skin clean to the tops of my thighs.

Still rolling my hips, I rise slowly, dragging my hands along my every curve, dipping into the narrow fabric nipping at my waist, and to the swell of my breasts barely covered by the thin black bodice held by nothing more than delicate strings tied in a bow at the nape of my neck.

I'll have to show them skin. That's how this works, but first, I'll make them helpless to do anything but take in my every dip and valley, one excruciating part of me at a time.

What if he was the one in the crowd, unable to escape, desperately trying to mask his forbidden reaction to me? I'd make him burn with the agony of wanting me. Giving him scandalous glimpses of the parts of me he's forbidden to see.

Every time I close my eyes at night, I will myself to slip back into the fantasy, the only place I have him now. Because to get near him again means surrendering to my father, and I'll die before I let that happen. But in my dreams... he's there and I'm free to touch, taste, and savor every last part of him.

And there, in that faraway part of my mind I escape to in order to rewrite my reality, he lets me.

CHAPTER

2

Konstantin

When I get my hands on her, I'm going to spank her ass raw.

She's fucking grounded.

Not enough. Exile.

Exile is good.

After I make sure I've reddened her ass so thoroughly she'll never bare it to another set of eyes again.

Nikoletta Maksimova Romanoff will live to regret every second she spends prancing her lithe body in maddening circles around that fucking pole. I'll make sure of it.

Years of dance lessons, private teachers, the best dance schools, and traveling the world with top-tier dance troupes and she's here. Inch after inch of her honey-kissed legs clean up to her waist on display with every movement.

Her dress hides nothing. Not one thing. When the light catches her just right—fuck—it only highlights her tight nipples.

It's too late to call off the meeting. The minute I entered this room, the plan went into motion. Tonight I sink the knife of betrayal in my best friend's chest.

What's left of him.

He will know I'm no longer standing at his side in any way, and in the war to come—I've chosen.

His second son.

I will stand at Nikolaj's side—because he's the right choice.

And it's the best way to protect her—the goddamn nymph seducing the ravenous crowd from the stage.

Devolving into delusions and mania, Maksim Romanoff's reputation frays under the war between his sons. If he isn't careful, his legitimate son and heir, Vladimir, will surely destroy his empire. The Romanoffs are one of only three Bratva families with origins dating back to the eighteen hundreds, and their vengeful and twisted first-born son is sure to ruin it all.

I've remained loyal to my best friend for thirty years. Three decades I've stood by my honorary brother's side, even when he didn't deserve it. When the woman we both loved fell for him, I conceded. When he repaid her love by marrying another, I stood by his side. When he bore children by both women and fostered animosity between his two sons, I kept my vows to our friendship. And when he had his little girl with the woman we both loved, named her for her mother, and asked me to be her godfather, I accepted my duty.

Even when I knew he did it to taunt me with what I could never have. His scathing jealousy and insecurity bled into our friendship until it ruled. The razor-sharp edges of his entitlement never failed to flay me wide.

I carry the scars of a life at his side, but it's the scars no one can see inflicted by my best friend that still ache to this day.

Despite being indebted to him for saving my life as a child, I should have walked away. I almost did.

But the day I held little Nikoletta in my hands before the altar at Old St. Patrick's Church right here in New York City, any chance I had of saving myself from a life of living in Maksim's brutal shadow vanished. My vows before God—to be an example to her, to guide her, to protect her—became the final shackle tethering me to his madness.

Eighteen years I've done my duty. I've shielded her, advocated for her, nurtured her—and despite everything I've done, she's here.

On display. Exposed. In more danger than she can possibly wrap that pretty little head around.

I want nothing more than to scoop out every set of eyes staring up at her, studying her, coveting her.

Her skin gleams and her muscles flex as she seduces a room full of ruthless killers tracking every roll of her hips.

Warring against possessive rage coursing through me, I force my hand open. My vision doubles before settling on the angry crescent grooves carved in my flesh from the violent dig of my fingernails. Pain I inflicted on myself the minute the hazy spotlight shone on her profile ripping the air from my lungs. The sting the only thing keeping me grounded in the moment and the worst of my fury at bay.

The sultry song fades away and a primal beat takes over, the sound wild and chaotic. Nikoletta's fingers skitter over the ridges of her collarbone and settle along the back of her neck where she gives one tie a firm tug.

Goddammit.

The heavy drum of my heart echoes through me into my skull, dulling the lusty beat of the song pumping through the club.

"Ahhh, now there's the look of a man who feels our Bee's sting. She intrigues you, yes?"

The image of my fist crushing his nose, driving the cartilage and bone straight into his brain with a satisfying splatter of blood over my skin is the only relief from the seething rage boiling my blood. The betrayal of my nickname for Nikoletta rolling off his slick tongue cutting me to the bone.

The roaring in my ears grows, and my jaw aches from the force of my clenched teeth. She used my pet name for her. For a moment, I can't speak. Of all the names she could have chosen... she chose one born of tenderness and love for the one light of my life. The need to punish her for sullying the purest form of affection I could give her engulfs me, leaving a red haze before my eyes.

"Where did you find her?" My voice is cool and even, despite the betrayal pumping through my blood.

"Why, she heard about my club, of course."

Pompous fucker.

"She brazenly forced her way past my men and straight into my office. Demanded a job." The slick son of a bitch leans back against the leather next to me like we're the best of friends.

One thrust of my blade between the ribs and I could watch him bleed out right here as he struggled for air through the lung I gleefully punctured.

"Ah, yes, full of fire in those golden eyes, that one. She's going to be fun to break," Silas says with a nod as he crosses his ankle over his knee, going for the hard sell. "She stormed in, shook her sleek hair back, puffed those incredible tits out, all confidence and bluster. But I saw her, the innocence she tries to bury with false bravado. You see it too, don't you?"

Step by step, she makes her way onto floor level. The way she moves to the animalistic beat, the slight hesitation before every step building the anticipation. She's a maiden lost in a dangerous, unfamiliar world. Travel worn, desperate, but still she clings to her pride. The air drips with sex. Primal and hungry, the darkness ripples. Men devour her every move, shifting in their seats, leaning closer. A hand darts out from the darkness, clasps the strings of her top, and pulls hard enough she fights for balance.

I grasp for every shred of my training to override my intoxicating torrent of instinct and possession, and stay in my seat.

With every glide, turn, and arm movement designed to give her a bit of modesty, she continues to dance, giving us all tantalizing glimpses of the sway of her breasts and those tight nipples just begging to be touched, pinched, and sucked until she's writhing... fucking hell. I shift in my seat and bite back a growl.

"Perhaps a closer look." Silas snaps and crooks a finger at her, earning a quick glare before she plasters a smile back on her face.

That's my girl. Right there.

She takes her time working her way over to us. Every second she makes Silas wait deepens the grimace on his face. The minute she's within reach, he wraps his fingers around her hip, his hand slipping beneath the high slit in her skirt.

I reach for him, but she beats me to it and grabs his wrist, sinking her nails into his skin until he lets go.

The look on his face promises retribution. "Touch her," he commands, the words rough with anger.

I swivel my head and pin him with a stare of pure hatred. Is this what he intends to do? Prance her around to these men, encouraging them to grope her, violate her, stain her.

He'll die tonight—screaming in a puddle of his own piss and despair.

Reaching for her hand, I turn her until her back is to me and stand. Her familiar scent teases me, the musky sweetness of jasmine and lemon that grows sweeter with the heat of her skin. I lean into her until her back is pressed against my chest. For just a second, I graze the crown of her hair with my nose and breathe her in.

A shiver courses through her and vibrates into me at our proximity, the liberty I'm taking with her right now cementing my place in hell.

Gliding my hands along her thighs, I catch the strings and raise them around the back of her neck, tying her bodice back in place. Shielding what's been mine to protect for eighteen years. What will continue to be mine for the half-million dollars my men guard at this very moment. Money meant to secure a shipment of guns for our arsenal in the upcoming war against Maksim and Vlad.

The minute I get her out of here, I'll have to get in touch with her brother to replace the cash before we have a more immediate war on our hands. No doubt Silas intends to hold this money for a time before turning it over to Nikoletta, if he ever had any intention of turning it over to her at all. Not that I'll let him keep a dime of it. But one problem at a time and right now, I need another half million to keep the whole deal from going sideways. If the boy is as smart as I think he is, he has it secured in a safe at his bar uptown.

And this is just the beginning.

Because she's supposed to be in Paris where Nikolaj is looking for her as we speak. The timing of this exchange is meant to keep Maksim and Vlad's attention off Paris and draw them as far from Nikoletta as possible.

I'm the bait.

And now... so is she.

But she won't be a plaything for these ruthless men who enjoy breaking pretty things. I'll protect her with my life as I vowed to before God, as I've been doing since the day she came into this world.

I motion my men, Dmitri and Grigori, forward from where they stand near the entrance with two briefcases full of cash, and commit to fucking our entire plan. "I'll take her."

She stills with a sharp gasp. Goosebumps race across her shoulders. She doesn't turn. She doesn't need to. My voice is as familiar as her father's and mother's.

She sways against me, her round full ass brushing over my shame straining against the metal teeth of my zipper. I wrap my fingers around her throat and tilt her head just so, exposing the slim column of her neck. Her pulse races under my thumb as my lips brush against the shell of her ear.

"You're in big trouble, *Pcholka*."

CHAPTER

3

Nikoletta

I slam my clenched fists on my dressing table, making the makeup and brushes rattle with the force. It's as if my fantasy conjured him out of thin air. Only now, he owns me.

Two years have passed since the last time I saw my godfather—my Konstantin. Two years since he picked me up clean off my feet to hug me, where I buried my face along his neck, letting his shoulder-length hair hide me from my father's harsh scrutiny.

Kostya, my nickname for him from the time I learned to talk, hugged me tighter and longer that day than ever before and I let myself fantasize that maybe the same feelings coursed through him as they did through me. Not that it mattered. Now that my father found out my secret, I was lucky to be going to Paris. There were far worse alternatives.

In the end, I choked back the lancing pain, like a part of me being carved out with a hot blade, and let him go before my father could suspect him of something. He'd been at my father's side my entire life—since they were kids according to the stories they told us growing up. His best friend, his right-hand man, the brother he chose. Kostya never broke my father's trust. Not once. But if my father got it in his head that he might have, that's all it would take. Bonds would break and blood would spill.

He'll take me back to my father now. Without a doubt. He'll tell him how he found me on the stage, selling my body —my innocence.

When my father finds out he bought me, he won't believe it to be coincidence. He'll go right back to that day when he found my diary—my fantasies right there in black and white. The ways I dreamed my Konstantin—a man thirty years my senior—would touch and take me.

Nothing will stop the wheels from turning in my father's head, and my godfather would pay with his life.

I have to tell him the truth. The mortifying truth before he can contact my father. At the very least, then he can protect himself.

His touch lingers with me even now. I sensed him in the darkness and told myself I was crazy. When he took my hand, my heart leapt into my throat, but I dismissed my reaction as nothing but longing. When he tied my bodice back into place, I thought I was hallucinating his scent, but then his voice, the deep rumble washed over me.

Every part of me came to life. For one singular moment, I forgot about the danger, the fear, the promise of a future mired in pain, and lost myself in the nearness of him.

Did he watch me the whole time? When I bared my breasts to them, did honor have him turning away? Did I disappoint him?

My heart pinches at the thought. He has to understand I had no choice.

"Save a little for the rest of us, why don't you. Slut," Stacy says as she makes her way past me.

I've been careful to control my temper, but with my nerves raw, my body awakened by Konstantin's touch, and the danger looming, my control fractures. A snarl bursts from my throat. Fisting my fingers around the metal nail file under my hand, I spin on her, snatch her by the back of the hair, yank her head down, and press the tip of the file into the delicate skin under her eye.

The chatter around us dies on a series of gasps. Someone runs out of the room, her heels clicking as she scurries away, no doubt running to Silas.

Good.

Anger and fear war in her jaded blue eyes. Her chest heaves and her fingers lock on my wrists like she has a chance of stopping me. I let her fear wash over me, relishing every second she cowers before me, wondering what I'll do to mar her beautiful face. In this moment, we're the same. Both facing looming uncertainty and the guarantee of pain.

This is the Romanoff in me. The part of me deep inside I'm afraid to let run free. The broken part of my soul desperate to turn away from everything good, ready to set fire to her dreams, and embrace her legacy of blood and death.

"Call me a slut one more time and I'll scoop that pretty little eyeball out of your skull. Understand me?"

A whimper breaks free and she nods carefully, the tip of the file biting into her skin just a bit.

Letting her go, she crumples to the floor and the other dancers rush over to help her up and drag her to the other side of the room.

Silas storms in and spins in a circle, making eye contact with each of us. Pushing his suit jacket back, he rests his hands on his hips. "What the hell is going on in here?"

I shrug a shoulder, grab my lipstick, and swipe a fresh

coat over my lips as though nothing happened. "Same old, same old."

KONSTANTIN

"Gentlemen. My apologies for keeping you waiting," Silas says as he finally joins us in his office. He runs a hand through his hair as he circles around his desk and gestures for us to sit.

"We'll stand. Is she ready?"

He scoffs. "Yeah—" He meets my hard gaze and stammers, "Uh, yes. Sorry. She'll be joining us in just a few moments."

Something has the man rattled. My lips twitch as I bite back a grin, wondering what my Pcholka might have done to knock him off-balance.

"I'll hold the payment for forty-eight hours. You do understand, I'm sure. I have to make sure she follows through on your investment before I compensate her."

"Understood." The money will be out of his possession by sunrise, but he doesn't need to know that. I flick a glance to the door. Where the fuck is she? There's no way she would abandon the money. Without it, where would she go? What would she do?

"I require a damage deposit. In the event you return her in less than presentable condition."

"Waive it." Eyes locked, neither of us blinks. Music thumps through the walls in a muted, dull thud.

"I'm a businessman. This is—"

I slam my palms down on his desk and loom over him. The words he's forcing me to say to get her out of here only adding to the promise of certain torture for him later. "She's a whore. You have half a million dollars, most of which is your fee, I'm sure. You have plenty to keep you satisfied no matter what condition I return her in. You will waive your deposit."

My men move into place beside me, their hands tucked in their jackets and on their weapons.

His eyes dart between them. When neither of them so much as blink, he snaps his gaze back to me and bows his head slightly. "As a courtesy for your first purchase and generous full price offer, I'll waive the fee."

Straightening before him, I smooth my fingers over the lapels of my jacket. "Excellent."

A soft knock at the door draws our gazes and seconds later, Nikoletta steps in wearing the same dress she performed in. How the hell am I going to get her out of here without someone spotting us?

Her blazing copper eyes meet mine and she juts her chin, proud and defiant. And thankfully quiet. Dmitri's gaze widens with recognition and slides to mine. I don't have to say anything. I don't have to so much as move. With one look, he knows to stay silent.

No doubt he's already piecing together a plan in his head which is exactly why he's always by my side.

We still need to get out of here before anyone recognizes her, because if we don't, we'll have a war on our hands. A cabaret full of men who'll be all too willing to brave snatching her to claim advantage with the Romanoff family. I like to know my opponent and here, there are just too many unknown variables.

"Jacket," I snap.

She dares to narrow her eyes on me, the little shit. "I don't have one."

"Find one."

Silas comes around his desk and curls his hand around her upper arm. "Behave." The word is barely audible, but punctuated with the way his fingers dig into her flesh.

I'll slice his tongue out first. Followed by each and every finger on those bold fucking hands of his.

She drops her bag to the floor and steps out. Less than a minute later, she's back with a cape.

A fucking cape.

Actually, that might be good.

Slipping it from her fingers, I wrap it around her, satisfied when the fabric swallows her whole, leaving very little skin exposed. Pulling the sides together, I cinch them in place with the belt. My lips brush her cheek as I lean in where only she can hear me as I draw the hood over her hair. "You'd do good to lose the attitude. The childish bullshit will only get us all killed or worse. You're lucky I'm the one who bought you."

She pulls back, hatred in her eyes. "So you can return me to my father? I'd rather die."

My little bee. Feathering my thumb along her cheek, the band squeezing my chest ever since her father exiled her to Paris and away from me loosens a fraction. She's lucky I'm the one who found her tonight. She's angry now. Trapped. Her plan thwarted, but she knows, deep down, she knows with every fiber of her being, I'll never hurt her. Her virginity will remain hers.

Cupping her neck, I bring her in where only she can hear me. "There's so much you don't know. Just know this. You'll never be your father's possession again, Pcholka."

CHAPTER

4

Nikoletta

"**W**here are we going?" My heel catches on the threshold of the back door and I stumble onto the cracked concrete steps leading down to a narrow alley. The scent of trash lingers in the air as it always does in the city, especially as the cold clinging from the winter fades away into the warmth of late spring.

With a firm tug, Konstantin whips me around to face him. He leans in, his face deathly serious. "Quiet."

It's the look I associate with danger, but after the way he found me, the way he looked at me and touched me—maybe that's not all it is. Good. If he's affected, I have leverage. "Not until you tell me where you're taking me."

Dmitri steps in, his gun firmly in hand, his eyes sweeping the area around us. "The best entry point is two blocks away near the five points. An ambulance and police cars one block over have everyone's attention. We can slip right by, and no one will know."

"Good. Let's go," he says with one quick jerk of his chin before dragging me along with him.

I yank my arm free, earning a harsh glare from Konstantin. A hazy light hanging from the back door illuminates his face and I stop breathing, stop hearing the sounds around me. It's just him, the way he looks at me twisting me up inside, wringing out every forbidden feeling I try to hide.

But it's there for him too, for the briefest second, I see it. Now I'm positive with him at my back earlier, tying my bodice into place, I felt it.

Truth and realization tumble in the space between us, leaving nowhere for either of us to hide.

He steps into me, looming over me, and in the light, I see just how much more silver threads his hair as it hangs in a tumble of waves, hiding his face. Two long years. The valleys bracketing his mouth are deeper. The wrinkles fanning from his eyes more pronounced. But my God, he looks even better than he did then.

Strong, cunning, and mine.

Looking at him makes it all but impossible to hold on to the bravado I've worn as an armor since the day I left him. Sadness and longing threaten to drown me right here on the spot, and despite everything I do to contain it, a broken sob slips free.

His grimace slips and his eyes sink shut. When he opens them, they're glassier than before. He's showing me his weakness for me. He always has. But his vulnerability to me has always been that of a godfather to his goddaughter. Not a man to a woman.

Cupping my neck, he lowers his forehead to mine and rocks his head from side to side, brushing his nose against mine.

"I made a promise before God to protect you, Nikoletta. Lord help me, I will keep that vow."

The sound of my name on his lips, not the nickname you

give a child, but my given name, has me dizzy and swaying against him. "I've missed you."

Sliding my hands inside his jacket, I clutch at his shirt for balance. His muscles jump at my touch, and he sucks in a ragged breath. Not just the kind that comes from fear of losing a loved one. No, the hiss from his lips—the sound he tries to swallow back is the visceral reaction of attraction and temptation.

Hope swells in my chest.

He feels it. I know he feels it now. This is different. We're different. I'm no longer that little girl and that desire for him only pulses stronger now than it did then.

"Trust me, Pcholka." The flash of awareness between us quells under his childhood nickname for me, but it was there, and it will be there again.

I nod and slide my cheek against his. "I do."

"Then we go."

"Where? He'll find us. There's nowhere—"

"Underground. We go underground and we don't come up until Nikolaj brings his army." He presses a kiss to my forehead, his fingers sliding from the back of my neck to my shoulders and giving me a reassuring squeeze. "Come now."

Taking my hand in his, he rushes me through the alley. His men, the same men he's had at his side since I was in grade school, check the street and give us a nod. Dmitri moves first, leading the way up the sidewalk along a series of wrought iron fences and Grigori slips in behind us.

My heel catches again, breaking clean off this time. I gasp, my hands shooting out in front of me, but before I fall, Konstantin's arm is there, locked around my middle, keeping me upright. "I hated those heels on you anyway."

"You hate that they make you see me as a woman."

With one swoop, he lifts me off my feet and just as he turns, I hear a soft click that has him going rigid.

"Leaving so soon, Malikov? Is that any way to start our new business relationship?" The voice drips with confidence and a hint of disdain. Each word is a taunt from the shadows until the man steps out into the light of the streetlamps, his gun aimed at Konstantin's head. "She must be valuable if you're willing to break our deal for her."

I keep my head hidden by the hood as the man moves in closer. I catch a quick glimpse of dark hair slicked back, a jagged scar trailing down his cheek that sends a shiver down my spine.

"The night is young, Moretti. Go back inside and get yourself a drink. Before you find the bottom of the glass, the deal will be done." The words rumble through the night, calm and sure, but I feel the change in his heart. The ominous thud in his chest as the adrenaline in his blood surges to a whole new level.

Moretti's dress shoes click in time with the clucking of his tongue. "This looks a lot more interesting." A cool hand glides over my calf. "Why don't you do whatever it is you need to do, and I'll keep the girl company."

"Hands off." A growl echoes from Konstantin's chest. With a quick jerk, he yanks me free, spins me, and dumps me in Grigori's arms.

The cat and mouse games die the minute Moretti laid a hand on me. With one move, Konstantin meets the challenge of battle and our quiet escape plunges into chaos. Shots split through the hum of the air as Grigori's feet pound the pavement.

"No! We can't leave him."

I push against his chest, fight him with everything I have,

but he only tightens his grip, a curse of frustration on his lips. "He's fine. Dammit. Stop moving."

Digging my nails into his flesh, I thrash against him, my every movement shifting the cape until it binds me while more shots ring through the night. Konstantin could be dying right now. In the street, alone, bleeding, and I never had the chance to tell him—to show him—what he means to me.

My lungs ache as I fight back frustrated tears. I can't stop tearing at his skin, his blood slick under my nails, his pain-laced hiss the only sign I'm having any effect on him. Within minutes, he's taking the steps two at a time and ducking into an apartment building.

Dropping me to my feet, he snatches my hands away from his neck and holds them up between us, his eyes widening at the sight of blood coating my fingers almost to my palm. "Fucking hell. Damn women. More fucking trouble than they're worth." With a grunt, he drags me over to the door under the stairs that lead to the second floor. Shoving me through, he drags it shut behind us, plunging us into darkness.

My heart hammers in my ears, the sound of his mutters blurring at the edges until they disappear under the thunder of my own panic. I spin around and reach out, searching for something, anything to ground me. My fingers scrambling for something familiar.

When I spin again, he flicks his flashlight on, the beam hitting me right in the eyes. The dull glow offers sweet relief from the darkness, and the panic threatening to sweep me under recedes, just a bit.

I blink down just as Grigori yanks open a panel in the floor. "Go."

There's no light, just stagnant air and silence.

I take a step back. "I can't."

Darkness, thick and warm from another time, another place closes in on me. I hate the weakness. I loathe the control those memories have over me. The power I fear they'll always have, reminding me that despite my strengths, I'm weak.

I fight for every breath, shaking my head, tears streaming down my cheeks. There's no way out and he's here. In the darkness. Waiting to touch me. Taunt me. Hurt me.

Vlad's torment breathes life despite the two years apart. Because of him and his torture, I will always be vulnerable, even when I'm strong.

"Nikoletta!" The urgency in Grigori's voice cuts through even as my vision narrows, and blackness creeps in along the edge until oblivion swallows me whole.

CHAPTER

5

Konstantin

I make my way through the cold stone walls of the tunnels to the crypt where Grigori was to take Nikoletta. Every second she's out of my sight deepens my sense of dread. It was all I could do to turn her over to him. It's not that I don't trust him, I just trust me more.

Hunched over and aching, I shuffle through the shortest, narrowest section of the passageway, the part that runs alongside the crypts under Old Saint Patrick's church. After I pass two more corners, I feel for the false wall that leads to the makeshift dwelling in the family crypt running along the south side of the property. The passage through to this section is a bitch, but it's the only section where we've managed to tap into the water and sewer system. At least then, if we have to lay low for a long period of time, we can survive.

When my fingertips snag on a rough edge along the painted stone walls, I stop. Digging my fingertips into the crumbled gap between the pseudo door and the concrete, I give a firm push. The fake stone slides into the crypt, the foam sealant we use to make it look like it's sealed giving way with a scrape.

My hand lands on my gun at the sight waiting for me. Grigori is leaning over Nikoletta's still body on the bed. Something deep and possessive snaps inside me at the sight of him looming over her and in two steps I've got him by the collar. Dragging him off the bed, I throw him against the wall and level my barrel at his forehead. "What did you do to her?"

Palms up, he cranes his neck where I see claw marks and dried blood soaked into the collar of the dress shirt and sticking to the fabric. "Easy. She passed out after she tore the shit out of my neck. I still managed to get her down here. You're welcome."

With a click, I tip my gun back. "Watch it." Grigori might get away with that sharp-witted tongue with me, but other members of the Bratva wouldn't put up with it.

"What happened?" I whip my jacket at his chest which he catches at the last second.

"Panic attack, I would guess. The minute we got in that closet she freaked, but when I opened the panel in the floor and she saw the darkness, she folded on the spot."

Dropping down on the bed next to her, I run my hands over her clammy, chilled skin. Her face is so pale and she's shivering. Jesus.

I get to work peeling the cape from her so I can get her tucked under the covers, but when I draw back the fabric from her shoulders, I find scrapes along her shoulder blades. Red, raw lines with dirt still caked in her skin. At the view of her marred skin, the swell of anger swirls with the adrenaline still surging through my veins and I have to will myself to stay where I am. "Where did these marks come from?"

Never in all the days I've spent protecting her has she ever looked like this and despite seeing no other way to get her to safety, I can't help but blame myself for it.

"I had to drag her through the narrow section of the

tunnel. I tried to keep the cape under her, but there's a couple pieces of rebar."

I shoot to my feet and advance on him.

He backs up and holds his hands up. "One of them caught on the cape, but not on her. I promise, boss."

This child—no, woman—she's a woman now. A reckless, impulsive, beautiful woman who will get herself killed taking risks the way she did tonight on that stage. To even step foot in the spotlight was beneath her, but to bare herself to the men there—over my dead body would anyone ever see her like that again.

We fucked up. We didn't prepare her for just how nefarious this world could be. No matter what recesses of the world she finds herself in, she will be hunted, a prize for whoever possesses her. She's vulnerable because we didn't teach her how to be ruthless, cunning, and disciplined. Passionate and spirited, she lacks control. And now, evil more sinister than we ever could have imagined is seeping through the cracks in this family, and she's ill-equipped to protect herself from it.

The day will come when Nikolaj will head this family with intelligence and responsibility. He'll be a fearsome force, but until that day, we're all hunted, Nikoletta most of all.

"You're alive," she whispers as she reaches for my face and rests her palm along my cheek.

My shoulders slumping in relief, my rigid muscles ache with the constant tension and worry for her. "You think so little of me that I'd fall so easily?"

"Guns. So many guns firing," she mumbles before licking her lips. She blinks, her gaze dropping to my arm, her eyes widening. "You're hurt."

"It's nothing." And it's not. I don't even feel it. Nothing

more than a flesh wound and nothing compared to the injuries I've sustained over the years.

"What now, Kostya?" Her gaze darts around the room where burning candles are scattered throughout.

"Nikolaj is coming. I got in touch with him on my way here. Moretti's dead and his men will be looking for retribution. So we stay here until we have reinforcements."

She pushes up onto her elbows, her thick waves sleek only an hour ago now a tangled mess framing her face. If this were any other time, any other place, she'd look like a woman thoroughly fucked from where she sits in the center of the bed.

With a wary gaze, she blinks rapidly, her eyes adjusting to the dim light as she gazes through the stark room. Not that there's much to see. A shelf of pantry foods that don't require refrigeration, several cases of water, a sink, toilet, and a claw-foot tub.

I've been in worse places with no food or water, surrounded by dirt and death. This room, despite being a crypt, is comfortable and dry—a paradise compared to where I've been, but I have to wonder what she sees. Raised in wealth, she's only ever slept on lavish sheets, a mountain of feather pillows—her bedroom alone bigger than most modest family homes. She travels by private jets and luxury cars with buttery soft leather seats and bulletproof glass.

This room is where her extravagant lifestyle dies.

Her bottom lip trembles, but she fights back the fear, her teeth sinking into the flesh to keep it still as she takes a few deep breaths. "It's so dark."

"We'll light more candles." I brush a lock of hair away from her eyes and settle my palm on her cheek. "When you're ready, we'll get you cleaned up."

"And you'll tell me what's going on. Why you're no longer at my father's side. Why you stand with Nikolaj." Her fingers lock on my wrist in a surprisingly strong grip, reassuring me she's coming out of it and she'll be fine.

I'm staring into the eyes of a Romanoff through and through, and despite her impulsiveness being enough to get us both killed, in moments like this, I have to remember, although having been taught to be demure, she's been bred to be ruthless in her own right, even if not like her brothers.

"We'll talk, Pcholka."

NIKOLETTA

The minute Konstantin leaves me alone to speak to Dmitri and Grigori, I shiver once again. The ceilings can't be more than six feet tall from the way Konstantin has to round his shoulders and hang his head.

His men glance at me on occasion, but before long, they head out the narrow, short opening, back out to the tunnels. Konstantin sprays the edges of the wall panel and slides it back into place.

"What is that?"

"It's a sealant. It spreads and settles, making it look like the crypt hasn't been accessed in years."

"Are we trapped in here?" My heart climbs into my throat, fluttering like panicked wings, making me lightheaded. I clench and unfurl my fist endlessly while I close my eyes and count.

"We're not trapped, but it's not safe out there. Not for you. So we wait."

This is the one thing that will crawl inside my head and fuck with all the recesses of my mind until I break.

How many years did Vlad torture me like this? Locking me in the dark. Sometimes a room. Other times a closet. The spaces growing smaller and smaller while he toyed with me, tortured me—filled me with fear of the unknown.

Every time, I waited for relief, for someone to find me while I wondered when he'd finally push it further. Screaming in the darkness, clutching at my throat, unable to temper my panic. By the time he and Nikolaj were sent off to a private school in Vermont, fear plagued me to the point I needed lamps scattered throughout my room to sleep at night.

But there are no lamps here. Just candles. How long before we have to douse those too? The heaviness in the room settles on my chest. There's not enough air and before I can stop it, the edge of hysteria takes hold and every breath feels like it might be my last.

My vision goes black, my body heavy, the only sound the blood pounding in my ears and Konstantin. His voice is muffled, edged with fear, and so far away.

Keep breathing. Keep breathing. Keep breathing.

My throat burns. Drained of every ounce of energy, my arms turn to lead next to me on the bed.

Warm arms lift me, and I want to curl into him, but the darkness won't release me from its grip. Seconds go by— maybe minutes—his warmth disappears and my body is lying against something cool and hard and slowly more light fills the room.

Tears spring to my eyes as my throat opens with a burn that makes it impossible to speak. Then there's water. Cold water rushing under me. My eyes snap open and he's there, with one hand under the water as it grows warmer, the other along my cheek.

Mouth tight, his skin pale, he watches me. I open my mouth to speak, but he cuts me off.

"Just breathe."

He lays his palm flat on my chest then, right between my breasts. The water on his palm soaks through the thin fabric and I shiver under his hand. His dark eyes leave mine, his gaze falling to the way he's touching me.

We're locked there, both focused on the rise and fall of my lungs. My nipples tighten painfully, and more than anything, I wish he'd touch me. The water rises, the skirt of my dress floating in the water around me, exposing my thighs.

"Did you bring clothes with you in that bag?" His voice is quiet and low. Pained.

"Yes." The word is a whisper on my lips. My skin is on fire, the blood rushing under it flowing to all the right places, leaving me throbbing and desperate to be touched by far more than just his hand. I squeeze my thighs together, the ache only growing with every passing second.

The grimace is swift and he yanks his hand away. I catch the glint of his knife in the candlelight before he fists the side of my bodice where it meets the slit above my hip and slices clean through. Gliding the tip under the straps, he slices them away too until the fabric sinks to the bottom of the tub under me.

"I hated that dress," he mutters, sheathing the knife once again.

I sink down deeper in the water, craving the warmth on my skin. "No, you didn't. You just hated that other men saw me in it."

He doesn't look at me. Keeping his eyes averted, the cords in his neck flex. "You're lucky, Pcholka. If it wasn't for your panic attack, I'd have you over my knee right now as punishment for what you've done tonight."

"Your idea of punishment would only guarantee I'll do it again."

He freezes next to me, his fingers turning white with the force of gripping the edge of the tub, the air pulsing between us.

When I settle my fingers over his, tracing along his index finger, his fingers flex—but then he's on his feet and walking away.

CHAPTER

6

Konstantin

Every minute she's in that tub is sheer torture. I refuse to turn around. It's bad enough I have her naked body burned in my mind.

I thought I could keep myself under control, but then I cut that fabric from her body and not even being right under the very church where I held her during her baptism could stop the lust flooding me.

She's always been mine, but not like this. We were never supposed to be this. As soon as she's safely under Nikolaj's protection, I have to leave. I won't risk stoking this new awareness between us. I won't encourage her. And I won't survive a lifetime of resisting her just to watch her with another man. I cannot bear witness to her having his children, loving him, building a life with him.

I've done it before. Her mother was everything in a woman. Beautiful, full of life, funny, kind, and I spent every day wondering how a person like her walked this world untouched.

Until Maksim broke her. Slowly, bit by bit, until that light in her eyes dimmed once and for all.

I thought Nikoletta's mother was the love of my life.

Now—I have a terrible feeling I was wrong. I wanted her with everything I had, but that was the want of a man in his early twenties. A man who, despite the abuse he suffered, didn't have one damn clue how dark this world could really be.

Twenty-six years have passed since she fell for my best friend—turned enemy. Never in all the years of watching them together did I feel an ounce of possession which takes hold of me now that I'm near Nikoletta again.

I want to punish all who desire her. The need to mark her as mine is a force sweeping through me. I want to spar with her in a way that's loud and vicious but will be so satisfying when she succumbs.

Every bond born of a godfather and goddaughter withers away with the awareness growing between us. How appropriate that it dies in the confines of this fucking crypt. Fear—a feeling so unfamiliar—flourishes here. Not for me, but for her, for what will happen between us and the damage it will cause to her.

No—less than twenty-four hours and Nikolaj will be here. I won't let it get any further than it already has. Once he has her, I'm gone.

The sound of water sloshing has me whipping around. Fucking hell, she's standing there, shivering, water sluicing over her skin, every inch of her bared to me.

"A towel, Kostya."

I mutter a curse and stalk over to the shelf just out of reach. "Here." I hold it out without looking at her, but I don't need to see her face to know what she's thinking. Her amused laugh, the kind of knowing laughter women possess, it's a part of her now and it is aimed at me.

"It's just a body, Konstantin. You've seen them before."

"Child, do not test me."

"I'm not a child."

This would all be a hell of a lot easier if she were. "You're acting like one."

With the towel tucked securely around her, she shakes back her wet hair and laughs. "No, Kostya. That's you. You're unbalanced. I kind of like this side of you."

The way she reads me steals every thought from my head. So instead of saying anything, all that comes out is a grunt.

She reaches out and settles her palm on my back. Next thing I feel is her forehead leaning against my spine and her jagged exhale. "Everything feels right when you're with me. It always has, but it's different now."

"It can't be different, Pcholka," I bite out, my throat thick.

"You're mad, but it's not at me. Maybe at yourself." She pulls away then and I can finally take a deep breath, just to have her steal it away with the words that follow.

"My father sent me away and you just stood by and let him do it. How could you let him do that?"

Little shit. Like I had any choice in the matter. She's not mine. Stalking to the door, I grab her bag and toss it at her feet. "You got yourself sent away. You hanging out with that stupid girl who liked to write all that fucking nonsense in that fucking journal about me. That's why you were sent away—because of the influences around you."

She jutted her chin and even though I stood a foot taller than her, it was as though she was looking down at me with that prideful lift. "The journal was mine."

The roaring in my ears crashes over me like a turbulent sea. No. This is not—no. She's—no. Just no. I can't form a single fucking coherent thought and if I can't even work this revelation out in my own head, we're not going to hash this out here. Out loud. With nowhere to retreat.

"We're done talking about this." Every word from those lips leads to a dangerous level of awareness neither of us can afford.

"No. We're not." Clutching the towel between her breasts, she takes a step toward me. "It was mine, Kostya. I wrote those words."

My fucking body is already reacting. Blood charges through me with every step. Despite averting my gaze, my eyes defy me and swing right back to her. "No. You have a crush. Nothing more."

"And what do you have? I felt you tonight. You were hard. You wanted—"

"No! I will not hear it."

"You will! We may be forced to hole up in this crypt, but I will not hide from you for one more minute. Do you hear me? I never wanted to."

"What are you saying?"

"I'm the one who wanted you. Dreamed about you. You're still the one I fantasize about. You're the man I was dancing for on that stage tonight and I didn't even know you were in the crowd. Every move, every touch, every sway of my hips was me escaping those roving eyes into the fantasy of you. Of us."

My chest heaves with the force I exert to stay rooted right to this spot. Tension skitters between us. I start pacing, hunched over, the candles flickering from the air I displace with every pass. Flexing my fingers, I do everything I can to keep my hands off her.

"You watched me. I bet you never took your eyes off me. Remember what you saw on that stage tonight and call me a liar. I dare you."

I've never been easy to shake. But tonight, I unravel with her verbal assault. Whipping around, I snarl at her like the caged animal I've turned into from being stuck in this tomb with her. "I've kept my vow. I've never done anything but honor you."

"Yes, you and that maddening honor. I'm an adult now so who are you holding on to that honor for? Me? My father? Or do you have a death grip on that honor to protect yourself?"

"You're barely an adult, and your recklessness makes you even younger than that."

"I seem to remember stories about someone reckless. A legend. And despite all the risk he took, he's still standing right here before me."

"I'm not a wo—"

She shoots her hand up between us and cocks her head with attitude. "Don't finish that. Don't you dare condescend to me because I'm a woman. I don't need a man telling me what to do. I only need a man for one thing. And you're the man who bought me."

"A technicality, Pcholka. And nothing more."

Her smirk slides into a knowing grin. "Are you sure, Kostya? All those young girl fantasies, all leading to here, to now, to us—alone."

Truth tumbles in the space between us, leaving nowhere for either of us to hide.

"You don't know what you're talking about."

"Then let's find out. One kiss, Kostya. Just one. I'm an adult now and one kiss will leave my virginity intact."

I sidestep her and make my way to the bed. "No."

"You're afraid."

Jesus Christ, she's everywhere. Relentlessly taking shots at my control. She's absolutely maddening. If it wasn't directed at me, I'd be proud. "It's not right."

"Says who?"

"God."

"God? So what's his opinion on the killing, the drugs, the illegal weapons, the whole foundation of our family being built on a life of crime?"

"You're trying every bit of patience I have, Pcholka."

"The same way you try mine." Neither of us blinks as the air grows thick with the challenge she's sprung between us. My knuckles turn white with the force of my closed fists as a war wages inside me.

She bites her bottom lip and drags her teeth along the flesh, a nervous habit of hers that looks a whole lot less innocent now. Now it only makes me want to shove my cock between those lips until she's choking on every inch with tears streaming down her cheeks as she gags on me.

Her fingers unfurl from the towel and a strangled sound comes from my throat, making us lock eyes on one another.

"Hold on, Kostya. I'm about to try your patience even more." Her hands fall away from the towel and just a mere second later, the terry cloth slides to the floor at her feet.

My control snaps under the weight of wanting. Any bit of resolve crumbles. I suck in a rush of breath, my shoulders swelling, and in one long stride I'm on her. Looming over her. Just one kiss. She'll still be a virgin, a point she proudly made. She won't be sullied by one kiss.

My fingers spearing through her hair, I yank her head back and drag her fresh mouth up to mine.

Slanting my mouth over her stubborn one, I plunder until my tongue takes command of hers with long, seductive strokes.

Blood rushes to my head and I sway on my feet as every taste of her only makes me greedy for more. Until I'm helplessly devouring her. A starving man who had no idea what wanting really meant until now, until she stands naked before me.

The helpless hungry sounds from her throat make my pulse pound behind my eyes as she leans into me, her full breasts pressed between us as I taste her over and over, her mouth imprinting on me, changing me, making it impossible to go back even if it's impossible to move forward.

Warm and wet, she gives as good as she gets with that mouth, making me wonder who taught her to kiss like this. Was it some guy in Paris? Another student? Maybe a dancer? I growl at the image of her in some pathetic kid's arms as he gropes her with no finesse, only reaching for his own selfish pleasure without worrying about hers.

In my mind I'm there, pulling him off her. Tossing him to the side and taking her for my own. Until I catch sight of us in a mirror. Her eighteen years to my forty-eight. The years etched on my face a stark reminder of who I am, who I'm supposed to be to her, and why this is all wrong.

"No. No." I let her go and she stumbles away from me, the stricken look on her face tinged with humiliation and rejection.

Her parted swollen lips are too much and I have to glance away. This isn't right. I made a vow to God. And yeah, she shot all kinds of holes in that promise, but what of the one I made to her father? Her mother? And now her brother?

This attraction has no life outside of the confines of this room. Now I just have to figure out how to control it because right now it's controlling me.

"Get dressed," I snap as I spin away from her.

CHAPTER

7

Nikoletta

An hour passed since the kiss and still the man won't speak to me. I feel his lips all the way to my bones. It doesn't matter how much he fights it, his mouth on mine, devouring me, it only bolsters my resolve. Even if he can't let himself consider a future with me, there's only one person I can imagine losing my virginity to, and it's him.

He *is* the one who bought me. Oh, the irony.

The candles flicker, straining to stay lit in the pool of melted wax flooding them. He's sitting by the door, his back to the wall, his gaze on me from as far away as he can get. When I look him in the eye, he looks away.

He's full of shame and for once, I have none.

He pushes to his feet and blows out the one nearest him. It's okay. It's just one. There's still more lit. I bite back the whimper when he blows out the second. Holding my breath, I pray that he'll stop, so I don't have to tell him the truth of my fear, but then he blows out the third and I wheeze out a lungful of air.

"Fuck," he mutters. I hear the sound of a lighter as I grip the edge of the mattress and focus on moving air in and out.

"Why are you so paralyzed by the dark?"

"Vlad."

Four letters. One name. And really, is there much more to say?

My oldest brother—half brother—has a taste for torture. Evil through and through, his only competition to be the most sinister of monsters is against himself.

"Your father indulged the little shit for far too long." Frustration laces his voice as he struggles to dig through a bin of supplies, then pulls out a couple fresh candles.

"My father covets him. He's exactly the kind of evil my father wishes he could have been."

"Nikoletta—"

"Don't. You know it's true. Besides, you have no idea the things he's done to me. No one knows."

"Tell me." He lights the first candle and sets it on a makeshift nightstand next to me.

"What part do you want to hear about? How he used to lock me in rooms in the dark and leave me for hours on end? Or maybe how he started locking me in smaller places when rooms no longer held a thrill for him." A humorless laugh scrapes from my throat and dies.

He crouches next to me and lights the next candle. Despite his proximity, the chill of panic reaches into the deepest parts of me and I shiver, wishing I could curl into him again.

"The best was the false wall in Father's wine cellar. A space no more than three feet tall and full of bugs. He shoved me in and locked me there for hours while he taunted me through the wall."

A slew of Russian curses cuts through the air. I'm stupid to take solace in them, but I do.

"As horrible as it was, none of it could match what came next. When locking me in small spaces no longer held a thrill, he locked me in the dark with him. And nothing is more terrifying than being trapped with Vlad in the dark."

He reaches for me then, smoothing the hair from my temple. His hands shake with barely restrained rage for which he has no target right now. "What did he do to you?"

"Whatever he wanted." I can feel him willing me to look at him, but now it's my turn to hide.

"Did he…" His words trail off and he swallows thickly. A giant of a man, my own warrior, and he can't bring himself to say the words.

But I know what he's asking. Every woman knows exactly what he's asking.

"Yes. He touched me."

A muscle ticks in his jaw. A growl of anger and agony tears from his throat. He grabs my chin, his grip almost punishing, and turns my face up to his. "He'll pay for this, Pcholka. I promise you. He. Will. Pay."

"When, Kostya?" My voice breaks and I hate it. I hate the weakness in the emotion. Anger is better. I cling to my dreams of revenge and when I speak, my voice is stronger. "When will he pay? How much more of me will he take before he does?"

Violence ripples through him, anger blooming in red slashes over his sharp cheekbones. "He won't take one more piece of you, Pcholka. He'll never get near you again."

I reach out while he's distracted by his need for vengeance and trace my fingers over his full bottom lip. His taste is a part of me now, nothing will ever wash him away. "He takes now, even when he's not here. He made sure of it. Made sure I can never really escape him."

He kisses my fingertip, all the reasons he clings to as to why he shouldn't seemingly forgotten for this brief moment in time. "Nikolaj will win. I have no doubt he'll win."

"Why do you have so much faith in him?"

He lifts his face, jutting out his chin with a hint of pride. "Because he's smart, cunning, and maddeningly patient. But also, he has a level of compassion for his family that is unmatched. He didn't get it from your father."

"Mama," I whisper. Nothing has been the same since I lost her. Since this life took her from us by whittling away who she was until all that was left was a shell of a woman plagued with paranoia. It happened so fast. In less than a year, she went from being full of life with endless energy and the best hugs to a hollowed-out version of herself with no life in her eyes. And just when I thought I couldn't take one more day seeing her that way, she ended it by throwing herself from a cliff into the sea at our vacation villa.

Women in the Bratva break. They always break.

I've never been able to look at the ocean since.

"Yes. Your mother." He lets go of my hand and settles against the wall next to me with a wince on the cold, mercilessly hard stone beneath him. The stubborn ass should just get in the bed. It's big enough for both of us, but nope. That fucking honor slides right back into place.

"But Nikolaj is still a man. Even if he wins and rises to power. I'm still the princess of the Romanoff empire—just a bargaining chip. If you don't think he'll default to those old fucking moves and reduce me to something that is passed between families, then you haven't been paying attention."

His gaze snaps to mine, his eyes full of challenge. "You think so little of me."

"You're one man against a centuries-old force, Kostya. One man." A smile teases my lips at the look of sheer disgust on his face. God, how he hates being reminded he's human. "And from where you've all kept me perched, I've had nothing but time to see what no one else can."

His body stills. He almost looks relaxed, but looks are deceiving. He's spent years softening his hard edges around me, protecting me from the brutalness of our world. But I've seen it despite the ways he tries to hide it. And sometimes, it's he who's hidden from me under the stifling darkness engulfing me.

"What did you see, Pcholka?"

"Tradition demands Nikolaj use me to attain power. He's formed from this same poison I am. And while we may be better than our brother, purer of heart, more honorable when it comes down to it, we will do what needs to be done. That's why I put my own price tag on my virginity. Because I know, if it came down to saving the empire, he would fucking trade me or sell me for what's mine. And I'm terrified I will fall in line just like the women before me."

I'm gasping now, the agonizingly slow death of my spirit over the course of the years looming before me. But this one thing... this one experience. It can be mine. I need it to be mine.

"To the rest of you, I'm a means to an end. Nothing more."

"You've never been a means to an end to me. Never."

"But is it enough to stop you from doing your duty?" When he grimaces, I shake my head. "Don't answer that. I already know. But hearing it from your lips would cut too deep, Kostya." I blink away the moisture in my eyes and meet his eyes. "My virginity was the one thing I had that I wanted to be mine and mine alone."

Exhaustion engulfs me and in the looming silence, my heavy eyelids sink closed, but it's okay. He's here. He's protecting me. Today I'm mine. Tomorrow, I just don't know. I sink under the covers deeper, stealing every bit of warmth I can for a chill that never quite escapes me. I have no money, no friends, nothing to help me in my escape, but none of that matters. I have to go. I just need one opportunity, whether it comes from their complacency or utter chaos, it doesn't matter. The unknown is a dark swath, but for now, I have the oblivion of sleep, where the dreams of him come.

The only place I can have him as I truly want him.

It's in this place without time, without space, where he sheds duty and touches me. Every glide of his fingers over my skin awakening my nerve endings before setting me on fire. I'm drowning in a sea of lightheadedness as his lips trail over me, tracing the path of his fingers.

Darting out his tongue, he drags along the valley between my breasts, his gaze dark, seductive, and never leaving mine.

The ache for him runs so deep it takes my breath away. Unable to bear another minute of his torture, I reach for the one place he's avoided touching. Wet and throbbing, the minute I find my clit, I'm grinding against my fingers, a cry tearing—

"Damn you, wake up!"

My eyes flutter open and he's there. Looming over me, his fingers digging into my arms with a rough shake. But he's not hungry for me, he's seething, his every breath tearing through gritted teeth.

"What's wrong?"

"You. You're killing me. Jesus, Pcholka." He lets me go then, spinning away from me, and I fall back on the bed. Sweat dots my temples, my hair clinging to my damp skin.

The ache from the dream, it's still here, and when I glance down, my hand is buried between my thighs behind my white panties.

Embarrassment is but a flash as I watch him seethe, realizing how something so natural had such a powerful hold on him.

"I can't control what I do in my sleep, Kostya. If you would just go to sleep, you won't have to see it."

He's pacing now with his hands balled in fists at his sides. His dress shirt hangs open, giving me a peek at his wide, hard chest. "I need darkness to sleep, Pcholka. Light means I'm exposed."

But it's not the physical exposure plaguing him now. It's the inescapable truth in his heart provoking him, pummeling him with a truth that won't hide one more second.

I swing my legs over the edge of the bed and stand, the t-shirt I put on to sleep grazing the tops of my thighs. I bite back a whimper at the feel of cotton gliding over my skin. Stepping into his path, I force him to stop. "I'm vulnerable in the darkness and you're vulnerable in the light."

"It seems so, yes," he growls, a sound of pure frustration breaking free.

"What if there's a solution?" I run my fingers along the buttons of his shirt and peel the fabric over his shoulders, careful of the wound he must have bandaged while I was in the tub.

Violent fingers grip my wrist. "What the hell do you think you're doing?"

"Making different memories of the dark."

His fingers clutch the back of my hair and he yanks my head back. "Bite your tongue."

"I'd rather you bite it."

Lungs heaving with a battle of wills inside him, he lowers his forehead to mine. "Damn you. You must stop this. This road doesn't end well for either of us. Blood and death. No happy ending. Is that what you want?"

Leaning up on my tiptoes, my mouth hovering over his, I cup his face. "I hate this life I'm cursed with, Kostya. Is it so wrong to want something for just me?"

"No, Pcholka, it's not. But I can't give you this."

"Fuck my virginity—"

His tortured groan takes me in a choke hold where all I want to do is soothe him.

"Sleep with me."

"Pcho—"

I press my fingertip to his mouth. "Just sleep. I can face the dark if I'm in your arms, Konstantin. Please."

He doesn't speak. His eyelids sink shut and his shoulders relax. With his nod of surrender, I take a step back and climb back under the covers while he blows out all but one candle. At the edge of the bed, the flicker of light illuminates the doubts raging through him and every second of looming darkness without him touching me plunges me into all-consuming fear.

"I'm exhausted, Kostya. Please."

He blows out the last candle and the swift rise of panic grips me by the throat. The complete darkness unlike anything I've known being in this crypt squeezes around me.

But then the mattress dips and he's there, lining his body up with mine. His bare chest a broad warm force keeping me anchored to safety. I lay my palm over his heart, reassured by the rhythmic pounding behind his ribs.

I focus on each one, counting them in my head until the bands tightening around me loosen, and my breathing grows deeper, my breaths longer. Unable to see, my other senses take over. The musky scent of his cologne, faint but still clinging to his skin. His forearms brushing over my shoulder as he threads his fingers through my hair tentatively, like he doesn't know what to do next or how to treat me.

Growing bolder, I trace my fingertips along his chest, the curls covering hard muscles and hiding a roadmap of scars he's picked up along the way. Some jagged and raised, others no more than a barely perceptible line.

"So many scars. How did you get them?"

He stills under my palm. "Protecting you."

The air stutters out of my lungs. "What?"

He takes my hand and runs it over the first scar. "When you were five, the Povlovs tried to kidnap you. I intercepted their men making their way up the stairs to your room while you slept."

Ignoring my gasp, he moves my hand to the next, a raised scar, more of an oval between his heart and shoulder. "When Vlad was attacked in the schoolyard, your father ordered another child's death, despite my protests. The family, in turn, went after you. This was the bullet they aimed at your head the next day at the park."

A soundless tear breaks free and streams down my face, tumbling into the hair at my temple. "How many scars are from protecting me, Kostya?"

"All of them." Tipping my face up to his, he brushes at the damp skin beneath my eyes. He can't see one single bit of me, but it doesn't matter. He's so attuned to my proximity, he doesn't need light.

He knows every square inch of me, without ever having memorized my body with his own hands.

Our history goes so much deeper than even I know.

"This is your love for me," I whisper as I finally understand everything... and perhaps nothing at all.

"Yes, Pcholka. You were born to your mother and father, but make no mistake, you've always been mine." His voice deepens, turning gruff and jagged with the words that follow. "What you're asking of me—it's not so easy for me to accept whatever this is between us."

"You know what it is, Kostya." His admission, even as he evades the stark truth, gives me a kernel of hope and for right now, it's enough.

With a snarl of pure aggravation rumbling from his throat, he snatches my hand from his chest.

"What—"

"I smell you, dammit." Grasping the fingers I had buried between my thighs, he brings them to his lips.

When his hot, wet mouth closes over my fingers, my eyes roll back in my head. The air leaves my lungs in a whoosh with every hum that vibrates over my skin. Each sweep of his tongue around each digit leaves me gasping and frantically clutching him with my free hand.

"What have we done, Pcholka?" His anguished murmur over my fingers sends me in a spiral of longing. I can't stay still, every part of me seeking, struggling to get closer to him.

Heat swallows me whole. When I cry out in sheer frustration, he's there, his mouth on mine, devouring all my sounds like he can collect them deep inside and keep me to himself.

I reach for him. With one brush of my hand, I find him hard and heavy between us.

"No. Not that. Not here."

"I swear to God, if you don't—"

At his deep anguished laugh, the words die in my throat. "You need relief," he murmurs, raining kisses along my throat.

"Please... I can't—" He bites the tendon in my neck, plunging me into desire so fast and hard I'm grinding helplessly against him, the sound of my whimpers mixing with our heaving, ragged breaths.

Curling his large, strong hand along the back of my thigh, he opens me, dragging my bent knee over his hip. So freaking close, but not close at all.

But then his thigh is lodged against the heart of me and his hand slides to my ass where he guides me into rocking against him to alleviate the ache.

"That's it," he whispers over the shell of my ear, sending a cascade of shivers down my spine and goosebumps over my skin. "Ride me, Pcholka. I can't give you what you want, but I can let you take what you need."

I hate his words, because they mean only right now, in this moment cloaked in darkness. I'm only to ride his thigh until I come when what I really need is to control my destiny. To not let something like my innocence be the pawn between superpowers.

And as angry as it makes me, every flex of his thigh grinding along my clit swipes at my ultimate goal. The torture of wanting him for so long is so great, I can't help but take this—take the little he's offering me.

My belly jumps as my need coils impossibly tight. In my eagerness to ride him hard, I'm bowed off the bed, but he's holding me, always keeping me from falling.

Even now, he's torturing himself, giving me just enough, but keeping us both from tumbling, and the truth of that burns through me as the first waves of my orgasm take hold.

I love and hate him for it.

As I break, as the sharp pleasure slices through me, I'm beating at his chest, thrashing in his arms, loathing how he's the last lock to my freedom. An immovable force sacrificing himself to keep me caged in a reality I detest with everything I am.

In the aftermath, unable to speak, unable to move, he smooths a hand over my leg and pulls me against him, tucking me right along his heart.

The heart that won't lie, and with every frantic beat tells the truth of just how much he wants me too.

CHAPTER

8

Konstantin

If I don't get out of here, I'm going to lose my ever-loving mind. My sense of time gets lost here, but my watch tells me I've been at the mercy of my memories of last night for the better part of today. The dinner hour is rapidly approaching and fuck if I can spend another night like this. I don't know what I'll do.

She brought clothes with her alright. More dresses. And now I know what she wears under those dresses. A flimsy scrap of cotton that barely covers anything and reveals everything when she's soaked and aching.

Come on, Nikolaj.

The crypt is filled with her scent, my mind filled with her cries of pleasure, and my chest and arms ache with the way her nails carved my skin as she lashed out while riding my goddamn thigh.

She succumbed to deep sleep after, never once struggling in the darkness of the single longest night of my life.

But the obscurity I always appreciated at night escaped me entirely. Instead, I replayed every moment in my mind, over and over, resisting the urge to stroke my cock for relief, or worse, bury myself inside her.

Everything we brought into the light between us mocks me, and God help us both, I don't think I'll ever manage to put it safely away.

Danger hunts her every day. Do the reasons matter? What if we both left? What if—no. I can't betray Nikolaj. He's worked too hard. He's been building his own empire to join with the one of his father's. For years he's nurtured relationships, cemented his place alongside the powerful, and I suspect he's even joined a secret society here in New York, giving him an admirable foothold globally.

How do I walk away from the promise I made him before he has a chance to change the course of this family?

As long as he's successful.

I shake away any doubt. He will be. There is no other option.

Now I'm cursed with the taste of her I stole from her fingers. That's my punishment for taking what was never meant to be mine.

The sound of the foam crumbling draws our attention. Gun in hand, I keep her behind me and wait. When I glance over my shoulder and raise my fingers to my lip, she surprises me by pulling a knife from her bag.

Of course she has a knife.

Question is, does she know what to do with it or is it just one more thing that will get her hurt or worse?

The one thing I do know... she and I are going to have a talk about it.

With a shove and a final scrape, the door breaks free and Dmitri makes his way in and nods. "Boss."

"What's Nikolaj's status?" Grigori stands outside the crypt, his back to us, no doubt keeping an eye out. Not that anyone would be down here. Restorations have kept the crypts closed to the public for two weeks or so now. The church above is closed to the public for one more night as they address a plumbing issue that may or may not have something to do with us tapping into the system. Not that it matters, Nikolaj compensates well for the inconvenience of the web of tunnels he's building that snake their way under the entire city.

"He lands in an hour. He'll be here an hour or so after."

"With reinforcements?"

"Oh yeah. The minute he found out she was here and not in Paris, he called in everybody."

"Good."

"There's more." His gaze darts over my shoulder to Nikoletta.

I glance back at her and damn that pride in her that has her shoulders pulled back, her chin jutting in the air, just daring me to shut her out.

"Whatever you have to say to me, you can say to her as well."

He nods. "Vlad also left Paris. He touched down for a brief stop in Madrid. We don't know where he was off to after that. At least not yet."

"Do we have someone keeping an eye on the airports in the area?"

"Absolutely."

He fills me in on the Moretti mess, how the authorities have already begun sweeping it under the rug. Moretti's family and men know better, and they know who he was to meet that night so we won't have a choice but to deal with their wrath in the future, but he reassures me there are no eyes on the church.

With the turn of events last night, I couldn't leave Nikoletta so Dmitri and Grigori handled Silas and retrieved the money. I only hope they did it as painfully as I would have. I find little satisfaction in his death, only resentment it happened by their hands and not mine.

Joining Nikoletta, I let myself get closer than I have since we woke up tangled in one another under the heavy weight of how far we'd let things go the night before. When I reach for the knife, she flicks her wrist, flipping the handle in her hand until the blade is tucked along the edge of her forearm.

"So you do know how to use it?"

"I'm not a child anymore, Kostya."

When I search her eyes, I see the challenge there, but also the quiet confidence. And love. So much love in those eyes for me. It's so deep and fathomless I have to glance away.

"How would you like to see the place I first held you?" The words are out before I can consider how bad of an idea it is, and the hopeful look flashing in her eyes keeps me from taking it back.

Her lips part and the smile stabs me right in the fucking chest. Up on her tiptoes now, she moves in to kiss my cheek, but I turn my head so our mouths are right there, just a fraction of space between them.

I'm a fool to take this risk in front of Dmitri. He may be one of my men, but to take the chance of anyone knowing beyond the two of us will only result in weakness.

She settles her lips over the corner of my mouth and the gesture is so fucking intimate, but also innocent in a way that renders me speechless and unable to move.

I can only want.

My frayed control lies in tatters and I swear to all that's holy, one gust from the Devil and I'll be doing the things I can't take back.

"Show me."

The timing of those two words from her tempting lips with the thoughts burning through my mind take another swipe at my control, but I nod with every intention on fulfilling the offer.

After what she suffered last night, after being so fucking brave facing her biggest fear, what choice do I have?

Taking her hand, I guide her out of the crypts, along the long hall that will take us to the heavy wood doors leading to the vestibule. The tension simmering between us slips away as she takes in the stained glass, ornate woodwork, and brass grates along the stairs leading up to the old cathedral.

She's all delicate touches and gasps of delight, closing her eyes as she inhales the scent of a long, unique history.

Maksim's decision to baptize her here stunned everyone. We'd been in New York for the better part of a month while he secured alliances throughout the boroughs of the city. He always gravitated to more lavish spectacles, but when Nikoletta's mother suggested St. Patrick's Cathedral in midtown Manhattan, he immediately turned it down.

Instead, he favored something more personal. Closer to the part of the city that welcomed immigrants. The place where the foundation for alliances and power soared.

I'll never forget that day. For once, we could focus on the family since we didn't have to manage security in the middle of a global tourist attraction. Maksim's wife and Vlad's mother, Elena, had not intruded yet on the day, and Maksim carried a smile that reminded me of the boy I knew all those years before.

For just a few hours, I was able to pretend we were those friends again, that he hadn't bound the woman I loved to him as he married another. I pushed all worry about the way he pitted his sons against one another out of my mind and focused on Nikoletta.

With confirmation from Dmitri that they have the entrances covered, I usher Nikoletta through the heavy wooden doors into the cathedral. My past and present collide with each step deeper into the place we began, and of late, our sanctuary. Right away, her gaze sweeps up stained glass windows spearing into the domed ceiling overhead.

Her gasp of delight draws a genuine smile from me. I slide my hands in my pockets and hang back a few steps, watching her every move. The way she's light on the balls of her feet as she flits through the pews, running her fingers over the aged wood with a content sigh on her lips.

I can't tear my gaze from the way she wraps her arms around the column and laughs at just how big they are and how impossible they are to encompass.

"It's stunning. I never want to leave." Her cheeks flush as she makes her way to the altar and for a moment, I'm reluctant to follow to the place where I held her tiny body in my hands so long ago.

But Nikoletta has never been one to let me retreat into the shadows. Running toward me, she takes my hand and drags me along as she jogs up the stairs and stops at the altar draped in purple.

She bends down and lifts the fabric and her eyebrows bunch. "It's a table."

I can't help but laugh. "Yes, but a marble one."

She gives me a shove that does absolutely nothing to move me. "Show me where you stood."

I shift into place, to the right of the altar, the toe of my shoe resting along the edge of the marble leg just like it did then. The awe fills me once again at being trusted with something so precious, so vulnerable.

I struggle to clear my thick throat. "You looking to recreate a photo or something, Pcholka?"

"Or something..." she trails off. The gleam in her eyes promises something I'm definitely not going to like.

Trailing her fingers along the fabric, she works her way toward me. When she reaches my side, she plants her palms on the altar and lifts herself onto the surface. Before I can do much more than suck in a gulp of air, she's sliding before me, right between my legs.

"So you held me, right about here."

The skirt of her dress settles barely past her hips, revealing her smooth thighs. There on the outside of her right leg, bruises from my fingertips from the night before.

The buzzing in my head grows and I can't tear my gaze from the spot where I've marked her.

I can't touch her.

Can't even consider touching her right now with the raw replay in my head. "Cut it out."

I take one step back, then another, leaving her alone on the altar under the massive cross suspended from the arched ceilings.

My sins are too many to count, but this was the one fucking thing I had that I could cling to. The good deed I could take with me in death to find some sort of forgiveness.

She raises her palms in surrender, the move so unlike her I flinch at the sight. "I'm running out of time, Kostya."

"You'll be with your brother. You'll be fine."

"Not if Vlad manages to get to me and if he does, I'll wish for the dark again." She gulps and the color drains from her face. "Because he's promised me to Ivan Petrov."

It's as though the confession was meant for this place. This very spot where I promised to do anything to protect her. Where we're both closest to God and the power of his protection.

Here, in this place, eighteen years ago—my vow changed

me. And today, under the threat of a road chosen for her, I'm changing once again.

Cold dread slithers through me and I can do nothing but stare at her. He would never turn her over to a Petrov. His own sister—he couldn't. But even as I tell myself he wouldn't, I see the truth in her eyes. She's not lying. She's been promised to Petrov and that means Vlad will stop at nothing to get to her.

"Have you seen what they do to their women? They carve them into ugly things for breeding." Her chin wobbles. "Every scar along their cheek representing each time they tried to run away."

At the fear in her eyes, something in me begins to crumble. There's no room for error because for her, the consequences are dire.

"Vlad stopped trying to break me the minute he made the deal. He needs me to hold on to what fire is left in me. Because the sick bastard wants to count over how many times I run by the gaping wounds they dig into my face."

Molten-hot rage pours through me. Images cascade through my mind of them raping her, beating her, cutting her open, and leaving her to suffer.

I can't speak. I can't take another step away from her.

Because now I know why this is so important to her. Time is running short. All we have is right here, right now, before our world closes in on us.

"Some of them only have one. They learn that lesson the first time. Some of them have four or five because their fight-or-flight instincts tell them they can still get out. So, they keep trying. Every act of survival is defiance to them so they carve chunks of flesh from their faces that disfigure them with every mark. That could be me, Kostya. You know I'll fight. I won't be able to help myself. It's been your greatest lesson. And I'll pay."

The sunset filters through the stained glass pooling behind her, so different than the day of her baptism. Like her innocence of that day is dying here, under the weight of an uncertain future, or by my hand.

How do I even make that choice?

"With you, I'm not losing something, I'm giving it willingly." One tear slides down her cheek born of anger, hopelessness, frustration—I don't know, but I can't tear my gaze away.

"Because I love you." Her voice breaks on her declaration of love and I break with it.

In a second I'm on her. Scooping my hand along her ass, I drag her against me. Prying her thighs open wide, I rest my aching cock against the place we were never meant to unite. Or maybe we were. Maybe this whole time, a force so much greater has been marching us straight into this moment.

With my hands buried in her hair, I drag her mouth under mine, but I don't kiss her. Not until she's looking up at me.

"He'll never touch you, do you hear me?" I shake her then, my rage and fear crashing into one, turning me absolutely feral with possession. "Never, Nikoletta."

Her pleading eyes meet mine as her childhood name dies on my use of her given name. With one look, I'm giving in to everything she wants. And maybe there is no better place to do this than here on this altar where I promised to protect her. The marks on her thighs that brought me shame just moments before are just the beginning. She's mine, goddamn them all.

Mine.

Diving my fingers between her thighs, I tear the panties away from her, the gasp of shock on her lips echoing through the sacred cathedral.

I don't know what she hopes for in this moment. If she wants soft words and declarations, she won't get them. She's had me on the edge for almost twenty-four hours. I need to feel her around me. I need to swallow her cries. I need every fucking tear that squeezes from those golden eyes.

Mine. All of her. Everything.

As much as I am and will always be hers.

Pinned there against me, I clasp her jaw and devour her as I tear open my belt. She struggles for balance under the assault, propped up on her hands as I bend her back. But she meets me stroke for stroke with that wicked tongue, her chest heaving in time with mine.

With my pants shoved down, my cock free and poised at the heart of her, I run the head along her soaking slit before forcing her to look at me.

"Eyes on me, Nikoletta."

She gives me a frantic nod as she dives her fingers into my hair, gripping me as though I might disappear. Her nails claw my scalp, her fingers twisting, anchoring me to her.

We have no time for finesse, so I drive into her, stealing a brutal scream torn from deep in her chest.

She clings to me, a mess of gulping sobs as I force myself to stay still, but fuck, the way she's choking my cock right now is every goddamn thing I never knew I craved.

"That was the worst of it. I promise." My words are low and calm as I stroke her cheek and she curls into me, seeking my comfort and protection even as I'm the one hurting her.

"I need more. Don't stop." She thrusts against me and gasps against my mouth. "Even if it hurts."

But I can't let it all be pain. There has to be something in it for her other than the choice of who she gives this part of her to.

God, she gave it to me. She'll go to her grave remembering

this day, this experience she can only have once—and she chose me of all people. The weight of that settles in my heart, revealing the cold hard truth.

I love her too.

Yesterday I loved her as a godfather to his goddaughter, but today, I love her as the woman she's become. It's all-encompassing, this fusion of love and lust. It's craving and powerlessness. It's succumbing to animal instinct and taking.

When I pull back and spot her blood streaked on my cock, something primal takes hold. I want to make sure every moment she roams this earth she feels me with her. Inside her.

I plunge deep once more, my focus fracturing before narrowing again.

Her nails score my skin and I want more. I want her to make me bleed just as I've made her bleed. Slanting my mouth over hers, I devour her. My growls and her cries a primitive raw song filling this hallowed place.

Tension eases from her with every thrust until she's not reacting to pain but chasing pleasure. Sinking her teeth into my lip, she draws blood, making me grin against her mouth before drawing back and locking eyes with her.

"Mmmm, that's it, little girl. Make me yours." I lick the blood away and her eyes dilate with pure fucking lust that has me pinning her flat to the altar and wrapping my hand around her throat.

I've heard her cries and longing through her mouth, but now, now I will take them all through every single vibration from her pretty little neck.

My fingers dig into her thigh as I pin her there. I watch the way she stretches around my cock, taking every inch of me, despite the pain.

Such a defiant little princess.

Dragging the scooped neck of her dress down, I bare her breast to me, to God, and dare him to watch how I twist the sacred vow I made. How every raw thrust is sacrilege to His house.

Curling over her, I take her rigid nipple between my teeth and bite until she jumps from the sting, impaling herself on my cock even more.

"Just like that, princess. Fuck me back."

She glares at me even as she bucks her hips against mine. The viselike grip she has on me is maddening, and I'm struggling to keep myself from coming far too soon in her sweet pussy.

Sweeping my thumb through her folds, with the stain of her virgin blood on my skin, I brush over her clit. Over and over, every glide robbing her of much-needed air and stealing all reason until she's thrashing under me, slapping her palms on the altar, and that virgin cunt locks on my cock so fucking tight I see stars behind my eyelids.

My balls draw up tight, and I'm powerless to stop myself from coming. Leaning over her, my forehead pressed to her thundering heart, I fill her, spilling every fucking ounce of myself into her until we're boneless and gasping with Jesus looming on a massive cross right over our heads.

CHAPTER

9
Nikoletta

I 've died. I must have. Because Konstantin has collapsed on me and I'm running my fingers through his hair.

I'm broken and sore, but God, I've never been more alive than I am right here, right now. I want to laugh, dance, sing, run the entire length of Manhattan.

He shifts above me, slowly pulling out of me, and I hiss with the sting.

Okay, maybe I can hold off on the running.

"Come here," he rasps as he draws me up with him and settles me against his chest. "I was rough with you."

"Yes," I say with a breathless laugh. "Thank you."

A rare sound of amusement rumbles through his chest against my cheek. God, I could spend every day listening to him, fighting with him, making love to him.

"The next time, I..." His words die on his lips, but his grip tightens on me. "This is dangerous."

I grasp his collar and stare up at the turmoil in those dark eyes. "Tell me anything about my life that hasn't—"

The first *pop* splits the air and we freeze, our gazes locked, until two more shots follow. The doors fly open as we scramble to right our clothes, but there is no hope for it. There's no way to hide what we've done.

"Well, well, I have to say, Malikov, you surprise me."

Vlad's voice turns my blood to ice in my veins. It resurrects the suffocating darkness despite the light. He doesn't need to lock me in rooms or tiny spaces anymore. He just needs to speak, that polished voice with a maniacal lilt has pure power over me.

I'm reduced to that stupid and scared little girl, helplessly flailing.

With one fluid motion, Konstantin shoves me behind him as he faces my brother walking down the center aisle of the church. At first glance, he looks like the ideal man—every woman's dream. Muscular and blond, clean-cut in an impeccably tailored suit, but inside he's an endless well of poisonous pain and greed.

"You actually fucked her. My father always said the day would come, but you know, I didn't quite believe him."

Konstantin says nothing. Instead, he keeps his eyes trained on my brother while he curls his palms around the guns holstered at his back.

Vlad comes to stop right before the stairs leading up to the altar. Shoulder propped against the pillar, he crosses his ankle over the other and slips his hands in his pockets.

"He's not alone," I whisper. Because Vlad would never be so cavalier if he were at a disadvantage. I'd be willing to bet he has an army outside and Nikolaj will be marching right into the slaughter.

"What? Nothing to say?" Vlad shakes his head, that smug grin on his pompous mouth eliciting a snarl in me. "If you don't want to talk about it with me, maybe you'll have something to say to him," he says, hitching his thumb over his shoulder.

Our gazes swing to the front of the church where my father stands. The smirk on his mouth is a never-ending reminder that while he may not be quite as sinister as Vlad, they are very much the same. Where Vlad relishes the opportunity to inflict pain and torture, my father covets the show.

Maksim Romanoff would never be so casual as to lean against a pillar. No, he stands tall as he makes his way up the aisle. Careful steps—not too fast, not too slow—before coming to a smooth stop at the bottom of the stairs. His gaze lands on Konstantin's hands and the guns he has ready there before sweeping to me.

"Nikoletta, I hoped when you managed to slip away from the watch we had on you in Paris, you were smarter than this. Such a pity. Your mother's daughter through and through."

And suddenly letting Konstantin hide me behind him fills me with shame.

I'm only as weak as I make myself.

So I take a step out from behind him. Followed by another.

"Nikoletta, no," Konstantin commands me in a harsh whisper.

But I need to do this. If this comes down to a fight and we don't have the manpower to win, I need my father to know exactly what I think of him.

"You can physically take me, but you will never possess me. Never."

"No?" My father cocks his head and evil lurks in his gaze. "I took your mother. I possessed her. And when she betrayed me, I scooped out every last bit of humanity in her until there was nothing left to do but discard her."

I'm shaking my head before he even finishes his words. He didn't kill her. I was there when they pulled her body from the bottom of the cliffs. "No. Mama was sick. She killed herself."

"But did she, child? Tell me, were you so naïve that you believed that?"

Broken and battered, I saw her. I—I meet his eyes then, the slow smile spreading over his face chilling me to the bone.

I saw exactly what he wanted me to see.

"No more." Konstantin pulls his shoulders back and stares my father down.

"And you... did you tell her yet, Konstantin? Did you tell her the only reason you loved her was because you were in love with her mother, but her mother chose me over you?"

No.

No, it can't be.

But I turn to him then and a flash of guilt so utterly horrifying flits through his eyes and I stumble with the truth of it.

"Pcholka," he says, laying a gun on the altar and reaching for me.

"Is it true?" My voice is deceptively calm despite the vicious staggering pain that seizes every cell in my body. I gave myself to him and the whole time—the whole fucking time—he's what? Been in love with my mom? Saw me as a version of her he could have?

My God, he called me by my name. When he fucked me—because I refuse to call it anything else now—he called me by my given name.

Her name.

"It was a long time ago." His eyes plead for me to listen to him, to give him a chance to explain. But this world is twisted in lies, drowning in deception, and the one person I thought I could count on is the last person I should have given myself to.

Weakness frustrates me.

But feeling stupid and small—cuts me open wide and leaves me bleeding endlessly.

Too stunned to cry, I stumble back another step just as a torrent of bullets rip through the front doors, splintering pews and shattering centuries-old glass. Vlad and my father dive behind marble displays, guns ready, but instead of worrying about us, they're aimed at the door.

The twisted sordid tale lies between us, and I should be grateful that I know before it goes too far.

A humorless laugh bubbles from my throat followed by a sob I'm helpless to contain.

Because it's already gone too far for me to ever go back, and it turns out the one man trusted to keep them from breaking me broke me most of all.

Konstantin doesn't cower. He doesn't flinch. Strong and sure, he reaches out to me even as the war arrives at our feet and our sanctuary crumbles in a hail of gunfire. "Take my hand, Pcholka. Right now. Take my hand and I'll go with you. We'll leave all of this behind."

CHAPTER

10

Konstantin

Memories mock me here. Despite the certain misery, I'm helpless to stay away. A full year, exactly three hundred and sixty-five days since I brought my goddaughter, Nikoletta, here and crossed every line existing between us.

When my every vow to her, to her family, and to God shattered and rained down in jagged pieces at our feet in the shadow of her virgin blood streaking my cock.

My gaze follows the same path hers did that day, sweeping up the parade of colors casting a glow through the stained glass windows. Rich smoke lingers in the air from the last mass. Warmth, hope, forgiveness live here—but not for me. Inside, my soul has plummeted into a deep freeze impossible to shake.

Fragments of memories, regrets, and wishful thinking whisper through the still air. Shadows flicker and dance where row after row of candles burn. My gaze lands on the altar, where I held her as a baby—where I took her virginity when she was barely a woman. I haven't let myself touch the marble since that evening... when I took her, when I broke her—and she ran under a hail of gunfire and her brother, Vlad's, maniacal laughter.

Vanished.

And in three hundred and sixty-five days, absolutely no trace of her exists.

Tonight I can't avoid the altar. My desperate heart rules, making it impossible to keep my feet rooted to the spot. Despite any remnants of our encounter having been washed away long ago, I need to touch the place where my oaths died, where I took someone precious who was never meant to belong to me.

The cross looms heavier with every step I take down the center aisle. All evidence of the violent shootout that day gone, taken care of by a heavy donation to the church. Just one more way Nikolaj has earned respect and increased his edge in the war for New York City against his father and brother, the ruler and successor of the Romanoff Bratva respectively.

Maksim, once my best friend, and for a brief time my competition in matters of the heart, slowly slipped into madness, a kind of madness Vlad, the legitimate, yet deranged heir stoked and manipulated. Over time, Maksim Romanoff, a name that instilled respect and fear, transitioned into uncertainty and terror.

His kingdom cracked and twisted into something unpredictable and venomous with each passing day. Vlad slowly taking the helm only guaranteed the Romanoff empire will feed on itself and destroy everything in its path until it plummet straight to hell.

Generations of power and wealth I helped nurture for the past thirty years, pissed away by a psychopath.

I promised Nikolaj I will help him build an army and take control. If we fail, my purpose will become singular.

Protect Nikoletta from Vlad's wrath.

Regret haunts me. The crushing guilt for all the time I spent protecting her and completely missed how she had been tortured right under my nose by her own brother. She'll never be locked in the dark by him or with him again. He'll never again touch her, abuse her, violate her.

If that means destroying the world in the process, so be it. If I die protecting her, I'll take his deranged soul with me.

I falter on the second step, my gaze catching on the leather book lying there. The air lodges in my lungs. My eyes roam the well-worn leather. A sense of dread consumes me from every direction until my gut hollows out and the hair on my neck stands up. I spin on my heel, scanning the sacred space with a shrewd eye, searching for the slightest movement.

The silence has a heartbeat, or maybe that is mine. Tingling skitters up my spine, my senses telling me someone watches from the shadows.

Or perhaps that is my own guilt.

Swinging my gaze back to the altar, I shoot up the rest of the steps and advance on the hand-tooled journal, embossed with an *N* in the center and a little bee in the corner.

Nikoletta's journal.

The journal her father found that had him sending her away from me. The pages where she confessed her fantasies of us while I was oblivious to the changes in her young, innocent heart for me.

Dropping my palms to the cool granite, I hang my head and squeeze my eyes shut.

Vlad.

This *gesture* has his name written all over it. He knows I'll never be able to walk away and leave it here. He knows if I possess it, I will eventually crack it open. I will fight it, but right about the point I teeter on the edge of madness, I'll devour her words as though they are the only way to thaw my frozen world.

Skilled in torment, he counts on his prey to succumb to their hearts. For love—an emotion he'll never been capable of—to make them weak.

My gaze catches on the corner of an envelope tucked just inside the cover. I slide it out to find my name in Vlad's handwriting scrawled across the front in jet-black ink.

I let out a slew of Russian curses and tear the envelope open.

Konstantin, Konstantin, Konstantin...

I hear his mocking voice in my head with every repetition of my name. I can't wait to kill him. Slowly. Painfully. Life gradually slipping from his evil eyes.

My father charged me with destroying this journal, but where would the fun be in that? Oh no... I decided I'd much rather hold on to the steamy little piece of Nikoletta until it could prove useful. What better time than when you're cracking under the pressure of not finding her. She's cunning. I'll give her that. You've slaughtered hundreds in your search and still, a year later, nothing. No signs of her anywhere.

My little brother must have so many regrets about choosing you to be by his side. The formidable Konstantin Malikov, reduced to an unruly liability. Taken down by pussy. I used to think of you as a challenge, but now I've crossed you off my list, because why bother...

You're doing a stellar job of destroying yourself.

-V

I slam my clenched fists on the altar, a deep roar of despair tearing from my chest. With a glare up at the cross looming over my head, I snatch the journal and eat up the distance, striding for the catacombs.

Straight to the crypt where my honor died exactly one year ago.

CHAPTER

11

Konstantin

I haven't lit the candles we used that night since. But tonight... tonight, I will recreate that night I spent with my goddaughter here. The night I cut her dress from her lush body, but maintained my honor enough to look away. The night she challenged that very honor by stepping out of the tub and baring her body to me.

The first time I tasted her.

And despite it all, I still resisted her. But my resistance was futile. Because Nikoletta always held tremendous power over me. From the moment I cradled her in my arms nineteen years ago, she'd been my compass through this life. My every move, with her, because of her, and for her.

My chest aches with every ragged breath as I light candle after candle. After shedding my jacket and dress shirt, I pick up her bundle of secrets and pretend her hands were the last to touch the supple leather.

I lie to myself, desperately grasping for the illusion of closeness and connection.

Because without her, I am a dying man. Every bit of me

withers under the loss. At first, I was able to hide it, but eventually, my men noticed. Then Nikolaj's men.

And finally Nikolaj.

Vlad's words hook themselves in deep because for once he is right.

They eye me warily as I crumble. The more I fall apart, the more bloodshed I unleash on the city in an effort to dig up even a scrap of information as to where Nikoletta may have gone.

Nikolaj will grow tired of cleaning up my messes. I've become a full-time job for him. The aftermath of my rage has burned up more favors with his politician connections and law enforcement than he can afford.

He gives me a wide berth, but it is only a matter of time before he'll be forced to take control. After all, his army had moved aboveground months ago. Soldiers settle, hidden in plain sight, in safe houses, only retreating down here to move about the city secretly.

I have my own safe house, a massive modern space with every convenience. Luxury even. Yet I can't help but retreat here to wallow in my memories–my regrets.

Silence envelops me, the isolation of it only making the roaring in my ears louder, rivaling the harsh beat echoing behind my ribs. My gaze lands on the claw-foot tub she bathed in that long ago night and the black dress I'd cut from her skin now draped over the edge.

I haven't allowed myself to touch it since. I've hovered over the material in an effort to draw her scent from the supple fabric, but I never let myself touch.

Madness pulses with life here. With my singular focus on her. It crowds the edges of my reason and threatens to drag me from the reality I fiercely cling to as I circle this tub over and over. The urge to caress and the fear of losing the little bit of her still clinging to the fabric creates a war within me that leaves me on the brink of insanity every night I come here.

Tonight, though, I need to see this all through her eyes. How that night played out in her head after I sliced through her clothing and left her bare before me. On the one-year anniversary of taking her virginity on the altar, only to lose her moments later. I need to immerse myself in my last memories of her and pray for relief from the pain of letting her slip through my fingers.

Stepping into the tub, I lean back, bending my legs, fitting my six-foot-six frame in the space as best as I can. My cock strains against my waistband in this position so I drag the leather from the buckle and peel open my belt.

Then in an act of depravity disguised as comfort, I go a step further and release the button and draw down my zipper.

Flexing my hips, I settle in with my pants low and my cock lying hard against my abdomen. I glance down and a memory flashes, of my cock, wet with her arousal, streaked with her virgin blood.

A glistening drop of pre-cum leaks from the tip and I squeeze my eyes shut, struggling to clear the haunting image from my mind.

Shame. There is always shame. Perhaps there always will be. But a tsunami of pure fucking heat and longing sweeps it away every time, telling me when I find her, I'll be helpless to keep myself from touching her again.

With a final deep breath, I flick open the journal. Her scent, just a hint of jasmine and lemon, an intoxicating combination of maturity tinged with innocence, ripples in the air as I fan the pages.

Colors flash past, the paper carved with a rainbow of shades with cool and vibrant themes throughout. Blue, silver, and black bleed her sadness onto the page. A fight with her father. Fear of Vlad. Her confusion and grief when her mother died.

Pink, teal, and purple paint her excitement for summer, spending time with her friends, her absolute awe looking up to her older brother Nikolaj, and dreams of adventures to come.

And in between... the red strokes.

Heavy and crimson.

A bold *K* at the beginning of my name. The kind of looped movement in the letters indicating a profound excitement to pour out every salacious detail.

Pcholka, why would you expose yourself like this with my name right out there in the open? How could you not realize the danger of this?

I snap the journal shut before I can read more than a few words and drop my head back on the edge of the tub. Fisting the journal in one hand and squeezing the porcelain with the other, I let out a torrent of expletives. My knuckles scream with the force on my clenched fists.

Blood sizzles through my veins, my heaving breaths filling the thick silence as I fight the urge to read her every fantasy. Rolling my head to the side, my cheek brushes against her dress and my mind flashes to that night. Nikoletta submerged in the warm bath, steam billowing in the air, and her dress floating around her. So much fabric, but because of the design, it covered so very little. The way my blade sliced through the bodice like soft butter.

Her gasp. The heat flaring in her eyes. The way rivulets of bathwater streaked along her lush curves when she finally stood.

When she challenged me to kiss her and I caved.

My cock throbs, the tip helplessly leaking until glistening

beads of pre-cum roll along the head onto the skin of my abdomen.

Fuck it.

Every crypt in the catacombs, save for this one, holds the dead.

This crypt... holds secrets. Secrets that will surely have Nikolaj putting a bullet in my head himself if he ever finds out.

As long as what we've done and what I'm about to do stay here within these walls, they cannot bring ruin.

Stopping at the first crimson page, my heart thunders in my chest as I devour Nikoletta's words.

Hey, it's me again...

I saw Konstantin swimming in the pool tonight. I've only ever seen him in suits. This was waaaayyyy better. Not that the suits aren't hot. They are. I'm just used to them.

I couldn't sleep. Thoughts of Mama kept me awake. With Vlad always ready to torment me, I knew it was a risk to leave the safety of my room, but I couldn't stay locked with her ghost anymore.

So I snuck down to the library and pulled out the book Mama used to read to me. Well, not the exact same one. She wasn't allowed in this house. Our stepmother hated her.

I was staring out the window overlooking the pool a few feet below when he stepped out of the shadows in ONLY swim shorts and a towel over his broad shoulders. I hid behind the curtain, peeking out to get a better look without getting busted. That's when he turned. Oh my God, his back... black angel wings rounded up over his shoulders, narrowing down on either side of his spine, the tips disappearing under his shorts.

My heart just about exploded out of my chest.

Nadia's going to die when I tell her!

But I'm glad she's not here to see him like this. That I can keep this just for me. Plus, she'd start talking about all the things she'd like to do to him, and then I'd be trying to not kill Nadia for crushing on my Kostya.

I already had a fascination with his arms. The bit of his arms I saw anyway. Thick, veiny forearms painted with ink. Was it any wonder the boys at school did nothing for me? With their skinny bodies, pale skin, and knobby elbows. Ick. Sure, some of them were good-looking and one day would probably be great-looking, but none of them could possibly compare to my Konstantin.

He dove in, his long arms cutting through the surface of the water, the angel wings disappearing beneath the surface. I held my breath, my heart pounding in my ears, waiting for him to come up. Finally, his fingers curled along the edge of the pool closest to the window and he hauled himself up just enough to put his full chest on display as he shook his head back, sending water spraying all around him.

And when his eyes opened, they seemed to focus right on me where I hid. Like he could see through the wall and curtain. With his elbows propped on the edge of the pool, his eyebrows slashed low over his eyes, like they did when I frustrated him. When his jaw clenched, tingles exploded through me from head to toe.

I froze there, unable to breathe with so many feelings coursing through me. I ached between my legs and clenched. Not that it helped.

Then he climbed out of the pool and OMG!!!

His shorts stuck to him like a second skin, showing everything. EVERYTHING.

How did women do it without feeling like they were being

torn apart from the inside out? Or maybe it was a good feeling?
I don't know, but a part of me really wanted to find out.

But only with him.

I remember the day. I lived in my own house on the estate, but I occasionally used the pool in the early hours of the morning when I couldn't sleep. That particular night, sleep eluded me entirely. Nastasya Vlasova, coveted only daughter of our Vlasova allies, had been delivered to her family's estate in pieces as an example of just what would happen if anyone betrayed the Petrov family again.

The same Petrovs Nikoletta had eventually been promised to by Vlad.

Every time I closed my eyes that night, I saw her remains, but the lifeless eyes with blood dried in rivulets down her face peeking through the body parts weren't Nastasya's... they were Nikoletta's.

The image burned in my brain stole every bit of peace left in me.

Then there was the feeling of being watched, staring into the window, waiting for even a fraction of movement.

I felt something. I felt her.

She had just turned sixteen.

Fuck.

I flip through to find the next entry, but the pages fan out faster than I intend and I land on an entry that has me grinding my teeth together.

Hey, it's me again...

I can't stop.

Every room I step into, I look for him first. When he guides me into the car whenever we go somewhere, the hand at my back, perfectly innocent to him, has me so worked up I can't breathe. More than once he's asked if I feel okay.

No. No, Kostya. I don't feel okay. I'm trapped in this car with you, with your spicy cologne teasing me. I can actually feel your body heat. All I can think of doing is climbing onto your lap and grinding myself against you until this ache goes away.

I'm wet.

Hot.

My skin is on fire all the time. My heart races whenever I even hear his name, let alone see him. All of a sudden the boys at school are looking more appealing. I could just keep my eyes closed. Picture him the entire time.

I'd regret it immediately. I know I would. If my dad ever found out, he'd have the boy and his family slaughtered. And me, what value would I have to him then? I know what he needs me for. A marriage of convenience. Anyone he promised me to would expect a virgin.

So, grinding myself against my mattress again it is. Sigh.

Fuck, all I can picture now is her straddling me, not the girl she'd been, but the version of her I found at Illusions Cabaret. The barely eighteen temptress who played innocent on the stage, dancing tentative fingers along the lone pole in the spotlight. When she put her virginity up for sale to a room full of ravenous, dangerous men. Where I bought her for half a million dollars to save her from her own recklessness. Only to succumb in less than twenty-four hours, by taking her virginity despite my every intention to turn her over to her brother, Nikolaj, intact where he could keep her safe.

That version of her, now branded in my brain, her dress pushed up to her waist, hugging my hips, that tight pussy dripping all over me as I freed my cock and took her. Those velvety thighs spread impossibly wide, her hips accepting the inconceivable stretch. My hips pummeled her so violently toward the end I had to release her thighs and gain purchase by seizing her soft round ass in my greedy hands to keep her tight to me. Eyes locked on mine, she took me balls deep over and over, her teeth sinking into that full bottom lip as she did. Goddamned right she'd regret fucking one of those boys.

Hey, it's me again...

My father had one of his parties tonight. The kind we aren't supposed to interrupt. But tonight he wanted me there. He bought me a beautiful dress and had a hair stylist and makeup artist help me get ready. He even bought a diamond necklace and teardrop diamond earrings for the occasion.

I felt like a princess. A real princess for the first time. Not just someone expected to be seen and not heard until I was useful. He must have said something to his bitch of a wife, fuck if I would call her my stepmother, Elena, because she was nice to me. Okay, not nice, but she smiled. So it was a fake smile. I'd take it.

He had me dance with a few of his associates' sons. He said it was to get to know them better, but I knew what he was doing. He was shopping me around.

So much for him wanting me there because he loved me. When will I ever stop hoping he'll care about me as more than just someone he can use to secure an alliance?

The night didn't completely suck though.

Konstantin asked me to dance. I know he was checking up on me, making sure no one was making me uncomfortable, but I pretended he did it because he wanted me.

The music was so loud, he had to lean in, his lips right next to my ear so I could hear him. I wanted to turn my head so bad. I could have done it, pretended it was an accident. His lips would have been right there.

But if anyone saw it, my father would send him away. I knew he would. He always used Konstantin to keep me in line. Told me if I didn't behave, he would find someone to protect me who wouldn't indulge me.

I don't think Konstantin indulges me. He just loves me. He's my godfather. He's supposed to, even if it's not the way I want him to.

So I kept my face forward. I smiled. Laughed. Whispered into his ear when he bent to hear my reply.

And when I went to bed, for the first time ever, I didn't wear pajamas.

That's when it happened. Really happened. Nadia told me she touches herself all the time, but I never have. I'd always been too afraid of getting caught. Until tonight.

I locked the door, but also jammed a chair under the doorknob just in case. If anyone walked in, I'd die.

And OMG, sleeping naked you feel everything. EVERYTHING.

How cool the sheets are. The way they move over your skin when you shift and turn.

My nipples ached, but the sheets dragging over them felt good. So that's where I started.

Brushing them with my fingers felt nice, but pinching them felt sooooo much better.

My harsh breathing fills the crypt. This is it. This has to be rock bottom. Taking her virginity on the altar where she was baptized should have been the worst thing I've ever done when it comes to Nikoletta. But as I slide my hand into my pants pocket and pull out the panties I ripped from her before taking her virginity, I know what I'm about to do is far worse.

I bury my nose in the material and drag in a greedy lungful of air. She lingers on the fabric even now, a blessing and a curse. My eyelids slide shut as the scent of her moves through me. Every day she remains out of reach, I grow more desperate to touch her. How the hell will I ever control myself when I see her again? The hunt turned me into a reckless version of the man I'd been as I tear through this world, leaving bloody corpses in my wake.

Reading my goddaughter's fantasies while burying my face in her panties, the ones I've kept in my pocket since the day I tore them from her... also is not rock bottom.

Not quite.

I fist my rock-hard cock, the cotton wrapped around my hand, and stroke.

Now this... this is rock bottom.

I reached between my legs and brushed over myself lightly. But after a few minutes, it just wasn't enough. So I pushed a finger inside. Just a little. Parts felt okay, but nothing like pinching my nipples, until I found my clit.

One glide leads to another, and another.

I had to slap my hand over my mouth to muffle the embarrassing sound I made. I buried my face in my pillow and did it again. I couldn't stop. After a few minutes, it almost hurt, but also didn't. I wondered what it would be like if Konstantin did this to me. Would he know just how to touch me to make me feel good? Would he kiss me while he did it? What if we were in the back of the car and he closed the divider so the driver couldn't see us, would he touch my thigh, his hands moving higher, until he touched me here?

I show no signs of stopping. No flicker of decency. My fist grows greedier, squeezes harder, my hips meeting my depraved, accelerating strokes.

Her name a whisper on my lips.

Just the thought of him while I touched myself had me thrashing. My heels dug into the mattress, my toes curling uncontrollably. I couldn't stop squirming and clawing at the sheets. Every time I sucked in a breath, the fabric rubbed over my nipples. In just a couple of minutes, I was biting my pillow and crying out. Then I was warm, so warm between my legs, and soaking wet. My fingers were drenched. I tasted them and didn't hate it. So I flicked my tongue along them again. I didn't stop until I licked them clean.

Honor dies when I scoop the cum dripping from my aching cock with my thumb and drag it over my tongue, tasting what her fantasies do to me. Much the way she tastes herself.

If he saw me do that, would he think it was gross? I don't think so. I can't possibly be the first person who tasted themselves, right?

. . .

Pride? I don't even know what it is anymore. I have none. I squeeze my throbbing shaft, her panties dragging along the veins of my cock with every pump.

Would he taste me then? Draw my fingers into his mouth and lick?

Good? The sliver of good I had in me has withered. In its wake? Bone-shuddering cold, leaving me brittle and empty. But reading her fantasies of us, of what she wanted me to do to her—for once I feel the flicker of heat. I pump harder, the picture she painted alive in my head.

Would he let me taste him?

Gold help me, yes. Yes, I'd let you taste me. I'd demand it. An image of her on her knees for me, her lips wrapped around my cock, her golden eyes wet with tears as she gagged on me, flashes through my mind. The tingling burn starts in my spine, my balls drawing up tight.

What would we taste like together?

I squeeze my eyes shut, my chest heaving. Behind my eyelids, she's there.

She's in my bed, splayed wide, my cum dripping out of her.

The fantasy, a movie playing in my head.

She licks her lips and I feel the swipe of her warm wet tongue to my bones. I sink two fingers into the place where our cum meets and scoop up a taste of us for her.

I want to live in this delusion of us forever.

Where her ravenous mouth sucks my fingers in deep, her tongue greedily swiping over my skin, collecting every drop of us I offer to her.

I want him to be my first.

I want him to be my only.

A jagged growl rumbles from my chest as I explode on myself, ropes of warm cum landing on my stomach, and on my goddaughter's panties, mixing the two of us after all, in the most torturous of ways.

CHAPTER

12

Nikoletta

"**H**eads-up. He's in a mood tonight," my friend, Faith, says as she pushes through the swinging door into the communal kitchen.

"When isn't he in a mood? The real question is, which one? A superior pain in the ass looking down on everyone? The touchy-feely used car salesman in a desolate town bringing all the 'Hey there little lady' energy?" I ask as I wipe my hands on the hand towel over my shoulder and drain the sink.

If my family saw me like this, they'd think we'd been sucked into another dimension. Nikoletta Maksimova Romanoff, the only daughter of Maksim Ivanovich Romanoff, head of the single most powerful Bratva family in Russia, and New York City—for now—running the kitchen in a commune for a crew of thirty.

For all I know, my brother Nikolaj managed to snag the power from our father's clutches, but I doubt it. Not that I will know either way. We only have one television in the main house and it's not like mafia business is reported on the six o'clock news.

No one knows my true identity here, or my history, other than Faith, and it took me six months to trust her with my secrets. And she had to trust me with hers first.

"That's the thing," she says with a quick glance. "I can't quite figure it out."

The way she wrings her hands tells me it is more than just a mood and at some point soon, things will take a turn with our new leader.

Fuck. "You, Lexi, and Alex stay close to me at all times then, got it?"

Her eyes meet mine, then drop to where I grip the knife I've just finished drying more like a weapon than a tool. She smiles, and her shoulders relax a fraction. "Got it. I'll help you dry the dishes and get them put away so we can get upstairs. I know they're sleeping and should be fine, but I don't know... I just don't have a good feeling. I don't want to be away from them."

I hand her a clean dish towel and we settle in to dry the mountain of dishes I've just washed. "Agreed."

When I met her a little over a year ago, my hair was a finger-brushed mess, my dress wrinkled with a tear in the skirt, and my eyes puffy and red from angry tears I'd spent a whole day struggling to control. What little cash I'd had got me out of the city before hitchhiking my way into Northern New York, where I planned to lay low until I could figure out my next move.

Anything that had me using my legal name in any capacity would lead my family straight to me. My brother Nikolaj being the best-case scenario, my half brother Vlad and my father, the absolute worst-case scenario.

As for Konstantin... I may straight cut his dick clean off if I see him again. Not sure what kind of scenario it qualifies as, other than a bloody one.

Almost a year and a half has passed since Faith spotted me coming out of the bathroom at the general store. Her eyes met mine and saw too much. When I hurried out, she followed me and convinced me to come here. She'd only been here for a month at that point, and was still under the illusion that this was a safe place.

For a time we both were.

She moved in next to me and propped her head on my shoulder. "Have I told you how grateful I am that you're here? I don't know what I would have done without you."

Affection like hers is new to me, but after a time, I've gotten used to it, and even look forward to it. She has my back. I have hers. I've never had that with anyone else in my whole life. Because of her, I've had room to breathe and time in private to feel all the hurt and betrayal from the one person I held above all others.

I smile and rest my head against hers. With her, I don't have to be the Bratva princess I'd been born to be. Instead, I embrace being blissfully normal, even when I know it can only be temporary. "Every day. But I'm the one who should be grateful, it's you who saved me." They are words I never could have imagined saying to anyone. They expose my vulnerability which in my world is weakness. Only, in our time together, we've seen each other at our worst, our most vulnerable, and if I didn't have her, I really don't know what I would have done.

I've had friends before, but all of them were carefully vetted, even Nadia, before getting access to me. They all had to have valuable connections for my father.

But Faith, she comes from different roots entirely. She ran away from home, from a father and brother who raped her repeatedly. She had a boyfriend at the time, one she had been intimate with because she just wanted to know what it felt like to be touched by someone who loved her. Then the unthinkable happened. She got pregnant and she didn't know which one was the father. Fearing her father or brother would do something to harm the pregnancy, or even kill her, she ran.

But not before telling her boyfriend she was pregnant. And he delivered the final blow to Faith's heart by questioning if the baby was even his.

Every man in her life has been a fucking disappointment. Something I understand all too well.

Despite our completely different lives, if Vlad had escalated just a bit more, if my virginity hadn't been as valuable as it was, I could have easily been her.

A country bumpkin to the core, Faith speaks softly, works hard, and finds happiness in the simple things despite her traumatic childhood. She gave me a crash course on cooking so I could be useful since everyone pulls their weight here. In return, I taught her how to wield a knife, ensuring she'll never be vulnerable again.

We've both been easy targets for the last time.

When Konstantin reached for me in the hail of gunfire, almost a year and half ago, promising me we would leave this whole life if I just took his hand, I desperately wanted to take it. If my father hadn't chosen that moment to reveal their old rivalry for my mother, I would have. In doing so, I would have unknowingly committed myself to a lifetime of lies and deceit from the one person I loved and trusted most. Whose deception had the power to destroy me.

God, I chose to give my virginity to him. Begged him to take it, even. My father, my half brother, and Konstantin had reduced me to easy prey and a fool.

Festering anger simmers deep inside me at the thought of seeing Konstantin again. His betrayal cuts deepest. After finding out I was nothing more than a replacement for my mother of all people. I've had time to process and gain perspective, but my scathing hot temper will not be tamed.

If Konstantin ever tries to touch me again, I'll put a knife in the son of a bitch myself.

"Help!"

The rapid beating on our bedroom door shakes the doorframe and has me launching out of bed to answer it before the babies wake up. With a swift yank, I wrench it open and slap my hand over the mouth on the other side.

It takes my eyes a minute to adjust, before I recognize Regan's wide-eyed frantic eyes. Curling my fingers around her arm, I drag her in the room. Feeling around the base, I flick on the small lamp on the dresser next to the door so I can see her.

"What the hell happened?" I say in a harsh whisper to try to keep from waking Alex and Lexi.

Lexi lets out a whimper and shoots a fist into the air, but Faith steps in and gently rocks the crib the babies share until Lexi lets out a little shuddering breath. In a matter of seconds, Faith has her settled back into sleep with her arms flung back and her fists on either side of her head.

"Elij—a—ah." Tears spill over her eyelids, trailing down her cheeks as gulping sobs take over.

Looking her over from head to toe, I spot a tear on the side of her nightgown, the seam torn clean up to her waist. My stomach bottoms out. Every muscle locks tight, rage igniting the urge to seek retribution.

"Hey," I whisper, mustering a sense of calm I don't feel as I cup her cheeks and tip her face up to look at me. "What happened?"

"He—he..." She blows out a breath and sucks in another. She curls in on herself, doing everything possible to make herself smaller. "He came into my room. W-when I woke up, he was o-o-ver me."

Blood running cold, I shoot a look at Faith. This is the mood she couldn't pinpoint. The creep grew bolder by the day and now no one is safe.

I thought we at least had a few weeks before he forced my hand. Time to at least formulate a plan between all of us. But time has run out and I have only one way out.

I can protect them—free them even—I just have to be willing to climb back into my cage.

"How far did he go, Regan?"

She dissolves into a fit of sobs once again. Wrapping her in my arms, I gently stroke her hair.

"Shhhh, you're safe now." Mussed strands cling to her clammy skin. Peeling them away, my hand freezes as my eyes land on the red marks around her neck. "That fucker!"

"I'm s-sc-ared," she chokes out.

I turn her face to mine and wipe away her tears with a tissue. "Did he rape you?" I fight to keep my words calm while my blood blazes a trail of fury through my veins.

She opens her mouth to speak, but nothing comes out. Her gaze volleys between us as she nods and confirms the worst.

Clinging to me, she weeps uncontrollably for who knows how long, her face buried against my shoulder muffling the worst of the sound. Her body shakes violently until she finally slumps against me.

She clutches at my nightgown then and peers up at me

with swollen, red-rimmed eyes. "I need to shower. I-I need to get the feeling of him off me—out of me—but I'm too scared to go out there."

I take her hand in mine and give her a reassuring squeeze. "I'll take you."

"Nikoletta!" Faith snaps in a harsh whisper.

"What?"

"You can't. What if he tries something with you?"

I shrug. "I'll gut him."

"And if he comes to our room?"

I hold Faith's stare. "Then you'll gut him."

Her mouth falls open and a few seconds later snaps shut.

Crossing the room, I take her shoulders in my hands. "You know how to use that knife. I taught you. And you would never let anything happen to those babies."

She glances down at their peaceful faces and her gaze softens. She bites her lip, turns back to me, squares her shoulders, and nods.

Motherhood will drive her. She's not that helpless teenage girl at the mercy of her father and brother anymore. I made sure of it. She's become a powerful mother which means Elijah doesn't stand a chance. "When we leave, you're going to lock this door and don't open it until we come back."

"And tomorrow? What will we do tomorrow?"

My lips curve into a smile of reassurance while I fill with cold dread. "I'm going to activate reinforcements." By tomorrow night, I'll face Konstantin once again. There is no doubt in my mind.

"How will I protect them while you're in town? What if he—"

"Elijah's coming with me."

CHAPTER

13

Nikoletta

"**W**hat happened to your hand?" Elijah asks, strolling into the kitchen the next morning where I finalize the grocery list. His fingers are tucked in his pockets, his thumbs hooked on the edge, a weak little man without a care in the fucking world. The smarmy grin on his face makes me want to slice his lips clean off and feed them to him. Like he hadn't revealed his true self last night by raping Regan.

The fucker looks as though he has no clue we know. He probably thinks by strangling her, he scared her into keeping her mouth shut.

Wrong, fucker. You are so fucking wrong.

I guarded her for almost an hour while she practically boiled herself with scalding hot water, crying from the searing heat, but helpless to stop scrubbing at her skin until her flesh became raw and swollen. Uncontrollably trying to scour away what he did to her, not realizing, there is no cleansing away this nightmare.

I glance down at the gauze wrapped from the center of my palm up to the edge of my wrist and let out a sigh.

Time to reel the rapist in.

"I caught my palm on a chef's knife drying dishes. Sliced the fleshy part at the base of my thumb clean open. I need to get butterfly closures for it when I go into town." I turn my hand over so he can see the section and the "blood" I had just barely soaking through there.

Amazing what you can accomplish with a little corn syrup, chocolate syrup, and red food coloring.

"Are you sure you don't need stitches?" His fingers ghost over the bandage and move to the inside of my wrist. He licks his lips, heated eyes on mine as he works his way along the inside of my forearm.

Keep touching me, bitch. Give me every reason to make your death slow and painful.

"I'm going to need help loading the van." I shiver... from pure disgust, but he sees it, so I peer up at him through my lashes with a hint of a smile, making it look like attraction.

Interest flares in his muddy brown eyes and he cocks his head. "Then I guess we should go together. Just the two of us," he murmurs as he draws lazy circles on the inside of my elbow.

Goosebumps rise on my skin and he bites his lip.

"Meet me at the van in about twenty minutes?" I ask quietly.

His hand travels up my arm, over my shoulder, before brushing my collarbone.

I allow my eyes to sink shut, letting him think he has me right where he wants me.

When his fingers curl around the back of my neck, threading through the hair at my nape, the image of the red marks around Regan's throat flash through my mind. My fingers itch to reach for my knife, but I resist.

All in due time, fucker.

"I'll be there," he whispers over the shell of my ear, his palm flexing possessively before dropping his hand and turning to leave.

Twenty minutes later, I find him leaning against the van, feet shoulder-length apart, and his leering smile firmly in place. His gaze drops to the skirt of my sundress where it flutters around my thighs.

Stepping into the space between his feet, not too far in, just enough to let him think I've taken his bait, I hold out the keys. "Would you mind driving? My hand is throbbing."

"Throbbing, huh?" he asks, staring straight at my tits. "For you, Nikoletta... anything."

God, he is easy. A total whore for just a fraction of fake-ass attention. If all goes according to plan, he'll be focused on getting in my underwear instead of violating one of the eight other single women living in the main house.

The army will be here before he ever has the chance to rape anyone else here.

I cross my legs, right leg over my left, angled just a smidge in his direction to show interest. I sneak shy glances, darting my gaze away as though embarrassed at being caught the minute he meets my eyes. When he reaches for the volume on the radio, I do the same, making our hands brush.

Demure and uncertain is the name of the game if I want to embolden him to make a move.

Longest. Ride. Of. My. Life.

Ordinarily, every Friday, I drive the commune's minivan to town and pick up our canned goods and pantry staples. One order at Cosco, another at Wegman's, and back up to the commune I'd go. Elijah has me place the orders online using his card so all I have to do is collect the orders. His penchant for control conveniently keeps me from skimming money off the grocery funds to tuck away for our escape.

With no options if we have to flee, I know at some point, I'll be forced to use my credit card. When my brother made me an approved user, I knew he did it hoping to keep tabs on me. That's why I've never used it. I always keep it on me, though, no matter what.

Even that fateful night Konstantin and I explored the church.

Explored... well, that is definitely a word for it. More like desecrated the holy clean out of it when he took my virginity on the altar where I was baptized.

When shit turned on a dime last night, despite what it will mean for me—for my future—I was I developed the habit of keeping it on me no matter what.

Elijah reaches into his pocket, pulls out his wallet, and places a twenty-dollar bill in my hand. "While I pick up the order, why don't you run in and get those butterfly Band-Aids." His fingertips linger on my palm. "Let's take care of those pretty hands of yours."

"I checked online to see if they had them before meeting you at the van. They didn't. But I can grab them over at the CVS." I close my fingers around his, almost holding his hand, coyly playing him. "I can walk and you can pick me up when you're done?"

He winks. "Sure, beautiful. I can do that."

I stalk down the sidewalk like the hounds of hell nip at my heels and struggle not to puke in my mouth. Popping through the automatic doors, I go right for the register. "Do you have a restroom here?"

"Sure do," the cashier says with a smile. "Straight back on the left by the pharmacy."

"Thanks." First order of business, scour Elijah's funk off my hands.

After scrubbing my hands with the hottest water I can get

from the sink, I dry them and grab three pumps of hand sanitizer on my way out.

I find the butterfly bandages first and head up to the pharmacy window, praying Elijah will keep his nosy ass in the van if he gets here before I'm done.

The pharmacist makes her way over and I take one more glance behind me.

"How can I help you?"

"I need Plan B," I say quietly.

"Of course, give me just a minute." She moves two shelves down and around the corner before coming back with a box. "Will that be all?"

"Yes, thank you."

She reaches out and wiggles her fingers. "Here, I can add those bandages too."

"Actually, these are a separate order. I'm paying cash for these and using a credit card for the pill."

Her smile slips and her eyes narrow, not with suspicion, but concern. She glances over my shoulder which has me turning around to make sure he hasn't come in.

"Why don't we get the pill out of the way first, then," she says, her voice little more than a whisper.

"Thank you... if I take it out of the box now, can you throw the box away for me, please?"

"Absolutely." The minute she scans the box, she opens it and snags the foil pack inside. Leaning over, she hands it to me discreetly. "Here you go, honey. You just get that tucked away now, okay?"

The tension in my shoulders eases and I give her a grateful nod. With one last look behind me, I pull up my skirt and tuck it in the strap holding my knife to my thigh.

Her eyes widen and she leans over the counter, getting

close enough to whisper, "I can call for help. The police can keep you safe."

"I assure you, there's only one person who needs protecting in this scenario, and it's not me." I give her a wink.

A grin tips her lips in return and she pats my hand. "Whoever he is, you just give him hell."

"That's the plan."

When she gives me the total, I reach for the machine, but pause. This is it. I won't be able to undo this. They will find me and my fate will be sealed. But in return for going with them, I can get Nikolaj to make arrangements to keep the people at the commune safe, no matter what it takes.

I shove the chip in the machine and enter the pin before I can change my mind, the sound of the beep telling me to remove my card, like a bell tolling for the dead.

Seems only fitting since life as I know it will die here today.

As will my freedom.

CHAPTER

14

Konstantin

My muscles bunch and flex with tension. The desperation I've been clinging to every day I try to find her, slowly slides into despondency. My men notice, eyeing me more and more warily, as though I may just jam the barrel of my gun to their forehead for looking at me wrong. Nikolaj sure as hell notices. And now, it has become so noticeable, I have no choice but to acknowledge it.

Even if only to myself.

Today has been the closest we've come. We finally have a physical lead. Someone spotted her a couple hours west of here, just inside Pennsylvania.

Wasting no time, me, my best men, and ten of Nikolaj's guys hit the road. Every mile closer only increases my agitation and anxiousness to hurry up and get there.

I'll be able to touch her again. Hold her. I'll know she is safe. That the fallout of what we did hadn't ruined her the way I fear.

Finding her is the only absolute proof Vlad hasn't reached her.

Because knowing what he knows now, witnessing the aftermath of when I took her virginity in the chapel above this crypt, he has no reason to keep her unsullied. With nothing to gain, she'll be at his mercy. Any perverse hunger he's harbored for her will now be free from what little confines bound his most vulgar desires.

Total annihilation. Her absolute ruin from his sadistic hands.

Watching her mother's spirit die, bleeding from her bit by bit, until her copper eyes dull entirely with lifelessness, had been horrid enough.

The same dead-eyed stare in Nikoletta's golden eyes would destroy me entirely. She believes she is just a replacement for her mother. No. What I felt for her mother was no more than someone coveting a shiny object.

One with no history, no character, no unique qualities rendering it unforgettable.

My affection for her mother had no depth. No spirit.

But my goddaughter has seeped into the marrow of my bones. My soul knows hers. Feels her warmth. Yearns for her closeness. Waits with bated breath for her sharp wit.

And shamelessly craves her fire.

So when we arrive at the hole-in-the-wall diner where Nikoletta had been "spotted" and found a brunette of the same height and body shape, almond-shaped golden eyes, and plump lips that look so much like Nikoletta's, yet nothing like her at all, I fight the urge to destroy everything in my path.

It is all I can do to temper the violence coursing through me.

How could they possibly think this was my Nikoletta? Where is the tiny dimple at the corner of her mouth when she smiles? The high cheekbones that create a subtle shadow under the apples of her cheeks? And where is the subtle crease running vertically along her plump bottom lip?

My Pcholka's eyebrows arch gently on her left and peak sharper on her right, as if perpetually calling you on your bullshit. Where is the freckle under her right eye? And sure, this woman technically has golden eyes. Only with streaks of bronze. But my Pcholka, her golden eyes, framed with a ring of copper, hold a kaleidoscope of amber. A shade rich and deep exploding throughout, burning with breathtaking intensity around her pupils.

Returning early this morning, I came straight here. Stalking the length of the crypt. Hunched, unable to stand at my full height here in the prison of my own making, I seethe as I tear up the narrow confines.

A roar filled with outrage and hopelessness rips from my lungs. I whirl on the bed I shared with her for one night and flip the mattress, getting no satisfaction from the way it tumbles along the rough floor.

Her journal mocks me from where it sits on the frame of the bed. I'd tucked it away, out of sight, giving myself distance from my obsessive need to read her every word.

But this morning, red-streaked pages are as close as I can be to her. I snatch it up and climb into the claw-foot tub again, a sure sign I've lost my fucking mind. Flipping to the second half of the journal, I seek out the next page of us.

Her next teenage fantasy.

Hey, it's me again...

My father had another party tonight, only this one, he didn't parade me around like a prize pony. Nope, he left me to mingle on my own. I'd find him checking on me periodically, like this was some kind of test to see if he needed to put me on a leash or if I could handle socializing myself.

I smiled until my cheeks ached. I complimented wives and gave a little extra affection to their husbands, in a charming way, of course. In a way that made them believe they held my every scrap of adoring attention. Their chests puffed up with pride at my interest.

They never once suspected my movement throughout the crowd had nothing to do with making the rounds and everything to do with watching Konstantin.

He stood taller than every other man in the room. His shoulder-length silver-streaked hair wild, yet dignified. His shrewd gaze took in everything around him, including me. My very own broody babysitter.

Fuck my life.

I had just decided to walk right up to him and demand he knock off the spy routine when a blond waif strutted up to him, her hands going right to his abs, red-tipped nails flirting with the buttons running up his chest.

She leaned into him and he did nothing to stop it. In fact, the way he smiled down at her told me he very much enjoyed the attention she lavished on him. Intimate. Familiar.

I hated her on sight.

I could see myself slicing off each of her pretty little fingers and shoving them straight up her ass.

She peered up at him through ridiculously fake eyelashes as she pushed her surgically enhanced tits against him, right in his line of sight.

His gaze flickered down for the briefest moment. Curling his fingers around hers, he spun her into his arms solidly before leading her in a slow, intimate dance between them.

Maybe I'd chop his cock off for good measure.

· · ·

And there was my Pcholka's fire.

Veronica Ellis. The last woman I'd spent any intimate time with before Nikoletta. A woman who knew the deal. Flirt, socialize, scratch the itch, and walk away until we met again. A distraction to pass the time and nothing more.

A distraction who inspired violence in my girl.

Interesting.

I couldn't watch anymore. Not without doing something that would get me into a heap of trouble. I climbed the curved stair-case and stopped, overlooking the crowd before a sound grabbed my attention.

Moaning.

I danced my fingertips along the wall as I crept closer, the sounds getting more crude. I found them in the atrium surrounded by glass, with the moon and stars winking over-head. The transparent walls overlooked the garden spilling off the grand foyer where the party pulsed with what had to be a hundred guests socializing and drinking below. They drifted in and out the wall of open French doors. At any moment, they could look up.

Wide shoulders blocked my view of her for just a moment. Then he fisted the hair cascading down her back and forced her to turn and face him while keeping her body pressed against the glass.

Her lips parted on a gasp and a satisfied smile tipped his lips as he tilted his head down to study her.

My God, what would that be like? To have Konstantin command me in a bold display of ownership, just daring the people below to glance up and watch him take what belonged to him.

. . .

Towering over her, I wouldn't grip her hair and turn her face to the side to look at me. No, I'd grip her throat, her gulp of excitement rippling against my palm, soaking up her every breath and moan. I'd tip her head back impossibly far, until she balanced on the edge of pain. Until she couldn't handle another millimeter without breaking. With defiance flaming in her cheeks, her golden eyes blazing, I'd devour her mouth and swallow her cries. I'd consume every ounce of want from her bow-shaped mouth.

My head swam as I panted against the sensations flooding me. Clenching my thighs, I tucked behind the corner, my nipples pressed against the wall barely offering an ounce of relief. I dropped my hot forehead and struggled to control my racing heart.

She cried out and my gaze snapped up. His huge hand held both her hair and the fabric of her skirt against her shoulders now exposing her from her heels to her ass. Legs spread, his hand disappeared between her legs, pulling back just a bit before he drove his fingers into her with a lewd violence I craved.

Pain. He brought her pain, but the kind that had her pushing her hips back, chasing his fingers every time he slid out of her.

My heart climbed straight into my throat. Wetness flooded between my thighs, burning me up. Panting and needy, I watched him take her, own her, and make her scream for him while her palms slapped against the glass and she thrashed in his hold.

My Pcholka liked to watch. I'll remember that. Oh, I'll remember that. And in a deeper part of her hid an exhibitionist at heart. She wants to be made a spectacle and I'm all too happy to give her everything she wants.

I'll give her the illusion of being watched. She doesn't have to know I'll slaughter the man who dares look at her while getting thoroughly fucked. Her body, her desire, her every release belongs to me.

Only me.

My cock throbs painfully behind my zipper. Weakness and surrender grips me as I tear myself free from my confines and grip my cock, giving it a series of hard strokes. Dragging my thumb through the cum leaking from the tip, I bring it to my mouth and suck it clean. There'll be more and I'll consume every last drop until its rightful place returns to me. In or splattered over my Nikoletta.

Nowhere else will do.

How many fingers can she take? She'd been impossibly tight, but the way she stretched for me—she will again. One finger will bring a whimper. Two, a needy gasp and moan from deep in her chest. Three, the pained cry tearing from her throat will end on a groan of helplessness and lust.

Even then I won't stop.

My hips have a life of their own, chasing the grip of my hand, begging with every thrust for me to hurry and finish this.

Four, with four I'll break her. I'll leave no part of her inexperienced cunt unclaimed. And she'll never run from me again.

"Jesus Christ." The words escape on a harsh gasp. I clutch the edge of the tub, fucking my fist until my balls seize up so tight, the tension grips my throat, choking out my ability to make a sound. My release sweeps violently through me, robbing me of all sanity and reason.

My head falls back, my chest heaving... the echo in my

head so loud I don't hear Grigori pushing open the door to the crypt.

"Uh, boss," he says, his eyes landing on me in the tub and sliding away as quickly as possible.

They already question my sanity most days, seeing me folded up in a waterless claw-foot tub, my gasping breaths leaving no doubt as to exactly what I've been up to.

He is just smart enough to pretend he doesn't know what I have just done.

"What?" I bark, my hand covered in cum that will definitely go to waste. Grigori definitely doesn't want to see exactly what I would have done with it.

"We found her."

"Another spotting by someone who doesn't know just what she looks like?"

"No. Not this time," he says, daring a glance at me, a smile curving his lips. "She used her credit card."

I shoot up, my fucking cock still in my hand. "Fuck."

Grigori holds up a hand, shielding his eyes. "How about I meet you in Nikolaj's office in ten?"

"Yeah, shit."

He slips out the door and I hurry to clean myself up and right my pants. In a matter of minutes, I exit the crypt and make my way along the catacomb to the false wall connecting a series of newly built tunnels. Nikolaj paid a small fortune and bartered a lifetime's worth of favors to build the intricate system. Snaking it as far up as the financial district where his bar, Evolutions, hosts some of the most successful businessmen in the city.

At any given moment, we can retreat underground through any one of our forty entry points, and move over about half of Manhattan.

The refuge made up of catacombs and tunnels offers

stealth protection when the odds stack against us. Until about six months ago, his army practically lived entirely underground. However, with alliances comes wealth and Nikolaj has an uncanny ability to draw even the most skeptical of the influential elite into his inner circle.

The connections allow him to secure five different safe houses throughout Manhattan. The thirteenth floors no one knows exist in high-rises, all with private concealed entrances.

Despite having one of those safe houses all to myself, with every luxury I can possibly want, I still spend the majority of my time underground.

In exile.

Torturing myself.

Clinging to a past I can't change.

But maybe today I'll find a way out of my purgatory once and for all.

Clinging to the steep metal stairs that lead to the storage closet of Evolutions, I pull myself to the narrow space tucked behind the hot water heater. Smoothing my jacket, I cross the hall to Nikolaj's office. My men stand on either side of the door, their hands folded in front of them, the absolute picture of calm.

Deceptive that view. Tension fills the room as Nikolaj paces with his cell pressed to his ear. When he hangs up, he glares up at me. "About fucking time, Malikov."

I'll let him get away with that because he fears for her as much as I do. "Where is she?"

"About four hours north of here. I called the store where she used her card. The pharmacist who checked her out said she was nervous. Looking over her shoulder a lot." He flattens his palms against his desk, his rigid shoulders rippling with tension. "She had no reason to think we'd found her so she's not worrying about us, but she's worried about someone."

We'll need more men than I took to Pennsylvania yesterday. If she is in danger, there is only one way to go in... with an army. "Do we have footage to be sure it's her this time?"

"Yes, and it's her."

"You're positive?"

Nikolaj's head snaps up and he shoots me a steely glare. "She's my fucking sister. What the hell do you think?"

Our eyes lock in a quiet standoff, neither of us relenting. I've held power in this family for too long to cower to Nikolaj, and he rides the confidence of knowing that he is second only to his brother Vlad.

"I have fifty men arriving in"—he glances down at his watch—"less than ten minutes and then we leave." He flips his laptop closed and pulls an extra gun from his drawer. I know he already has one at his back and another strapped to his ankle.

"We?"

He doesn't look at me, just continues to prepare. "Yes, me and my men."

"What about your meeting tonight with the governor? He flew back just to meet with you. You good with him thinking you just fucked off and didn't give a shit?"

"It's family. He'll understand."

"And I'm not family? Blood never mattered between us before, but now it does? I was good enough to spend three months tearing apart Paris looking for her through every connection she had while going to school there. I was good enough to go yesterday, the first time we actually had a potential sighting, but today, no? What the fuck's going on, Nikolaj?"

He shoves a hand through his dark hair. "You locked yourself up in that fucking crypt again," he bites out.

"What the fuck does that have to—"

Sharp, hard eyes flash and settle into a glare that has made many men at Nikolaj's mercy piss themselves in fear.

I am not many men.

"Since we lost her, if you're not in that fucking crypt, you're leaving a swath of bodies in the wake of your fucking rampages. You're out of control. And when you're not, you're distracted and off-balance. Angry."

Grigori's eyes flicker in my direction. The bastard.

I hate that Grigori saw me spiraling. I'll never be able to forget what he witnessed. Nor will he. But that is a problem for another day. Today, I need a win. I need this. After all, I'm the one who drove her away to begin with. Now Nikolaj wants to steal it from me.

My fists clench at my sides and my teeth grind, together surpassing a snarl. "You're goddamn right I'm angry. There's no 'we lost her.' I lost her!"

"Fine. How can I count on you to not lose her again?" His voice has gone deathly calm, the picture of control while I have none.

In two strides, I have my fingers locked around his neck and he has a gun to my forehead. "Fuck you, kid."

She belongs to me. She always belongs to me. Even if she never lets me touch her again and we bury what happened between us... she'll still belong to me.

Fuck.

I let go of his neck, but he never wavers with the aim of his gun.

"If you fuck this up, Malikov... I swear, I won't think twice before putting a bullet in your head myself." He drops his weapon, laying it flat on the desk between us. "I'm trusting you one last time. Now fuck off and get our girl."

CHAPTER

15

Nikoletta

I spot the pinched expression on Faith's face, the worry bracketing her mouth, and know exactly what has her on edge. Leaving the babies alone. When Elijah and I get back, I nod to her as confirmation that I've done it. I activated reinforcements, calling for help the only way I can. Not knowing when they'll arrive adds to anxiety already thrumming through us from what Elijah did to Regan last night. Faith's intuition screams at her to stay with those babies.

Her every instinct thus far where they are concerned has been spot-on, so I have to trust in this.

I reach for her, giving her a quick, hard hug. "Regan and I can get the dishes tonight, go up to Lexi and Alex. I'll be up soon."

We'd spent endless nights talking into the wee hours when Lexi and Alex were first born. She hammered me with endless questions about my life as a Bratva princess to keep herself awake while she nursed. She'd had the benefit of distance listening to these stories, but soon, the buffer will be gone. Best to enjoy some quiet time now.

Mafia families fight a common enemy or enemies who

conspire against us from beyond our massive gates. Our family is no different, but it is the war my father set in motion on the inside keeping us balancing on a knife's edge at all times.

My father hates his wife and covets his lover, mine and Nikolaj's mother. Elena hates him right back. She definitely hates me because hearing my name—the same as my mother's—never lets her forget that marrying her pussy was a business deal, not desire. Vlad, the child between them, hates anyone he sees as a threat to his birthright.

A fact he never lets his half siblings forget.

The tension between Nikolaj and Vlad had been fed and stoked every day, a game of sorts for my father's entertainment. Maybe that's why our father had insisted we live with him full time. To amuse him.

I never quite figured out if Vlad had been born a demented fuck or if over the course of time, little by little, this relentless, poisonous competition bled into a normal heart and turned him into the complete monster he'd become.

Faith's eyes lit with excitement listening to every sordid detail as though being read a dark fairy tale before bed. My experiences created an almost innocent fascination. Her distance from my harsh reality, the impossibility of it all, lulled her into a sense of safety.

Despite what her father and brother had done to her, she's lived a sheltered life. She's never had to live within a gruesome game of chess where the pieces on the board have heartbeats, and removing the defender means spilling real blood, leaving behind stains impossible to scrub clean. She's never lived bound by the twisted power constricting her year after year, until it becomes impossible to fill her lungs.

I should have prepared her better for this. For what is to come.

"Faith..."

With a hand on the newel post and her first foot on the bottom stair, she turns.

"When they get here, follow my lead. Don't say anything." I have no idea who will lead the charge. It should be my brother, Nikolaj. Accepting my fate will be a whole hell of a lot easier if it is him.

But I know Konstantin. He'll go to great lengths to take the lead on this. To be the first one to get his hands on me. I'll only know how to play it when I lay eyes on him again, his face telling me everything I need to know.

My gut plummets, as though shoved over the first drop on a roller coaster, at the thought of seeing him again. Looking him in the eye after I told him every vulnerable truth about my feelings for him. Only to have him lie, tell me what I wanted to hear, and take what I offered.

And still the look on his face, the absolute wonder and possession I can't get out of my head softens the sharp edge of betrayal and sets butterflies fluttering through my stomach.

Oh, fuck him. Fuck him all the way to hell for taking me so fucking completely, there is no way another man can touch me without my comparing the two. Only to have anyone other than Konstantin come up severely lacking every single time.

She nods and gives me a soft smile. Maybe the last soft smile I'll ever see grace her face. Because my world devours goodness like hers. It tears a huge chunk away at first... a warning of what is to come, shocking the naive out of the safety of the life they knew before. Then it gnaws bit by bit, tearing every bit of innocence and hope.

Soon... very soon, she'll learn firsthand the bitterness of raw poison flowing behind the shiny veneer. And all evidence of the fairy tale she's built in her mind will disintegrate before my eyes.

NIKOLETTA

An hour later, with the last of the dishes put away, I walk Regan up to our room where we have kept her since Elijah raped her. With a promise to be back in just a few minutes, I head for the kitchen and begin gathering hand towels, linen dishrags, tablecloths, and oven mitts to run through the wash.

It all seems so foreign to me now, the chores I've grown used to, knowing this will be the last time I'll do them. They'll come tonight. My brother will never risk leaving me here until dawn. He'll know that using his card is an absolute last resort and time is of the essence.

My ears prick for the slightest unfamiliar sound. Goosebumps rise on my skin as my sense of hearing heightens until even the most quiet hum turns into a loud buzzing in my skull. The sound of the refrigerator compressor kicking on makes me jump to the point my hand shoots straight to my thigh where I keep my knife.

I listen for a few more seconds and shake my head. I'm being stupid. My body is already on edge, preparing me for the transition from this formerly peaceful, secluded life to a violent world bathed in greed and blood. Ice drops into the bin from the ice maker, but this time, I take a deep breath, holding on to a sense of calm. I'll need my senses soon enough. I sure as hell don't need to waste them on the hum of appliances.

Fresh mountain air blows through the open windows facing the hillside. The subtle breeze carries the chorus of crickets, giving a sense of peace I've grown to appreciate. The sound is foreign compared to years of my life living in estates with hundreds of staff on the grounds with occasional stints in the sophisticated cities.

Rustic floorboards creak charmingly with every step, in direct opposition to the luxury I grew up with. This is real. No striving for perfection, just simple beauty with rich history.

For a second, just a second, I know what it feels like to be small in the world.

I know peace.

A hand curls around my hip as a lewd hiss echoes next to me. "I knew you'd wait down here for me."

Elijah's smug voice floats over the shell of my ear, his fingertips digging into my skin so hard I know he'll leave bruises.

I bite back my initial reaction, ignoring the itch in my fingers to draw my knife and take a chunk out of him. With him at my back, the swipe will be weak. Virtually meaningless.

No. I'm Bratva. We bide our time and strike when we can inflict the most damage.

Elijah will not get off that easy. Not after what he's done. Not after what Regan will carry for the rest of her life.

His pathetic cock presses up against my ass and I meet the force with pressure of my own. Luring him in. Making him think I want this—that I'm helpless but to chase after more contact.

When his fingers slide between my thighs, making their way higher, hesitating just short of my underwear, I shudder as disgust sweeps through me. Cocky fucker he is, he laughs, then hums in my ear, mistaking my disgust for lust.

"So hot for me," he gloats, as though he is some magnificent catch and any of us would be lucky to have his undivided attention.

Spinning in his arms, I lean back against the table's edge and curl my fingers into his shirt, dragging him closer.

His eyebrow pitches in a smug arch as he glances down at the grip I have on him. "I knew you wouldn't be like the others. You're not meek, are you, Nikoletta?"

The others... the need to avenge his victims—who knows how many—takes over. Luring him in with flirtation dies as the echo of Regan's sobs come back as though we are back in the bathroom where she scrubs herself painfully raw.

I want him exposed and vulnerable when I turn my violence on him. Dropping my hand to his waist, I flick the snap of his jeans and peel down his zipper.

With greedy eyes, he watches my hands work his jeans and underwear free, with a feigned eagerness, as though I can't bear another minute without his cock.

Fighting the shudder of disgust, I peer up at him through my lashes and offer a smile that feels so brittle I'm sure he'll recognize it. But basking in his own confidence, he misses the clues, the ones promising painful retribution.

Oblivious to the perfect storm of absolute rage building in me, he grips the base, his scrawny cock looking like an overcooked hot dog. One that has been nuked in the microwave just before bursting and left to cool and shrivel for hours on the counter. With an arrogant smirk tilting his lips, he thrusts his hips and smacks the pitiful-looking prick against my cheek.

A taste of the humiliation Regan had to have suffered spikes in me and his words—*like the others*—reminds me there are more women he's left hollowed out and shamed, carrying stains of him they'll never wash away.

My Romanoff blood and upbringing choose wrath. I let it sweep through me, embracing the violence, feeling more like myself than I have since I arrived.

With a jerk of my chin, I strike, sinking my teeth into the fleshy top of his thigh until the coppery taste of blood blooms on my tongue. He screams, the high-pitched sound ending on a whine before I grab ahold of his balls and dig my fingertips into where the delicate skin connects to his groin. My nails, although short, still have a bite. I grip him in my fist, digging them into the fragile area where they meet his body. The feral look I aim at his pain-filled eyes has him fighting to scramble away, but no, he won't get off that easy.

I hear it then, a sound I can't identify, but foreign all the same. As though the night has come to life, rippling with chaos and intent. If I want to make him pay, I have to do it now so the suffering inflicted is my trophy, and mine alone.

Elijah stumbles back, coughing and wheezing, his hands frantically pushing against mine as he fights to break my grip.

"You raped her," I say through gritted teeth.

"No, I—she wanted—" His scream of pain cuts off his denial as I twist, sinking my nails deeper into his skin.

"She wanted?" I shove him back by his balls until he drops into the wooden chair. "Don't you dare try to tell me she wanted it."

"I—"

"No." I slide my knife from my thigh, the light glinting off the blade before I press it into the skin of his neck, the pressure just enough to promise pain.

"She wanted her body to be her own," I seethe.

"She wanted the fucking choice." The skin on his throat splits under the pressure of the blade resting against his vulnerable skin. It takes everything in me to hold back. To keep myself from ending him quickly. Slicing into his artery is a mercy I'll never give him.

"She wanted it to be for love." I lean over him, his blood staining my lips, trickles of it drying where it runs down my chin. My words end in a vicious growl. In a fraction of a second, the knife at his neck is gone, flipped in my grip. I smile at him then, an evil smile that has him making one more futile attempt at lunging away.

Then everything happens at once. My ultimate power and my greatest weakness converging.

Soldiers swathed in black burst through the windows, leaving a shattered spray of glass in their wake.

The pounding footsteps of the army surrounding the building echo through the night.

The front door flies open, Konstantin's massive height and wide, powerful shoulders dwarfing the doorway as he bursts through, guns drawn, eyes absolutely savage and locked right on me.

Pain slashes at my heart.

Every betrayal delivered by my father, Vlad, and finally, the man possessing me with his gaze alone, right at this very second, merging into a tight ball of hatred.

I channel my rage and stab my knife into the space between us. Pure instinct guiding my aim.

His eyes widen in battle between shock and terror, until shock wins, giving him one last reprieve before agony robs him of breath.

The blade drives through Elijah's shriveled pathetic cock, before piercing clean through his balls, where it lodges with purpose and irrepressible violence in the wood under him.

My heart thunders in my chest, the only sound now of Elijah's crying and my heaving breaths until Konstantin's deep voice, like delicious grit over velvet, utters three words I both hate and love.

"That's my girl."

CHAPTER

16

Konstantin

Dark-espresso hair I'd recognize anywhere hangs tousled down her back, the light gleaming off the strands. Shorter pieces frame her face, clinging to her bloodstained lips and the rivulets trailing down her chin.

Her searing gaze snaps to mine. Golden eyes narrow and flash with pure hatred.

Angry, powerful, and... alive.

Relief sweeps through me, burning over my skin, making my head swim with the rush. Whether she is aiming the hatred at her victim or both of us, I can't tell. We'll find out soon enough, and sick bastard I am, I hope a good dose of hatred is mine. Oh, the ways I want to spark her fury just to watch her turn her into this.

Stripped bare, at my mercy... and me at hers.

Always at hers.

Chaotic energy brews within me, a combination of helplessness, betrayal, and fury, building with every day she's been gone. Now it rules me entirely. Having her before me should have quieted the storm, but no—I remain trapped between two souls. One dark, the other pitch-black—vying for control in one body.

But on one thing, those opposing forces agree. They want to punish her for running.

"If you've made it your mission to be the single biggest pain in my ass, child, you've succeeded."

Her eyes narrow to slits, an angry hiss sliding from her lips.

Ah, so she doesn't like being reduced to nothing more than a rebellious kid. Like she gave me a fucking choice. If I don't, she'll know just how much she means to me and how deep she'd cut me, by running away.

To give her any of those truths will be handing her power when she already has far too much over me. Power I will take back.

My men fan out along the perimeter around us. I keep both guns in my hands, but lower them to my sides. Keeping my eyes on her, I take measured steps behind her victim. Stopping directly behind him while she stands directly in front of him, I give her a devious grin. The very next step I take, she mirrors my movements in the opposite direction.

We slowly circle her victim and each other. Hunter to predator, predator to prey. A rather delicate hierarchy.

My eyes trace over every part of her. Her sundress caressing sun-kissed skin and hugging new curves that have blossomed during our time apart. The material brushes her thigh, just above her knees as she moves.

Late summer in the country looks fucking phenomenal on her.

My palms itch to teach her a painful lesson about taking off without a trace. Fucking off to wherever she damn well pleases in a world where she is hunted, but too naive, too fucking stubborn to realize it.

A lesson leaving her bare ass red, the flames of hell licking at her skin from the thrashing I'll give her.

The mutilated man at her mercy has finally stopped screaming. His pleading eyes meet mine as his chest puffs out with some sort of authority. "You've gotta help me, man. These whores are crazy... and she's the worst one of—"

A buzz skitters over my skin. I bare my teeth and lunge, my gun aimed right at his head, making the words die on his lips. "The fuck did you just call her?"

I catch movement out of the corner of my eye. Before I can shift my focus, Nikoletta reaches around, yanks the knife free from the man's balls, and aims the lethal, bloody tip of the knife right at me as she approaches.

"He's mine," she snarls, her eyes burning with deadly warning. She takes one more step and settles the tip of her blade against my belly, pressing it firmly into my jacket. "If you kill him, I kill you. Got it?"

My gaze drops down to the mutilated flesh between his legs before meeting her gaze once again.

What has he done to bring out such savageness in her? Spilling blood where he is most vulnerable... has it always been there, brewing in the recesses? Or has something, or someone, sparked this viciousness in the time we were apart?

Jealousy slices through me. The idea that anyone else can claim credit for this side of her has rage curling in my gut.

Ruthlessness is born out of education or desperation.

Under me, it would be an education. Under him... I study him, his position, the wounds.

She has him at her mercy. Powerless and small. An eye for an eye.

My blood runs cold.

Desperation.

Rape.

Burning hatred slithers through my gut. The thought of anyone touching her, having her—stealing from her, sends a surge of rage coursing through me so far beyond anything I've indulged in during my darkest days.

I search over her with new eyes. Looking for clues to the truth of it, but she's changed in the time she's been gone. She stares blankly at me, with slightly hooded eyes, her bored gaze fueling my temper. She's mastered keeping her mask firmly in place no matter what or who blindsides her.

She may have purposely tipped us off so we could find her, but we'd be stupid to let that detail trick us into thinking she is powerless.

It was a calculated decision.

God, look at her. Just when I think I've seen all of her, every single side, I find her like this. Coiled with deadly aggression, ready to strike.

Bathed in blood and completely unshakeable.

She is no one's damsel in distress.

Now that I know this version of her exists, a modern-day Pandora's box of sorts splits wide open. I'll be helpless to stop myself from warring with her, anything to seek a taste of her wrath.

I'll let her spill my blood just to use it to anoint her full lips.

This Nikoletta will never be reduced to dressing up in elegant gowns, her ears dripping with jewels. A pretty ornament on display in our Bratva world.

No.

She'll demand to stand with us. And if she chooses to do it wrapped in extravagance, she'll do so because the posh elegance makes for the perfect mask.

There'll be no keeping my distance. Fuck loyalty. I took her virginity. I'll take every other first too.

If she has any left.

Because what if he stole them? The precious firsts that should have been hers to give. The ones I would have made mine, until my collection is complete.

Respecting her right to exact vengeance stops me from lashing out for my own satisfaction on the heels of my worst nightmares playing out in vivid color in my head.

Her screams. Tears. Excruciating pain. An inescapable humiliation diminishing every experience in her future.

The monster lurking in me, the beast I fed every day she's been gone, refuses to recede into the shadows even though we found her. The man she knew, stoic with honor, bound to duty, died on that altar with her virginity. I've morphed into something new. Darker. Grittier. With nothing to lose, I've become an aggressor to the core.

That sick fiend, haunted by what might have happened to her, wants to see what she does next.

I lower my gun and take a step back. "Don't let us stop you, Pcholka. How does it end?"

I want her violence.

I crave her reckoning.

For him. For me.

Not one to give the enemy an advantage, she pierces the knife straight down between his legs. He screams, the high-pitched sound piercing our ears as the blade stabs through his cock and balls, impressively close to the holes she left the first time.

Blood pools under her enemy, but not enough to signal his impending death.

She glances down at her handiwork, a look of dissatisfaction crossing her face. Her hostile gaze crawls from his mutilated cock and balls up his chest before landing on his sniveling face. A look of contemplation lights her features.

Her eyes narrow in a glare, lingering on his fingers, then his eyes.

My pulse kicks up. I suck in a breath, my chest expanding, my shoulders straightening as curious energy zips through me. I need to see her in action, the carnage she leaves behind when she metes out punishment.

Take the eyes, Nikoletta. Do it.

A wicked smile curves her lips as her slim fingers grip the knife once again. Grasping a hunk of his hair at the crown, she yanks his head back. Staring straight into his eyes, she rocks the blade back and forth as though she needs the scissoring motion to free the knife from the chair under him. But there is no way she needs to move it that much.

No, she is torturing him. Keeping him nice and distracted.

If Nikolaj were here, there'd be hell to pay for allowing his sister to do something so barbaric. Something reserved for the men in our world. We've kept her sheltered for so long and he'll never have the chance to see another side of her. But I've had a glimpse, the night she put her virginity up for sale so she could leave this world behind. So desperate to escape, she plunged, bleeding, into shark-infested waters.

We've been wrong sheltering her. We should have been training her. Nurturing her untapped potential. Turning her need to flee into a desire to stay.

The knife pulls free. She flips it in her hand with deft fingers. Wasting no time, she sinks the tip into the corner of his eyeball and pops it from the socket. With a slash of her arm, the orb slides free from the tip of the blade and tumbles to the floor.

Nostrils flaring, she drops the knife between his legs and slice into his thigh. Hot blood gushes from the gaping wound. Proof she hit the femoral artery.

Pride tilts her chin as she throws him to the floor, one eye still intact, so he'll have no choice but to see what she's done to him. He slinks pathetically away, fingers groping the wood, his gushing leg dragging behind him. His final moments, he spends searching for the eye she plucked from the socket.

When he collapses, what little energy he has left spent, Nikoletta rolls him over onto his back and kicks his feet open. With a gritty snarl more animallike than human, she delivers a nasty kick right between the legs.

The rest of my men begin filing in then, bringing with them the residents they've collected. Gazes land on the mutilated corpse, a few gasps break free, but beyond that, no one seems surprised to see the destruction before them.

If anything, most of them look... relieved.

I swipe a hand down my face. What a fucking mess.

A pretty pink blooms on Nikoletta's cheeks. My palms itch to reach for her. To claim her. But these men have no idea the lines we crossed, leaving us in the confines of goddaughter and godfather.

Adrenaline rules in the aftermath, leaving her pupils blown and her breaths coming in rapid pants.

Oh, she'll be in this position again. I'll make sure of it. But this time, without an army of witnesses. Only the two of us... and I'll tap into the perfect storm brewing and fuck every last drop of energy out of her.

"Nikoletta..." Her name, almost rusty with disuse, cut through the thick silence. The first time I've uttered it since the last time I saw her.

Her golden eyes lock on mine at the sound. Her head tilts and her jaw clenches tight. Tension rolls off her as she takes a step toward me. And then another.

Six in total.

The final step is punctuated with her closed fist delivering an uppercut directly under my chin that sets my teeth rattling with the force of it.

Gasps fill the room and my men grow more rigid, more alert, never taking their eyes from her. She may be the mission, but they won't stand by indefinitely and let her show such disrespect.

"Don't you ever say my fucking name again." She delivers the warning with a dangerous edge. The girl she had been, dead and gone, leaving her bitter and hostile.

We face off, her feet planted wide apart, her hands curled into fists at her side with no sign she felt the contact her knuckles made with my jaw. She is good. I'll give her that. Not even a flicker for the ache sure to be radiating through her hand for days to come.

I should have known she'll never deliver an open-palmed slap. It would be too predictable. So incredibly pedestrian and beneath her.

Physically weaker... sure, but she won't let it deter her from hanging with the big boys and delivering payback in the same crude way.

Stepping into her, I force her to tip her head back if she wants to maintain her warning glare. I snake my fingers around the back of her neck and bury them in the hair at her nape.

My fury for the cheap shot and relief at touching her for the first time in far too long war within me. The force of my grip surely causes pain where my fist locks in those silky strands.

Settling my cheek to her temple, I suck in a deep breath, my chest expanding, lungs filling with the scent of her.

She stiffens, a gasp lodging in her throat.

I close my eyes for the briefest moment as a hum of pleasure escapes me.

So. Fucking. Affected.

By me. By my touch.

We'll hash out our attraction soon enough, but first... the rabid little shit needs to be reminded exactly who is in charge here.

She's the one who led us to her. If she wants to remain in control, she should have stayed lost to us. If my putting her in her place delivers pain, so be it. She's lucky I don't inflict more.

Oh, and I will... just not here. Not before prying eyes.

The hurt I'll deliver won't be a fraction of the agony I've been through searching for her.

"Be very, very careful, little girl," I say, watching goosebumps bloom as my breath caresses her silky skin. "You're not the only one who's changed since we saw each other last. Push me hard enough and you may just find out the man who indulged you no longer exists."

Her fingers curl into my shirt, the only thing keeping her nails from scoring my flesh. "I'm not my mother."

I discreetly trail my nose along her hairline from temple to the shell of her ear. Her breasts heave with her rapid breaths, the round swells splattered crimson and straining against the edge of her bodice.

Blood rushe below my belt and I swell impossibly hard, the evidence of my want concealed between us. I discreetly press my length even harder against her stomach.

"No, Pcholka... you're not. Not even close," I say, knowing she'll misunderstand my words, assuming I find her lacking when compared to her mother. The woman I thought I had loved, but it turns out, was nothing more than an object between two prideful, competing men.

Her breath catches. When it breaks free, she snarls with hatred. But it is the shaky exhale, the way she bites down on her lip as she pierces me with lust-filled eyes that give her away.

The encore? The feel of her body discreetly thrusting against my hard cock.

She can pretend she hates me, but her primal reactions to my proximity expose her for a liar. My goddaughter's body craves me inside her.

If it comes down to a battle of wills between her head and her base animal instincts, those animal instincts will win every single time.

With every thrust, she'll question if I'm fucking her or fucking the idea of her mother. And still, she'll spur me on. She won't be able to help herself.

Scenting the blood coating her, the urge to drag my tongue through the deep valley of her breasts swiftly follows. I yearn to savor the reckoning she so beautifully delivered, now a masterpiece painting her skin.

"You are so much more than your mother," I say quietly, the words only for us. "You're magnificent." Releasing her from my painful grip, I tip her chin up just a bit more with my thumb. "Now, we go."

She pulls her chin out of my grip with a firm shake of her head. "Not until we make arrangements for them."

"Pcholka...

"No!" She yanks free of my grip and glares up at me. "Elijah owned this property... with him dead, these people will lose their home. For some of them, the only home they've ever known. If you want me, you have to protect them."

I snake my hand out in a flash and wrap it around her wrist. With a quick yank, I spin and tug her back against me. Her back to my front. "You can march that sweet ass of yours out there, or I'll haul you out in the least dignified way I can think up," I promise, grinding my cock shamelessly against her with every word. "Either way, you are coming with me."

Craning her neck to the side, she glares up at me and makes sure she looks me dead in the eye. My fierce little goddaughter will not hide, not from anyone. "You're not the boss of me. You're just my ride out of here."

Tightening my hold, only our thundering hearts between us, I drop my voice low with warning, my lip grazing her ear, making her shudder in my arms. "Your ride? Just your ride, huh? You just wait, little girl. I'll show you exactly what kind of ride I am. Now move it."

A sexy little whimper breaks free. She tries to smother it with a frustrated growl. "Not without a promise from Nikolaj that he will make sure this land goes to them. Call him," she snaps.

I maintain my hold on her, though I know if she attempts to break free and run, she'll never make it past my men who have every exit protected.

Her pulse in her wrist hammers under my fingertips. Her golden eyes blaze with pure belligerence. I hope they'll do the same when she stares up at me from her knees, with my cock choking the air out of her as I fuck her throat raw.

Because I will definitely fuck that throat raw, her tears and spit mingling before rolling down her chin under her jaw.

She'll love every single minute of how I plan to filthy her up.

With the touch of one button, still holding her wrist, I wait for Nikolaj to pick up.

"You better not be calling to tell me you lost her," he warns. The meeting with the governor sounds more like a dinner party in the background, which definitely explains his surly disposition.

"Your baby sister..." I begin, enjoying the snarl bubbling

from her throat with my use of 'baby,' "... is making bold fucking demands. You meet them or she doesn't leave."

"You're over six and half feet tall, Malikov. You outweigh her by at least a hundred pounds." The tension in his voice flees with the confirmation I have her in my grip. "But to get her out of there, after she deliberately alerted us to her whereabouts, you need promises from me? You losing your edge, old man?"

"You want me to throw her over my shoulder, her bare ass hanging out from under her dress for all of our men to see, just say the word."

"Jesus! No. Fuck." He mutters a few more choice words I can't make out. I picture him shoving his fingers through his hair in exasperation.

This is only the beginning. Wait until he gets a taste of who she's turned into. He may just tear his own hair out.

"Dammit... put her on."

I thought he might see it my way. Not that I'll ever let a single one of these men get even the barest glimpse of what is for my eyes only. Not without them paying for the glance with their life.

She snatches the offered phone from my hand and spins away, getting as far from me as she can.

I catch a few words here and there, 'you will do this for me,' 'set them up,' 'five hundred thousand'... the number that always seems to crop up since the long-ago night I bought her virginity at the cabaret for the same amount.

That fucking number, a curse and a salvation, mocking me with its existence.

Her cheeks flush more and more with her every demand. She keeps her back against the wall, just as this life taught her long ago, her gaze sweeping the room as she speaks.

Pride fills me watching her like this... her tactical stance, assertive in her commands, strategic with what words she uses to play on emotions and get what she wants. Even knowing she worked me over the same way almost a year and a half ago, and will surely work me over again, I take great satisfaction in the forceful woman she's become.

Finally, a satisfied smile curves on her lips. Her glance sweeps up to the balcony, landing on two women standing there with wary expressions on their faces and sleeping babies in their arms.

The hair on my neck stands up.

My skin prickles.

The weight of dread settling in my chest.

Fucking hell.

I already know where this is going when I hear her words clear as day. "I'm bringing friends."

CHAPTER

17

Nikoletta

Four hours in the car and still my hands shake as restless energy snaps and skitters through my veins. I can't stop shifting on the seat. My skin throbs where I mercilessly scrubbed it in the shower, much in the same way Regan had the night before.

Both of us stained by him in such different ways.

The occasional light flickers in from the streetlamps along the Hudson, dull beams cutting across my lap. Stretching out my fingers, I spot the dark lines under my nails where I haven't managed to scrub his blood clean. The glimpse takes me right back to my handiwork.

Elijah's skin splitting when I hadn't even meant to cut him yet, but satisfaction filling me just the same as blood trickled down his neck and fear lit in his eyes.

Seeing the knowledge in his eyes that this was the end, even as his body instinctively fought for survival, only made me want it all over again.

The music of his animalistic scream when my blade sliced through his flesh like a hot knife through butter, nailing him to the chair. Leaving him at my mercy.

Open. Vulnerable.

The brief taste only made me crave more.

More of his blood. More of his begging. And all of his pain.

For once, no one ruled me. I made the decisions. No more pretending to be the pretty princess or the lost little sheep trying to prove herself useful because she had nowhere else to go.

I fight to hold on to the satisfaction of payback, but the flood of feelings Konstantin's arrival brings overshadows all.

Hate, loathing, regret, and so much want I can scarcely breathe at the thought of it. And how stupid is it that I still have to fight the instinct to touch him?

My throat aches from holding back tears.

Every look from his intense dark eyes, every word from his deceptive mouth, his actions, reactions, motivations–his love for me, all of it poisoned by the cold hard truth.

I am a replacement for my mother. Worse, I am a replacement and the best form of payback at my father he can possibly get his hands on.

He must have secretly loved when I begged him to take my virginity. Oh sure, he used that honor he paraded around to feign resistance—but it was all for show. I'd been handing him more leverage than he ever could have hoped to gain. The rush of victory he must have felt when my father and Vlad walked in right after... bastard.

At least with Elijah, we all knew what we were getting. Konstantin's betrayal was a masterpiece nineteen years in the making. Thousands of lies layered one on top of another, each paper thin and delicate on their own, but together, breathtakingly destructive with their strength.

He left a gaping wound behind. Impossible to heal and always aching. He cheated me. He tarnished my first time, but it went so much farther than that. His lie by omission stole every happy memory I had of him in an otherwise oppressive, often terrifying childhood. Thousands upon thousands of deceptions—everything he taught me, every hug, every forehead kiss... all a means to an end.

Even if we never had more than our one time together, at least I had a lifetime of memories filled with him.

But now with this glaring truth exposed, I have nothing but this anguish I can't shake no matter how hard I try.

I want him to bleed for it. I want to shred his heart the way he shredded mine. Only in the aftermath of his betrayal, I have to wonder if he has one at all.

Pressing my knife against his gut ignited a twisted fantasy. One where I make him bleed. A fantasy I haven't been able to get out of my head since. My heart wants his pain and punishment, but my body, the fucking traitor... just wants him.

My skin prickles, heating with awareness. Before I can stop myself, I glance up and lock eyes with the snake.

The intensity I find there brings me right back to that altar, with his fingers flexing on my throat when the thin thread of control snapped and he possessed me, taking anything and everything he wanted.

I close my eyes, and like every other time they closed since that day, he is there. Rough and wild, drinking me in, unblinking as though he can't bear to miss a second.

Tearing myself from the vivid memory, I squeeze my thighs together, looking for relief. Forcing my eyes open, I find him still staring, only this time awareness flares in his eyes, a flush spreads over his cheeks as though he's been in my head with me the whole time.

He could learn a thing or two about subtlety.

His eyes have burned through me at least two of the four-hour ride into Manhattan. Now this. And every time Konstantin fixes his gaze on me, Grigori aims a curious one at him.

His man is putting the pieces together, and the more people who know something had happened between us, the more danger we'll be in. In this world, not only is he my godfather and once my father's best friend, which is forbidden enough, but I was promised to another man. Once word spreads that I am back, they'll expect the promise to be fulfilled. It doesn't matter how long I've been gone or what has happened in that time.

It won't matter that Vlad made the promise, despite my being under Nikolaj's protection. To the Petrovs, a family rooted in antiquated traditions, I am nothing more than a piece of property unfairly kept from them. Either Nikolaj turns me over to Ivan Petrov, or Ivan will bring a war to Nikolaj's doorstep.

Does he have the men he needs to win that kind of war? Or will we be forced underground indefinitely? I glance down at Lexi's soft, rosy cheek and take in the peaceful expression on her round little face. How can we bring these babies underground with no fresh air, no sunlight?

City lights come into view, looking deceptively far away. We'll be winding between skyscrapers in less than ten minutes.

Tugging the elastic free from my damp hair, I shake the heavy bun loose and massage my aching scalp. Grit coats my eyes, making them burn. A dull ache pulses in the back of my skull, the throb growing stronger with every passing minute.

I loathe the idea of talking to him. I definitely am not ready to hear his voice, the deep, sexy rasp always on the edge of more. Like he's constantly on the prowl, waiting to be prodded into letting loose a roar.

But I have to know. I have to prepare now if we are heading into the dark. "Where are we going?"

His hard eyes meet mine in the mirror. "Somewhere safe."

I swallow the ball of trepidation creeping up my throat and hold his stare. I will not show fear, dammit. I just carved up a guy and here I am, on the verge of panic at the thought of the narrow pitch-black entry point Grigori led me to the last time. "Underground?"

Fuck.

My voice wobbles just a fraction, but I feel it and the way his eyes soften tells me he sure as hell hears it.

"No, you'll have all the light you need, Pcholka," he says quietly.

My heart pinches.

Don't you dare make me feel anything for you, you bastard.

My throat grows impossibly thick as stupid girl tears I overpowered before come rushing back. Tears that won't change one damn thing. Tears I absolutely refuse to give him. Fixing my gaze out the tinted window, I watch the Hudson disappear from view as the city rises up around us, swallowing us whole.

Konstantin makes a call, likely getting security clearance before our arrival. I take the opportunity to lean over and shake Faith awake.

"Hey, we'll be there soon," I whisper.

"Already?" she asks, pushing herself upright. Her focus goes straight to the babies. "I swear I just blinked."

I give her a reassuring smile. Alex and Lexi's safety is the one thing I'm sure about at the moment. They won't remember a thing and one thing I know to my bones, these men, no matter how I feel about this world, about them— they will stand before the enemy and take a spray of bullets before they ever let anything happen to a child.

Faith turns in her seat to face me. "So, are we headed underground?" Her lips twitch and no doubt the details I told her of my night in the crypt with Konstantin plays in high def through her mind.

"No. This will be new to both of us." Just as I say the words, Grigori slows and turns into a parking garage under a massive high-rise that has to be at least eighty stories. Concrete closes in around us. I wince, waiting for the sound of the roof scraping when we bounce over a bump, but Grigori winds his way through with confidence, and the sound never comes.

Around and around corners we go, winding down until we have to be at least three stories underground. My heart creeps up in my throat. I'm not convinced this is better than the dark hole Grigori prodded me down the last time.

He pulls to a smooth stop in front of a set of elevator doors. When they slide open, six men, almost as big as Konstantin, step out. Not an easy feat since he is over six and half feet tall. Clearly, Nikolaj made impressive progress in building his empire and army while I've been gone.

Lining up shoulder to shoulder, three on the right, three on the left, they form a corridor of sorts from the car to the doors. Not a sliver of a gap to be found. Their shrewd eyes endlessly sweep the area around us.

Konstantin climbs out, his eyes narrowed, his jaw locked. Tension rolls off him, turbulent and stifling, serving as a wordless warning. We aren't safe. Not yet.

He opens the door and motions for us to exit.

"We just need to unhitch their seats," Faith says.

He reaches out his hand to Faith. "Babies last. They're safer in the vehicle than they are out here while you climb out."

Her inner hussy surrenders to the gesture. Next thing I

know, she lays her palm in his and steps out all regal and shit with a smile on her face.

Charming bastard.

"Once you're both in the elevator, I'll pass them to you," he says as he reaches for me.

Instinct has me complying, but I freeze, my fingers just inches from his. "Don't touch me."

The muscle in his cheek jumps, but he doesn't push.

Hands braced on the doorframe for support, I jump out and turn to help with the car seats.

"Elevator, Pcholka," he bites out, popping Lexi's carry seat from the base before reaching back to do the same with Alex. "I've got it."

"How do you know how to—"

"You seriously have to ask that?" he tosses back at me with a smirk.

Apparently, he's used up all the charm on Faith, leaving me with this prick. Good to know. His attitude douses any thawing my heart may have done when he reassured me I wouldn't be trapped in the dark.

Sarcasm, a language I understand well, is exactly what I need to cling to right now. I huff out a breath. "Oh, shut up."

Dark eyebrows slash over his eyes in the way that makes me itch to land another punch. "Ass in the elevator. Now."

Preferably a punch right where the bruise has just begun forming from the first one.

I jump across the threshold, all dramatic movements, and spin back toward him, then jut out my hip. "Happy?"

"Little shit," he mutters.

"What? I didn't hear you," I say, turning my head and cupping the ear closest to him.

He opens his mouth, but whatever he planned to say dies

in his throat, the sound of squealing tires cutting off his words.

Men all move at once, shifting formation in an instinctual way until two form a blockade in front of the elevator and the other four surround the SUV.

Faith gasps next to me. I squeeze her hand and find a small gap between the men where I can just barely see what is happening.

Konstantin yanks the second car seat free. For such a big guy, he moves in a flash, bringing the babies before him side by side, where he curls over their tiny little bodies, shielding them with his.

A red sports car filled with rowdy teens careens around the corner, their hands waving out the window as they scream their way through the parking garage.

No one moves until they are out of sight. Konstantin last, and only when Grigori reassures him they aere clear.

With the men forming a corridor once again, Konstantin sweeps between them, a car seat in each hand, only handing them to us once he joins us in the elevator and the doors have closed completely.

A side panel slides open then, leading to a long, straight passageway. "We're not staying here?"

"No. It's just another entry point."

"So Nikolaj has tunnels above and below the city now?"

"Technically no, we're still under the city," he says with a hint of laughter in his voice.

The fucker.

"You shielded them like you've done it a hundred times before," Faith says as she brushes her finger over Alex's cheek.

"I have." His deep voice echoes with his answer.

"But for who?"

Glancing over his shoulder, his dark stare holding mine, the heavy silence serves as his only answer as Faith glances back and forth between us.

"Oh," she says quietly.

The minute he turns around, I let out the breath I've been holding and turn to Faith who mouths the word "sorry" to me.

Was any of it real? At least in my infancy? A memory of my mother throwing her head back and laughing flashes through my head and I have to swallow down the bile rising in my throat.

He tainted my memories of her too. Now I agonize over whether she ever felt the same for him, if they kissed, if they did more than that... my mother, the idea of her, her ghost, turns into some sort of twisted rival.

He stripped me of every bit of happiness I'd had to cling to and here he is, just leading us to who knows where, where he'll have complete access to me whenever he wants. Oh, how fucking satisfied he must be with himself right now. His victory will be temporary. I'll make sure of it.

We had to have walked at least half a mile, Konstantin offering multiple times to carry Alex and Lexi, before arriving at a nondescript gray hallway with a private elevator at the end. Konstantin presses his thumb to a screen, then his right pinky, left middle finger, his right index and ring finger at the same time and finally his left thumb.

Okay, so no one is getting in. Good to know.

The door slides open with barely a sound, everything about it screaming high-tech security and designed to draw as little attention as possible. If anyone even manages to find it.

Konstantin presses the one and only button with no designation, setting us smoothly rising. In just seconds we come to a stop, the doors sliding open to a hallway almost identical to the one we've just come from.

Another panel, a different pattern of fingerprints later, and we are in.

Soft light fills the massive room. Okay, more than a room, this is one whole corner of a single story in a high-rise.

Floor-to-ceiling windows face the mirrored windows of the building next to us.

"Um, can they see us in here?" Faith asks.

"You can see out, but they can't see in," Konstantin assures her. "I'll give you the tour after you get some sleep."

He leads us to the first bedroom and pushes open the door. Lamps burn by the bedside. Light spills into the room from the en suite bathroom, illuminating the edge of a crib in the corner.

"Another crib will be here tomorrow as well as anything else you need. Will one do for tonight?"

Faith's shoulders slump with relief. Her chin wobbles and her eyes fill with tears. "Uh, yes, um, thank you. So far they've always shared one crib so this is perfect."

Side by side, we unbuckle Alex and Lexi from their seats. When we pick them up, they both do the same baby stretch where they arch their backs and stick their booties out.

I tuck Lexi into my elbow while she makes a suckling motion with her lips, just waiting to see if she will wake up, but with just a few brushes of my finger along her cheek, she settles into sleep once again.

My heart thunders in my chest the minute we get them down. There is no avoiding this anymore and Faith's worried gaze only confirms she knows it too. She glances at Konstantin leaning against the doorway, his jacket over his forearm, his hands in his pockets, like this is the most normal thing in the world.

Her arms shoot around me, squeezing me tight. "You'll be okay, right?" she whispers.

"I'll be fine. I don't know if he will be," I say, pulling back. "I promise not to commit murder tonight. Well–another murder."

"Nikoletta will be in the room at the end of the hall. Last door on the left."

My shoulders go rigid and a fiery haze fills my vision.

He did that on purpose.

"So much for that promise to not commit another murder," Faith mutters. "Just maim him a little maybe? I kinda like him."

"Yeah, well, don't get attached."

I don't meet his eyes as I pass by him in the doorway. If I did, I might just drag what nails I have down the side of his face.

CHAPTER

18
Nikoletta

Without a word, he leads me down to the room at the end of the hall and pushes open the door. I resist sinking my elbow into his gut as I pass, but barely.

The door closes with a solid thud, but there is no way he is on the other side of it. Not a fucking chance.

Next comes the sound of the lock, the click so final, so ominous in the thick silence.

The harsh pounding of my heartbeat fills my head, but beyond it, I swear I can hear his too. Our unfinished business looms heavy between us, reducing the massive bedroom to a stifling cage.

I don't want explanations or excuses. I want to go back in time and never give myself to him. To erase the truth revealed that day.

When I learned I was completely on my own.

Not one single person cares for me or loves me just for me. They all need me for something. I am a means to an end, nothing more.

With my mouth open, ready to unleash every bit of hurt I've turned to venom in our time apart, I spin on him.

He lunges, his fingers spearing through my hair, locking on both sides of my head. A growl rises in his throat, his forearms flexing like he is fighting to hold himself back. Pressing his forehead to mine, he sucks in a deep breath, his chest swelling wide.

No, no, no, no, no... damn him.

His warm, spicy scent fills my lungs. With every exhale, his breath brushes over my lips. At his first touch, he transports me right back there, on that altar, him between my thighs, everything I ever wanted in my hands.

Just to end up the only one in the room not in on the joke.

They made a fool of me.

He made a fool of me.

I reach for the knife at my thigh, only to have him anticipate my move. Snatching my wrists, he binds them behind my back with the steely grip of one hand.

His other hand goes to my jaw in a savage hold, forcing my head back and my face up to his.

I drop my head back even farther. He doesn't get to run this shit.

"I. Hate. You," I bite out each word, waiting, hoping to see each one cut him deep.

His eyes narrow to slits as he leans in and drags the tip of his nose over the bridge of mine. "I can work with that, Pcholka." His fingers flex where they hold my wrists, the adjustment relieving the ache. "Hate means you still feel something for me, and I'm just selfish enough to take it."

He seizes my mouth in a bruising kiss. Tongue sweeping across mine, he steals total control, the way he devours me obliterating my anger and plunging me into overwhelming sensation.

The profound ache I carry finally starts to abate and I hate him for that too. Hate him being the fucking cure to my pain when he is the one who delivered the excruciating blow.

My skin burns to feel his hands on me. Shivers snake up my spine until my scalp tingles deliciously. Head swimming in him, I can't help but succumb. I'd been the one to push him in that crypt, the one to try his patience in the church.

But here and now, he is the one out of control, helpless to stop himself.

The broken part of me clings to the power in that.

A jagged growl rumbles through his throat, every single hot inch of him pressing into me. His hard chest, thick arms locking me in his hold, his hard cock driving into my stomach, even his feet cage me in, keeping me trapped against him.

Longing makes my eyes burn with hot tears. He resurrects dormant, excruciating memories of safety and love that slash ruthlessly at my heart.

My grip on my indignation slips with every glide of his firm, warm lips–embers of that foolish girl I'd been, flickering to life somewhere deep inside me.

I can't let him see her. Won't give him the satisfaction of knowing she exists somewhere. To do so will give him power and I am done giving men power over me.

He pulls back, just enough to look into my eyes. Sucking his bottom lip into his mouth, he tastes me as he cups my cheek, this thumb gliding back and forth over my skin.

Lowering his head, he brushes a reverent kiss over the corner of my mouth that has me sucking in a shaky breath.

"Nikoletta," he whispers.

My gasp ignites something in him and he plunders again, but everything inside me, all the feverish sensations racking my body turn into shards of ice, stabbing through me with a viciousness that threatens to take me to my knees.

I want him to hurt. Need him to bleed.

Pulling back just a fraction, I sink my teeth into his bottom lip and only stop when I taste his blood.

A feral growl rises out of him. He jerks away, but I haven't let go of his lip yet, so it only makes the gouge on the inside of his lip deeper, longer.

Coiling his fist in my hair, he yanks my head back.

The balm to my pain... the beautifully stunned outrage on his face.

CHAPTER

19

Konstantin

The taste of copper fills my mouth, the sting of her bite turning into a throb with a heartbeat of its own.

Nikoletta grins up at me. With a curl of her sexy pointed tongue, she sucks my blood from where it stains her pretty white teeth.

I march her back by my fierce grip on her hair, until I pin her against the wall. Dragging my thumb over the broken flesh inside my bottom lip, I come away with a thick swath of blood. "Try to suck me clean all you want, little girl, there's more where that came from."

Pinning her thigh between mine, immobilizing the weapon strapped there, I settle my thumb on the subtle dip bisecting her plump bottom lip.

She gasps, her hot breath fanning over my skin, making my cock jump against her. What would it be like to have that hot little mouth of hers wrapped around me? Her heated, rapid breaths skimming over my tight skin. Those sharp teeth dragging along the veins of my cock, tempted to bite into me until she draws blood.

Pain is all I know.

Biting me?

That is just a flicker of foreplay.

I skim down her lip, tugging it before letting it snap back. Eyes locked on the fire in hers, I anoint her with my blood. First, along the divot under her mouth. Then over the curve of her chin. Finally, streaking crimson along the underside of her jaw to the column of her throat.

"Spill my blood and I'll just paint you in it so you don't forget who you belong to." I dip my mouth to the hollow at the base of her throat and lick, slowly working my way along the trail I left, every swipe of my tongue bathing my blood from her velvety skin.

When I reach her bottom lip, I stop and study her. Daring her with my eyes to lick the last vestiges of me from her flesh. Locked in a silent standoff, I search for a flicker of the woman who wanted me just over a year ago. The one who begged me, refusing to take no for an answer.

"You can't find her, can you?" she asks with a quiet confidence she'd found in our time apart.

This proud little seductress crawls straight into my head and taps into my greatest weakness, taunting me with it.

"Pcholka…"

"That stupid, gullible little girl you're looking for—she's dead."

"She was never stupid or gullible," I murmur, my eyes roaming every last inch of her face and stopping at where my blood had begun to dry on her lip. "But she is dead… because I killed her."

As much as this woman before me slays me in every possible way, I grieve for the piece of her forever lost— destroyed when I surrendered to this hunger pulsing between us.

I gave her father and brother a way to devastate her. What I did, no different than had I put a loaded gun in Vlad's hand with my blessing to end her entirely.

Her increasingly glassy eyes slide away, telling me despite what I ruined, she hasn't gone completely cold to the world around her. That is something.

For tonight, it will have to be enough.

Relaxing my hold on her hair, I cup her face, my thumbs lazily gliding back and forth over her cheeks. When her tears threaten to spill over, I press a kiss to her forehead, breathe her in one last time, and leave the room before I can see them fall.

Because if I witness them, she'll just hate me for that too.

I find Grigori at the island in the kitchen, a highball glass of whiskey tipped to his lips and another beside him.

Taking a seat, I wrapped my fingers around the glass, and he pounces.

"She's dangerous for you," he says quietly, his inquisitive gaze flicking to me.

I knock back two solid gulps and relish the burn searing down my throat and warming my belly. "Protecting her has always been dangerous."

He grunts and turns back to his drink, his silent judgment hanging between us.

"Whatever it is, just fucking say it."

He drums his fingers on the granite, every cascade of his fingertips grating on my nerves. "That's not what I meant and you know it."

"So what did you mean?" I slam my glass down, sending the liquor sloshing over the rim and down my hand. "Now's your chance, Grigori. For the next minute, I'm not your boss. You have exactly sixty seconds to say whatever the fuck it is you're desperate to say. You go a second over, I'll cut your fucking tongue out right here and make you watch as I grind it down my garbage disposal."

He tilts his head, his eyebrow shooting up, completely unaffected by my threat. "You love her."

"Of course I love her, she's my goddaughter. You just lost three seconds stating the obvious."

"Nice try," he says with a mocking laugh he'd never dare aim at me had I not given him this chance to lay it all out in the open.

"You stopped loving her as just a goddaughter in that crypt. I didn't need to see it to know what happened. You fucked her, and you still want her. But she just as soon put that knife she carries in you than let you get close. The question is why."

He slides off the stool and downs the rest of his drink. "She's not the girl she was. You saw what she did to that guy. She's a killer. Maybe more of a killer than any of us. So now you have her, but to what end? She'll kill you, or Nikolaj will find out and he'll kill you, but not before this new war costs lives."

Without another word, he sets his glass in the sink and heads for the door.

Nailed it in one. Fuck.

The minute he slips out, I hang my head in my hands, drag my fingers through my hair, and turn my gaze to the hallway leading to her.

Don't do it. Don't you fucking do it.

I refill the glass, this time to the rim, planning to get stinking drunk so I don't cave to my instincts to go in that room. Instead, I head for the sofa. The cushion yields under my weight and I lean back with a sigh.

Exhausted but too keyed up to sleep, I flick the small peg tucked under the upholstery along the arm. The secret compartment I had custom built into the side slides open, revealing a Glock, three spare fully-loaded magazines, and Nikoletta's diary.

I definitely have my work cut out for me if Faith will be here for any length of time with her babies. They look to be only a few months old, but soon they'll be crawling, then they'll be into everything. Which means I have about twenty hidden guns in this place that need to be secured to protect them.

Head swimming with my impending to-do list, I reach for the soft bound journal, but stop just inches away. My ears prick, listening for the sound of water running or the soft muffled sound of feet padding across the floor, any movement, but only a dead silence greets me in return. The chances of Nikoletta coming out here where she knows she'll have to face me are slim to none. Sheer stubbornness alone will keep her sweet ass in that room. So, I take advantage of the last bit of privacy I may have for a long damn time.

Settling back, I turn the lamp up a notch and run my fingers over the cool, supple leather, holding myself back. When I finally open the pages, her will would tease the air. A form of torture I seem to crave.

Whiskey clutched in my hands like a safety blanket, I hold the journal on my thigh and fan the pages. A sick satisfaction fills me every time that rich, bloodred ink flashes by. I've been so focused on reading the entries about me that I haven't noticed the pages with pink hearts until they streak past.

Setting my drink aside, I flip page after page, backtracking, curious what got my Pcholka drawing hearts with such flair.

When I finally find it, my gaze locks on three words that have me going rigid with a swift flood of jealousy.

My first kiss...

I have no right to be jealous. None. I never thought of her like this at the time. I never would have. But fuck if my heart doesn't despise the three-decade divide between us that means some rites of passage holding a place in her heart will not include me.

With my better judgment off somewhere cavorting with the liquor I've consumed, I start reading.

Hey, it's me again...

Do you know how hard it is to have your first kiss when you're the most guarded teen on the planet? Yeah, well, let me tell you... it means that you have several near misses and then finally, FINALLY, you get the opportunity, but... with your brother's best friend of all people.

Okay, let's be real... everyone would freak if they knew. He's like eight years older than me.

Try ten, you little shit.

Although, if they knew who I'd been crushing on all this time, they'd welcome Logan with open arms.

So, ummm, can we talk about this guy for a minute? Because wow!

Logan Rhodes is the definition of Mister All-American. Gorgeous. Smart. Athletic, and, well, powerful. He's a member of the secret society Nikolaj joined in college and that alone earned him a good dose of respect, a healthy amount of fear, and a mountain of opportunities beyond what he already had.

But he's not an asshole about it. He's quietly observant and understated. Loyal and protective.

Being in this family, constantly imprisoned, you'd think I'd avoid powerful guys, but there's just something about him. He does everything with confidence, but he's not so affected by that power. He's all easy humor and encouragement that makes you feel like you can do anything too.

This was his first time coming to a family event, just to come across me fending off Callum Heath's wandering hands and his way too eager mouth. I never should have gone to the gardens with him, but for a minute I thought I could just go, get my first kiss out of the way, and move on.

Plus, it was my sweet 16 and Vlad was off on some trip to who knows where. Probably schmoozing on some yacht. I was riding the high of not having to fend Vlad off at every turn. And with how fucked up Vlad is, was it any surprise that I'd miss the signs of Callum being a boner on legs?

He seemed nice enough, good-looking, but the farther we got into the garden, the more he sipped from the flask he'd stolen from his dad, and by the time we made it to the fountain, he'd turned into a raging jackass.

Callum is a goddamned dead man walking. And where the fuck was I when all this was going down? Her sixteenth birthday had been kind of a shit show full of distractions. But also, Vlad wasn't there, so maybe I was too lax.

Logan stepped in, all affable, with that unassuming smile of his, but the look in his eyes... lethal. It was a quick flash, but holy shit! #Drool

I'm not proud that it's that look that does it for me, but here we are.

Anyway, with Callum taken care of... meaning leaving with

a broken arm, Logan sat me down for a talk, but not in a condescending way.

"What are you up to, Nik?"

I loved how he called me that. Like I could hang with them. I wasn't just some helpless Bratva princess daddy would be peddling off to expand his power.

"The way it's going, I'm not going to have my first kiss until my wedding and I just can't live with that."

He studied me for several silent minutes. Finally, he sighed and for a second I thought he was going to dismiss me, but then he stood, took my hand, and said, "Your brother would kill me for this... and rightfully so."

Not. Just. Her. Fucking. Brother.

It's all burned in my brain from that point on and I cannot stop playing it over and over. I'm not going to sleep tonight. I'm just going to keep hitting the rewind button.

He tugged me to my feet and with his index finger to the underside of my chin, he pushed my mouth closed.

"First rule, find your chill. Don't look so amazed that someone is going to kiss you. You're beautiful and smart. It's not a stretch."

"No one has dared yet."

"Yeah, well, kissing you is dangerous. But if the choice is me or another Callum, it's going to be me." He took my arms and dipped his head, looking me in the eye. "You've been playing with boys. Boys grope. Men, a real man worthy of you, won't. He doesn't need to. He can make you feel with nothing more than his hands on your face. If he can't make you feel by touching you from the neck up, he sucks, and

when you're ready and you go there, the sex will be an even bigger letdown. Anything less isn't worth your time. Remember that."

This smooth fucker. But he wasn't wrong and I really resent the fuck out of that.

When he cupped my jaw, tipped my head up, and grinned down at me, I had no fear, no hesitation, no worry that I'd suck at it and he'd laugh. Because with just that look on his face, he assured me that it didn't matter what lack of skill I brought to the kiss, he'd control it and it would be amazing.

I could not hate this journal entry more.

He tasted like summertime and lemon. My mouth just naturally opened under his. I wasn't sure that's what I was supposed to do, but it felt right. If the way he stepped into me was any indication, it was.

I loved the feel of his fingers flexing on my jaw, like he had to fight the urge to take it farther. I felt powerful and finally in control of my fate.

When his warm tongue slid along mine, I almost fell over. Lightheaded, my skin tight and hot, I grabbed ahold of his belt loops and steadied myself.

The minute I found my balance, though, I walked my fingertips right up his sides, over his ribs, and slid them around his back.

His muscles went rigid under my hands, his kiss deepened,

and his dick... welp, let's just say it was noteworthy. The minute I felt it, he pulled back.

"Remember what I said Nik," he said before running his thumb along the skin meeting my bottom lip and coming away with a smear of lipstick. "Anything less is not good enough. Don't be afraid to go after what you want and don't settle for less than you deserve. Ever."

I snatch my glass of whiskey, sending it splashing over my hand, and medicate myself with a massive gulp.

So why, if Logan was all the amazing things, did I go home and touch myself with Konstantin in my head, and when I came, his name on my lips???

I swallow hard. My heart hammers behind my ribs. Every rough breath strains my tight chest. The wave of grief from being a voyeur, peering into another time and place, threatens to consume.

Knowing her first kiss was just as shaped by her love and desire for me, means it belongs to me too, even if I wasn't the first to breach her soft, full mouth.

God, I hate that he tasted her. He had no intentions of pursuing anything with her. This was just a means to an end. A way of making sure her first kiss didn't come from some selfish, clumsy kid who didn't care about or love her the way she deserved. But did he think about their kiss every time he happened to see her since? Will he continue to think about it when he sees her in the future?

What the hell am I even thinking? Of course he will. How

the hell do you look at her and not think about the way she tastes and how she moves under you? How do you forget the sounds that bubble up from deep in her throat when sensation drowns her?

You don't. I've tried. God, how I've tried.

Those doubt-filled nights my soul agonized over the idea of never finding her, despair carved me apart, stealing a piece at a time, until I didn't think I'd survive another day.

And when the sun came up, and air still filled my lungs, I buried the all-consuming anguish in wild carnage.

From the day she ran, I'd begun forming a strong association between the warm, fresh blood I spilled far and wide searching for her, and her.

Now I see the connection for what it was... foreshadowing.

I toss back the rest of the liquor and head for her. She has to be asleep by now and I have to make sure she is okay.

I have to assure myself she is mine. Just mine.

And the possessive, bloodthirsty monster in me has to know if my blood still remains on her lip or if she scrubbed me free.

I'll peek in, see her with my own eyes, and I'll go.

The handle moves freely. Not locking the door behind me has to be a good sign. If she really wanted to keep me out, she would have. Mustering up every bit of patience I have left, I turn the handle agonizingly slow, the sounds of the latch slipping free, barely a whisper of a sound.

Leaning in the doorway, my hand on the handle, I study her. The lamp next to the bed burns, the soft glow caressing her face. As my eyes adjust, I make out the tracks of dried tears streaking down her cheeks.

And there on her mouth, my blood still stains her bottom lip.

Pcholka, Pcholka, Pcholka, what are you trying to tell me by leaving my mark on you?

With all of her ferociousness at rest, her face softens the way it does just before her smile lights up a room—before her charming laugh draws people to her.

Much in the way I pictured her looking at Rhodes right before he stole her first kiss.

I silently cross the floor to the side of the bed where she is lying with her back to me. She stirs, burrowing her face in my comforter with a soft sigh.

Seeing her nestled in my bed, where she belongs, rouses something raw and possessive inside me. How much blood will she spill of mine if she finds out? Just the thought of her slicing me open ignites a strange fascination in me. A craving for her brand of pain that has my cock hardening even more, aching as it strains against my zipper.

Rhodes may have had her first kiss, but he'll never be able to handle *this* Nikoletta.

But pain is all I know, and if she wants to slice me to ribbons, I'll let her.

My knuckles throb under the force of my clenched fists as I fight my overwhelming urge to reach for her. I itch to rub the silky strands of her hair between my fingers. But if I start there, I won't stop. I'll pin her wrists over her head, tear away the scrap of warm, damp cotton covering her tight pussy, and take. Take until she screams uncontrollably, and I won't stop until I reduce her to whimpers and sobbing my name.

Grigori's ominous warning echoes through my head, and still I don't leave. Instead, I retreat to the cushioned chair in the corner, tucked away in the shadows. I watch her sleep like the fucking creep I've slowly morphed into more and more with every time I exiled myself to the crypt. My laser focus fixes on the steady rise and fall of her shoulders with each peaceful breath until my breathing pattern matches hers. Ears prickling, my sense of hearing heightens, homing in on every delicate sound she makes. Her breathing, sighs, the occasional soft mumble.

Every version of Nikoletta lives here, between her in the flesh and every rendition of her in my memories. All facets of her converge. The girl I've protected from birth. The teenager from her journals. The woman I found enticing men on that fucking pole. The woman I took on the altar. The killer she's become.

I drag my hand down my face. What the fuck am I doing in here watching her? Jesus. Every time I think I can't get lower, I rise to the occasion. Dropping my hand in my lap, my palm cups my cock and before I can tell myself to stop, I stroke myself long and hard over my zipper.

Fuck.

I've already hurt her. All but destroyed this girl she'd been. I refuse to be this. To do this to her. Disrespect her by getting off like some fucking freak in the corner when I'm supposed to be keeping her safe.

That means keeping her safe from this new, warped side of me.

Before I can change my mind, I cling to the man I'd been, her protector before it had all turned to shit. Without another glance in her direction, I leave the room as silently as I crept in.

CHAPTER

20

Nikoletta

S calding-hot water pummels my skin from six showerheads. You could have an orgy in this disgustingly ostentatious shower and still have room left over.

Maybe that's what it was designed for. Konstantin doesn't strike me as a big ole whore, but then I never would have guessed he only fucked me because he had a boner for my mother, so what do I know.

I squeeze my eyes shut against the tears threatening to well up. God, will there ever be a day that knowledge doesn't hurt?

Despite the buffet of options, rainfall, handheld sprayer, or the multiple showerheads hammering me now, nothing washes away traces of him lingering despite the half hour I spend under their spray.

His scent haunts me. The smoke-tinged leather, with a hint of pepper and bergamot, luring me in and pissing me off at every turn. The naive girl who lost her virginity to him— the one who still stupidly wants him, is so fucking hopelessly drawn to the rich, spicy smell.

I want to straddle his lap, tuck my nose along the crook of his neck, and breathe him in. More than that, I long to drag my tongue along his skin and relish the taste of him bursting on my tongue.

Knowing his sounds now has me salivating. Hearing them again last night when he kissed me, his erratic breathing, the desperation in the way he held my face–it took every bit of willpower I had in me to fight the way I wanted him and instead embrace the fury. I crave hearing them again. The growl of a man struggling to hold everything back, followed by a gasp and a groan of surrender. The echoing in my head has me squeezing my thighs together.

I muster all my willpower and try to shove the craving and memories away his smell invokes.

Only his cologne wraps around my childhood memories of him as well. A time when I associated his scent with safety, making the push and pull between betrayal and devotion excruciating.

Resting my forehead against the tiles, I close my eyes and take slow, even breaths through the pain pinching my heart. He devastates me, and still this yearning will never end.

I'll never shake him.

Not even twenty-four hours into my life sentence of being in close proximity to him, and already, I'm about to go out of my damn mind.

I have no interest in leaving my sanctuary of the shower, but if I spend much longer, he'll think I'm hiding from him and I can't live with that.

Sure, a part of me wants to hide, but the other part—the louder part—wants to be in his face at every opportunity until he experiences a fraction of my misery.

Fuck if I know which me I'll be when I finally make my way out there this morning.

I shut off the water and reach for the plush bath sheet I found in the linen closet. Gathering the terry cloth around my shoulders, I scrub at the ends of my hair since I hadn't been able to find anything even close to the size of an ordinary towel to wrap the dripping strands in.

Swiping my forearm over the mirror, I choke on the air I draw into my lungs. My gaze locks on Konstantin's blood still staining my bottom lip. I scrubbed all traces of him from my skin, yet I didn't touch that spot.

Unable to tear my gaze from his mark, I swipe the spot with the tip of my tongue. The metallic flavor is muted. Subtle. Before I realize what I'm doing, I'm sucking my bottom lip into my mouth and scouring every last bit of his flavor remaining on my lip.

Mine.

I'm condemned to him always tasting like he's mine.

Releasing my lip, my stare lands on the now clean, glistening spot. A profound sadness takes root with his mark gone and stupid tears well in my eyes. Pain moves through me, leaving a pulsing ache in its wake.

I want to succumb to being his. Despite everything, I yearn for it. Even if my pride doesn't demand I keep my distance from him after his betrayal, my path forward does. Power means controlling my future, demanding respect, upholding consequences for betrayal, even if those consequences leave me bleeding too.

And he left me bleeding more than any of them.

Heart aching to the point breathing became almost impossible, I turn away from my reflection. I grasp for the mundane, hoping one foot in front of the other will take the edge off the fucking despair eating me alive.

In a matter of minutes, I have to be on, immersing myself in the part I need to play, my mask firmly in place.

Digging through my bag, I pass up my favorite dresses and snag a pair of jeans. I love the freedom of a dress. I especially love the access to my knife while wearing one, but right now, with him, a dress leaves me too exposed. A vulnerable feeling that also has me reaching for my cardigan to top it all off. Warm and soothing, I burrow behind the soft knit.

With his kiss still alive in my mind, his taste seared on my tongue, my nerves snap with awareness. Even the caress of the denim along my skin threatens to transport me right back in that crypt where he held my hips as I rocked on his thigh in the dark. Desperate for any part of him he'd let me have.

Let me have...

My back snaps up straight.

That was the stupid, innocent girl in me.

I no longer settle for what men let me have. I take. I seize what I want with as much confidence and force as men do, as much as a Romanoff, making sure they won't overlook me again.

Tossing my hair up in a messy knot on my head, I take one last look in the mirror, square my shoulders, and prepare to face whatever waits for me outside this room.

I pause at Faith's door and listen for a moment to her muffled voice on the other side as she sings to Lexi and Alex. From the sounds, she is putting them back to sleep so she won't be joining us anytime soon.

So much for a buffer.

My fingers itch to turn the handle and slip into the sanctuary of our friendship, but it will only delay the inevitable.

The hallway opens up into a massive living area. Or at least massive last night. Today, Nikolaj's mood judging by dark eyebrows slashed over narrowed eyes and the hard line of his mouth, shrinks the space to a shoebox.

A toddler shoebox at that.

He lounges on the couch with deceptive ease, but I know that look. He uses it as a tool to keep associates and enemies off-balance.

Like a snake ready to strike, his sharp gaze locks on me. The fingers he's been drumming on the end table go still.

"Nikolaj."

He doesn't know what to do with me. Especially not when I greet him with just his name. The last time he saw me, I was in Paris. A teen girl, drunk on the independence from my family, even if it was a way to punish me and keep me from Konstantin.

We spent four days exploring the Louvre and Monet's Gardens, followed by a dizzying amount of champagne tours and dining at my favorite places throughout the city. It was the last time I felt a sense of true peace.

Standing before him now, I no longer resemble that girl.

At the time, I had unlimited access to the finest salons and spas, and no end to funds for only the best designer clothes. My only care in the world had been my appearance.

But now, my outfit from head to toe cost me under a hundred dollars. My nails, while neat, are a modest length and bare. My hair hasn't seen a real salon in a year and a half.

"Lettie." The affectionate lilt to my nickname brings with it sweet memories of running through the gardens with ice cream melting down our hands in the hot sun. Lazy afternoons of him teaching me to fearlessly let go of the handlebars of my bike and throw my arms up in the air. The first time a boy made me cry calling me a vile name, only to have Nikolaj knock out his two front teeth for the slight.

I force my feet to stay rooted to the floor as the instinct to run up and hug him washes through me. He is the last bit of family I can trust, whatever trust means to a Romanoff, but more than a year has passed and the divide looms wider than ever between us.

Longing fills me until my throat grows thick, choking back the sense of loss. The edge I've honed in my time away softens with his use of my nickname.

No path back to that bond exists. We only have whatever connection we build moving forward. The little girl counting on her big brother to pursue justice no longer exists.

I seek justice for myself.

He, no doubt, has a mountain of questions. For the first time in my life, I can't give him all the answers. Not without detonating a bomb in what is left of our family.

Konstantin strolls in from a hall on the opposite side of the room, his coffee mug tipped to his lips. His gaze swings between us, his expression utterly unreadable.

Uncertainty swirls in my gut. Heightened awareness skitters over my skin as I study them to gauge the silent communication of their eye contact.

The air grows heavy with everything the three of us choose not to say. Destructive secrets. One between Konstantin and me. Likely dozens between Konstantin and Nikolaj forged in the bond they nurtured in the time I'd been away.

Now I stand on the outside looking in when I had always been the one who ultimately drew them together.

With a shake of Konstantin's head and the tense flex of the muscle in his cheek, he ends his perusal and heads for the island, breaking the spell.

"I take it you're not getting any ass, big brother? You're looking grumpy as fuck." I sail past him behind the armor of snark. Snagging a bottle of water from the fridge, I lock eyes with him over my shoulder. "You should do something about that before it becomes a medical condition."

He raises one dark eyebrow but makes no move to stand. "The only medical condition I have is the pain permanently lodged in my ass from your antics."

I drop into the chair across from him and toss one leg over the other. "I'm an adult, and even if I wasn't, you're not my father. My antics, as you call them, are none of your concern."

He launches to his feet then and looms over me, his jaw tight. "When you put me in the position of having to buy your virginity for half a million dollars, it's my damn concern."

Pausing with the water bottle halfway to my lips, I tilt my head and focus on the vein next to his temple. "As I recall, Konstantin was the one who bought my virginity."

"With my money," Nikolaj growls, his hands balled into fists at his sides.

And there it is, the pulsing vein, just like our father. Nikolaj won't appreciate the observation for good reason.

From the corner of my eye, I catch sight of Konstantin, alert and ready to step in.

"I didn't ask for either of you to butt in. There were plenty of other buyers."

I don't need to see Konstantin's glare. It takes on a life of its own, tracing over me, promising retribution.

Good, I welcome the chance to make him bleed again.

Agitation rolls off him as he snags his suit jacket off the couch and shrugs it on. "I have to go out. I won't be long." His gaze locks on Nikolaj, but I don't miss the oddly dignified smirk on his face. "You're on babysitting duty."

He ends the words with a smug smile. I want to punch it right off his square jaw.

Keep stacking up the transgressions, asshole.

I shoot daggers at his retreating back, Grigori slipping out just behind him. When the door clicks shut and the lock engages, I turn my gaze back to my brother.

"That was chilly," he says, his brow furrowed, a questioning glance aimed at the door.

"You want me to be polite? Fine, but you two first." My water becomes my lifeline as I suck down a third of it. Maybe if I keep my mouth full, I won't say something that will come back later to bite me in the ass.

He tilts his head and cups his hand around the back of his neck, kneading the tension there. His hard eyes soften as his gaze travels over my face. "I didn't come here to fight with you."

"No, you came here to control me. You just didn't expect me to fight you." I can practically see him cataloging the changes in me over the past year. Konstantin sees my changes through the eyes of lust. His men, if they note my changes, are wise enough to keep their mouths shut and their faces impassive. Time will tell. I wasn't exactly focused on them when they charged into the commune.

But Nikolaj, it is as if he's found two sets of puzzle pieces scrambled in one bag. The pieces of each, similar enough to make it all but impossible to separate them into two piles, but he tries anyway.

"What happened to you?" he asks quietly, a thread of worry creeping into his voice.

"This family happened to me." I turn to the windows where rain falls at a slant, fat drops spattering the glass, obscuring a whole different world out there, just beyond my reach.

Clear walls give me an unobstructed view, but they are walls just the same.

"This family happened to all of us, Lettie."

He will not minimize this to just something we go through being Romanoffs. "It's always different for the vagina." None of them have any idea what it is like to be a commodity. Even our mother never had to suffer this. She had choices. Two men wanted her, loved her, and she got to choose.

"Don't make this about gender."

"I didn't." I fight the urge to cross my arms. I have his attention. If I look like I am on the defensive, he'll dismiss this as nothing more than childish acting out.

I need him to hear me. To see me. I may be back in my cage, but I've made the choice. My cage is no longer a cell.

They'll never find comfort in my confinement again. They'll learn to never turn their back on me.

If they try to make my cage a prison, I'll drag every single one of them into that prison with me.

"Our family made this about gender generations ago. Our grandparents, parents, and now you. You just don't like that I'm not conforming to it."

Nikolaj all but deflates before dropping back down on the sofa. "Jesus, if I didn't know better, I'd say some guy did a number on you."

"Not just one." But it is just the one who delivered the final blow.

"We can't escape our legacy, Lettie."

"You don't think I know that? I know it better than all of you. I'm the bargaining chip. I know about being trapped better than any of you."

"I won't let the Petrovs have you." His sharp words vibrate with harbored rage. I love him even more for it.

I can't let him in, but I will secretly covet the little tells in his voice, his mannerisms, proving his love for me. "You can't stop it."

"You underestimate me."

"No, big brother, you underestimate them." His eyes flash in warning, but I ignore it, knowing he will never act on it with me. He may take a hard line, but he isn't cruel like Vlad. "They're driven by their pride and arrogance, and you don't have a stronghold on the family power yet. They'll come for me. And even if you manage to protect me the first time, they'll come for me again. At least if they manage to get me, they'll get far more than they anticipated. I'll carve into them just as much as they carve me."

He hides it well, but I spot the slight wince. The thought of them hurting me, hurts him, whereas Vlad would only find excitement in the prospect.

"What if I have a solution?"

"And what would that be? Marry someone they're afraid of?"

The corner of his mouth twitches. "Actually, yes."

I throw up my hands and huff out a breath of sheer frustration. "How did I know the solution still involved a man in the family pawning me off in marriage? So who are you hoping to tempt with my magic pussy now?"

He jerks back, like he's just taken a bullet to the chest. "The fuck?"

"Which part of my question did you take exception to? Me comparing you to the other men in our family or my magic pussy?"

"I take exception to all of it, but the magic pussy is what's going to haunt my nightmares for years to come," he says as he pinches the bridge of his nose.

"Good. If I have to suffer, so do you."

"So what if it was up to you?"

"What's that?"

"Who you marry." Intertwining his hands, he steeples his index fingers and taps them against his chin. "Look, there's no getting around the fact that marrying the right man, one with enough power and influence to instill fear, will protect you. It's not like we can decide the rules are different, send out a decree, and expect everyone to fall in line. If we can't change the rules, let's use them to our advantage. You pick."

"How do you suppose I do that? The minute the Petrovs know I'm here, the clock is ticking. That doesn't exactly leave a lot of time for dating."

"No, but you're not marrying for love, are you? There are plenty of influential people looking for a mutually beneficial arrangement, instead of love." He leans forward and props his elbows on his knees, a confident smile spreading on his lips. "As a matter of fact, there's a party tonight."

I'd rather chew my tongue clean off than admit his idea has merit so I tamp down the thread of excitement making my heart pump just a little faster with hope.

Drawing up my legs under me, I pick at the frayed edges of my favorite jeans. "Sure, I'll just put on clean jeans, no problem. Get real, Nikolaj. I have a half-filled duffel bag of casual clothes and split ends. And it takes an army to move me around the city right now. How am I supposed to shop, find a salon at the last minute, and be ready to go by tonight?"

"Leave it to me and I'll bring the shopping and the salon to you. You don't have to go anywhere. All you have to do is say yes. So what'll it be?"

Marriage of necessity, but on my terms. And a chance to distance myself from Konstantin. I swallow the lump in my throat that tells me I'm not as happy with the prospect of that last part as I should be.

No more heated stares. No more stolen kisses. No more impossibly close proximity to someone I want with every fiber of my being yet can't have.

Maybe I'll find some peace and these memories will finally fade, taking the worst of the pain with them.

And before I go, Konstantin will have no choice but to

watch me. Watch me flirt and watch men make moves, relegating him to a distant bystander as I forge a path without him.

Out of his reach for good.

"Who exactly is going to be at this party of yours?"

"It's the society... friends, allies, politicians, old money, new money—basically every power player on the East Coast."

"No mafia?"

"Some, but no one I wouldn't approve of." His eyes lock on mine and a bit of my brother slips away before my eyes only to be replaced by the formidable man he's become. "The Ophidian Society will always overrule the mafia, Nikoletta."

Konstantin will hate every last minute of this and that holds the most appeal of all. "Deal."

CHAPTER

21

Konstantin

After three hours and two SUVs full of everything I can think of Faith may need for her babies, I finally make my way back to the safe house. Demitri and Grigori don't know shit about babies which meant I had no choice but to take the lead on a task I would have happily dumped on them otherwise.

The mere mention of baby shopping and Grigori's eyes darted around in panic. A man who's buried countless bullets between the eyes and broken thousands of bones for a living brought to his knees by the idea of diapers and bouncy seats.

Demetri, on the other hand, had a damn look of excitement on his face. Like this was a fucking field trip with a gift shop stop at the end and a limitless credit card.

He'd come back with bullshit gadgets and toys—ones he might share with the babies, or not—and I'd still be running out for the basic necessities.

No doubt Nikolaj has a few scathing words for how long I've been gone.

Try me, son.

He has no one to blame but himself. He's the one who caved the minute his sister put the pressure on to bring a *friend*.

A friend with infants.

This isn't a fucking field trip. It is life or death. Faith doesn't look old enough to vote, let alone to have twins. And Nikoletta marched all three of them right into our world of crime, balanced on fragile alliances, all on a river of blood.

And those fragile alliances, the crime—that is the best case reality for the established power system within the Bratva, which we aren't. We are the hunted... a fact my little Pcholka seems to have forgotten in her time away.

Maksim will never stop coming for us as long as his heart remains beating and the minute it stops, Vlad will take over entirely and carnage will ensue. Nikolaj, his number one target, and me, a very close number two.

Vlad loves the power trip, but he craves playing deadly games more. He has no real awareness of how easily his life can be snuffed out with one wrong move. Instead, he gambles as though he's made a deal with the Devil to live forever.

With no rhyme or reason to his actions, his next moves are impossible to predict.

Nikolaj has killed hundreds of men in the time he's worked to build power. As a member of The Ophidian Society and the illegitimate son of the pakhan, the body count is just the tip of the iceberg. He's maimed far more than that. A formidable opponent for Vlad, but under the influence of his sister, his edge wavers, leaving room for catastrophic mistakes.

He needs to shore up his defenses—and fast.

Pushing my way through the door, I jerk to a stop, my eyes going straight to the center of the room where Nikoletta stands on a small riser, a shimmering gold gown cascading down her every curve.

My gaze lands on the wisps of hair breaking free of the messy bun on top of her head, brushing over the soft skin of her neck. Blood rushes to my cock and I clench my teeth as I take in the expanse of skin exposed as my eyes trail down her spine.

Gut churning, I close my eyes against the glimpse of back dimples in full view, barely an inch above her mouthwatering ass. The slightest shift and she'll be revealing a hell of a lot more than her sexy back.

I hate the fucking gold gown as much as I want to bow at the feet of the designer for their fucking brilliance.

My knuckles ache from how hard I squeeze the handle of the door. Jesus Christ, my heart cannot take this.

If she wants to keep me away, she is doing a shitty job. In that gown, she's all but guaranteed I'll have my cock grinding against her ass the whole time the dress graces her body to hide what is mine, goddammit.

Our tailor, Ahmad, kneels at her feet, pins pinched between his lips as he adjusts the length of the dress. He keeps his head down. Smart move or I may just have to put a bullet in his skull for seeing her so exposed. Fuck rationality.

Next to them stands three clothing racks with everything from casual clothing to designer gowns.

On the living room rug, Faith coos at the babies lying on their backs on a plush blanket. Their little legs kick as they squeal with the softest of giggles.

Just last week, this place had been silent as a tomb. Now —I can't even begin to process the now. It's the goddamned fashion district meets daycare center.

When not chasing leads on Nikoletta's whereabouts, me and my men spent our time here studying an array of monitors from our surveillance cameras to keep an eye on our more volatile new allies.

Nikolaj never goes straight to the top to make deals and attain power. He starts at the bottom. Rather fitting for an unofficial Bratva mafia operating underground.

He forges subtle bonds with the soldiers. Earns their trust. A small favor here and there. Making connections for them on occasion. Saving their asses when they screw up. He earns enough respect, he doesn't have to find an in with the leaders of their syndicates, the soldiers do it for him with a word here or there, in his favor, to their superiors.

Those new, tentative alliances need nurturing—and babysitting.

Me and my team are quick to eliminate problems before they can bite us all in the ass. I like it that way.

Within the first few weeks watching, we knew who would be the most useful, who would be an asset—but a messy one, and who needed to be snuffed out almost immediately. Every day his allies grow and before long, I know we'll outgrow this space for surveillance.

I didn't know we'd start busting out of the seams like some fucked-up versions of *Three Men and a Baby*.

My safe house became a prison... one holding a woman who has swiftly turned into my greatest temptation—and most destructive secret.

Nikolaj strolls in with his hands in his pockets, coming from the direction of the office where he no doubt spends a good deal of time scouring those monitors himself.

"About time, Malikov."

"The bigger the mess you make, the longer it takes me to clean up. You're welcome." I toss my keys on the island, cross my arms, and nod my head in Nikoletta's direction. "You want to tell me what the hell is going on?"

"A party," Nikoletta chirps from next to me like I hadn't watched as she dripped blood while she practically sliced and diced a guy the night before. "You are familiar with those, right, Konstantin? It's where people—the ones without sticks up their asses—mingle, laugh, drink, dance, you know, have fun." Nikoletta aims a razor-sharp smile at me before turning away under Ahmad's direction.

Keep it up and you're going to have something up your ass, little girl. "No."

"No, you don't know what that is?" She tosses over her shoulder with a smirk.

"No. You're not going."

She tilts her head in a mocking way, reminding me just how young she is. "Funny—you actually think you have a say."

Just as they did that long ago night in Illusions Cabaret, my fingers itch to redden that sweet ass of hers until just the idea of sitting makes her whimper.

Nikolaj gives his sister a warning glance before turning to me. "We have a plan. She's going."

"A word, Nikolaj." I aim my index finger at Nikolaj and then the door to my office as I stride past him, ripping my jacket off along the way.

"Oh, not without me, you don't." Nikoletta gathers the skirt of her gown in her fingers and scrambles off the riser.

I hold the door for Nikolaj, but the minute he crosses the threshold, I take great satisfaction in slamming the door in her face.

Propping my shoulder against the wood, I hold it shut and flip the lock. "You want to explain to me why the hell she's going to a party when she's a walking fucking target for the Petrovs, Vlad, not to mention anyone else who might have it out for you?"

The door vibrates under my shoulder as she beats on it from the other side.

"Let me in, dammit!"

Nikolaj's lip twitches with amusement as he glances at the door and back at me. "It's a society party... no one will touch her there."

"Konstantin, damn you, open this door right now or you'll live to regret it."

Oh, she'll get touched there. With all the skin she has on display in that fucking gown... it is a goddamned guarantee.

And I'll have to stand by and watch men through the evening touch what's mine.

"Mafia will be there and you fucking know it."

"A few, yes, but they won't dare cross The Ophidian Order. I've already made it clear that she'll be there with me and she's not to be touched. They'll honor it."

"I swear to God, you better open this door right now or the minute you close your eyes, I'm slicing your balls off."

Nikolaj rarely shows surprise. He'd learned to school his features as a boy to keep from giving his father or brother the satisfaction of knowing anything they said or did affected him. But the minute *balls* comes from his sister's mouth, his eyebrows rise.

"Listen to her out there. She's been gone for a year. You didn't see where she was. I'm telling you, she's not ready for society."

"She'll be fi—" A whip and thunk echoes through the door, cutting him off.

Silence fills the air. I flick the lock and open the door to Nikoletta's furious red face glaring at me. Her chest heaves, practically launching her breasts from her dress with every gulp of air.

The knife she used to carve up Elijah sticks out of the wood of the door, eye level—my eye level.

"Does this look ready for society to you?" I ask Nikolaj, pointing at the knife. "The only place she should be going is to a hospital for rabies testing."

She blows out a breath, sending the errant strands of hair falling on her face out of her eyes. "Of course, that's what a boomer would say to a woman demanding to have a place in the conversation, you know, a conversation about her."

I clench my fists, a thin thread of control the only thing keeping me from throwing her defiant ass over my shoulder and hauling her off to her—my damn room for a time-out, adult style. "*Boomer*? I'm forty-nine, you little—"

"What the hell is up with you two?" Nikolaj winces, pinching the bridge of his nose. "You're like a couple of kids snarling at each other. Jesus."

"She's not ready for this, Nikolaj. She's a liability."

She yanks the knife from the door and pauses with it pointed right at me. "Oh, you can fuck all the way off, Konstantin."

"You," Nikolaj says, pointing right at her. "Leave the knife at home. And you," Nikolaj continues, pinning me with his hard stare. "She's a liability? Fine. It's up to you to make sure she isn't. Handle her."

Handle her? If he only knew my *handling her* is the reason she is like this in the first place.

"First, where I go the knife goes." She lifts her gown and slides the knife into the sheath strapped to her thigh. Next to it, another knife.

Hell.

The hand-tooled leather bites into her skin just enough to remind me how soft and round those thighs were when I was fucking her on that altar.

They look even softer now.

Thicker. Mouthwatering. Fuck.

Before I can stop it, the vision of my fingertips digging into her flesh flashes in my head, making me grit my teeth.

Feral. Just remember she's feral now.

Except, I'm pretty sure I like her this way more. Fucking her would be a blood sport—violent, angry, and absolutely devastating in the best fucking way.

Our mutual rage colliding would shake the souls under this city from their resting places until all peace has been obliterated.

"And second, handle me? What the fuck, Nikolaj. Whose side are you on?"

"Yours... always yours, which is why you're going. But right now, you've been too busy snarling to keep in mind what you have to lose in this. You have..." Nikolaj glances at his phone. "Six hours to get your shit together and remember what's at stake here. The minute you arrive at the party, the clock starts ticking. The Petrovs will know you're back before your head even hits the pillow tonight."

"A list of every attendee. That's the deal, Nikolaj. You want me to keep her safe, I need a list of every single person who'll be there from guests to bathroom attendants. Within the hour."

Nikolaj narrows his eyes but nods. Our relationship still suffers the growing pains of a man who grew up with me as an authority figure, his father's best friend, protection and counsel to his family. With his growing power, my authority transitioned into something different. Our playing field leveled somewhat. For now.

However, as he rises, even if under my guidance, he'll seize ultimate control and my life will be in his hands.

In some ways, it already is.

He steps up to her then, his gaze sweeping over her from head to toe. His expression forlorn, like he finally sees the little girl who looked up to him so much is gone, leaving a woman—a hardened one at that—standing in her place.

"You turned into a lioness when I wasn't looking. Learn how to control that power so it doesn't control you." He cups her cheeks then and kisses her forehead. "Be smart, Lettie."

CHAPTER

22

Nikoletta

The last party I attended was Christmas of senior year. Seventeen, and home from abroad for two weeks, I was desperate to be taken seriously. I'd tried everything I could think of but was dismissed at every turn. So that night, I wore my hair in a high ponytail. Sleek and severe, I chose the style so I'd look more grown-up.

A girl then, I naively thought I could achieve something so crucial with the most basic decision about my appearance.

I certainly caught attention. In doing so, I hovered on the fringes of important conversations with powerful people and studied.

In a matter of hours, I learned being noticed and taken seriously were two very different goals. Being seen was trivial, and fleeting at that. If I wanted to be taken seriously, it required far more than what I presented on the outside. It took more than being noticed. What I chose to say with my mouth, my eyes, and my demeanor, played crucial roles in the outcome.

It was knowing when to say nothing at all and listen instead.

Something I'd been getting good at before Konstantin impaled me with that unforgettable fucking dick of his. Now that we'd crossed all the lines, he is the ultimate distraction I can't afford.

Deep breath.

I need to channel that energy and hold on to it with everything I have. Collect all those lessons I learned and implement them flawlessly, the impression I leave behind tonight nothing short of unforgettable.

He'll be watching me for hours, scrutinizing every expression, my body language, and how everyone reacts to me. My job? To let him without giving him a reaction. I have too much at stake to do anything else.

The last thing I need to do is show any sort of divide within our own. Fuck if I will give Vlad or my father even a spec of help figuring out how to hit us the hardest and cause the most damage, or anyone else for that matter. Because Nikolaj will have other enemies there tonight. While their loyalty to the Ophidian Order may keep them in check, as well as their fear of his power being both Bratva and society member, they'll be looking for any sign of weakness. Details they can hold on to until an opportunity arises to strike.

Nikolaj is right. Marriage is the way. It's not what I want, but having control over who I marry is far more than I would have gotten otherwise.

Taking in my reflection in the full-length mirror, I smooth my palm over the crown of my hair. The stylist worked wonders. After washing, deep conditioning, shaping, trimming, and drying, he gathered the mass loosely at my nape and wove the strands into a loose flower French braid, guaranteeing my back remained fully exposed.

Feminine and soft, when I am anything but.

I glance at my mother's solitaire pearl diamond necklace I

used to wear and bite the inside of my cheek to chase away the tears. At one time, I thought death put the ultimate distance between us, but this twisted love triangle that defied logic proved me wrong. Exposed truths sucked the soul straight out of my childhood memories and shattered my dreams moving forward.

So I'll have to forge a new path, find new dreams.

With the lotion I've slathered on my skin finally soaked in, I slide my revenge gown off the hanger and step into the opening. The fabric glides snugly along every curve on its way up my thighs and over my hips. Ahmed nailed the alterations beautifully. The bodice plunges into a deep V held in place by nothing more than a delicate clasp on the thin straps behind my neck.

Amazing how such a simple piece holds everything together.

I smooth my hands over the soft, shimmering fabric on my way to secure the short zipper hidden in the ruched fabric cascading over my ass.

An evil little smile curves my bloodred lips as I turn left, then right, watching the thigh-high slit I'd had Ahmed add expose not just my thigh, but a generous glimpse of my hip.

Tonight is going to be brutal for my godfather, and after everything, it is just a taste of what he deserves.

A deep knock draws my gaze to the door. It has to be Dimitri or Grigori because Konstantin, the cocky bastard he can be, would have just walked in. Plus, he disappeared into his lair as soon as the information he demanded from my brother arrived and I haven't seen him since.

I fix a smile on my face, after all, it isn't their fault their boss is a shithead, and open the door. My eyes collide with Konstantin's broad chest where the tie of his tux hangs loose.

Shoulder propped against the doorframe, he holds a gold Christian Louboutin box on his upturned palm.

Leaning my hip against the door, I tilt my head. "Career change at your age? I'm not sure delivery boy was a wise move."

His jaw clenches.

Direct. Fucking. Hit.

The minute I reach for the box, he tugs it back and holds it over his shoulder and out of my reach. Unless I want to climb him. Which, to be fair, I do. Or at least, my lusty vagina does.

I itch to trail my fingers over the grooves deepening between his eyebrows with his growing anger. He glances down the hall, shakes his head, and steps right up to me, front to front, forcing me to back up.

Kicking the door shut behind him, he flips the lock and wraps his hand around my throat, sending a goddamn shock straight up my spine. His fingers flex along the sides of my neck as if he fights the urge to choke me. The increased pressure ignites goosebumps over my scalp and a flood of shivers from head to toe.

He drags his nose along my cheekbone in that way of his, his mouth stopping right by my ear. "You didn't seem to mind my age when you were begging me to fuck you, little girl."

"I did not beg." The words sound weak to my own ears.

He hears it too, but he doesn't gloat. He doesn't need to. His deep laugh along the shell of my ear does it for him. "Yes, you most certainly did. And you will again."

Fat fucking chance. I'll be married in a matter of months tops. And then maybe he'll know a fraction of the hurt he's inflicted on me.

He walks me back until I stand in front of the full-length mirror again and drops down onto one knee before me.

Flipping the lid off the shoebox, he tosses the red draw-string Louboutin bag aside. Strong fingers curl around my calf, smoothing down over my ankle and under my heel before lifting my foot onto his bent knee.

Heart in my throat choking out the hostile 'fuck you' I should have been delivering, I watch in rapt fascination, this side of him I've never seen.

The sexy heels pale compared to the sight he makes—all six-foot-seven of him on one knee—submissive, but only voluntarily so. Taking in the view of us in the mirror, a whole other scenario flashes in my mind, an unattainable fantasy I once clung to when anything more between us than our connection as godfather and goddaughter seemed impossible. A young girl's dream. One that conveniently glossed over any dangers of crossing the forbidden line between us.

Has he ever proposed to a woman before? Hasn't he dreamed of having a family of his own? Just the idea of him on his knee for anyone else has me volleying between violence and vomit.

I glance down at him to find his hot gaze locked on me—his eyes trailing over my skin from my face to the valley between my breasts. The brief flash of longing in his expression—longing for my mother or me, I can't tell—spears straight into my heart. Missing the part of me who loves him, it lands in the black corner poisoned with self-doubt and jealousy.

Embracing the bitter taste of knowing Konstantin has never really been mine, my mouth, as sharp as my knife—at times, sharper—delivers another blow. "Did you offer the same services to my mother when my father decided to toss her some dick crumbs and sent you to fetch her?"

The hand holding my foot goes impossibly still. The only

sound in the charged air is of his harsh, angry breaths. I am so focused on the ominous silence, the sharp smack landing on my ass makes me yelp, leaving a swift sting in its wake.

Without thinking, my fingers reach for my knife, just to come up empty. The sheath mocks me from the ottoman a few feet away, where I left it to apply lotion.

His gaze follows mine. "You go for blood and you'll just end up with a ruined dress, brat."

My mouth falls open, scathing barbs perched on the tip of my tongue, only to slide silently away as his palm stays planted on my ass as though it belongs to him. Only now, he rubs and squeezes, chasing away the sting. "I don't know what you need more, a brutal spanking or savage fucking— probably both—but your brother will be here in ten minutes, so for once, fucking behave."

His words set off an ache that throbs through me from head to toe. Or maybe it is the way his hand has gone back to caressing my ankle, then my calf. Subtly, he moves higher, setting off fireworks so powerful, it takes every last bit of resolve to hold back the whimper.

After peeling back the paper wrapping the shoes, he pulls out the heel and turns it over in his hand, examining it from every angle.

"You're just asking for a broken ankle in these."

"You just don't like how I'll look in them."

"Mmmm," he hums, his deep voice only diving deeper as he undoes the clasp. Silent but for our heavy breaths, I sway on my feet as he slides the shoe over my toes and up over my heel.

"I assure you, that's the part I actually do like," he says as he secures the delicate strap around my ankle before brushing a light kiss over the skin just above the clasp, "It's anyone else seeing you in them and getting ideas that doesn't work for me, Pcholka." He trails his fingers over my knee and along my thigh, hooking his finger under the slit of my dress.

I suck in a sharp breath, all of my senses anticipating the back of his knuckle brushing over my pussy. I'll never survive foreplay with this man. *Never.*

For this fleeting moment, I embrace the fantasy where nothing stands between us. A brief taste of what it would be like if our history didn't exist and he could be mine. In this room, we're just a man and woman, insanely attracted to one another, getting ready for a glamorous night out.

Maddeningly deliberate and with cunning precision, as though helpless to get closer to the heat emanating from me, he glides his finger farther behind the fabric bit by bit.

Like Icarus, but instead of being an overambitious boy flying too close to the sun, he finds the narrow path between the sun and sea, giving us both what we need, but pulling us back from our total annihilation.

How appropriate for my protector to find the balance. How fitting he has a set of black wings carved in ink over the length of his back and beyond.

"You're going to need to work hard to keep this obscene split closed tonight."

His gruff voice washes over me, leaving me throbbing and desperate. I'll take our destruction over his restraint. "That defeats the entire purpose of having Ahmed add it."

Dark, brooding eyes flash up to mine. Mouth tight, his hand clamps on my ankle, locking my foot on his thigh. The hand he used to explore the slit in my gown just seconds earlier, now reaches into the drawer of the nightstand. "Maybe a bit of motivation then."

I barely catch a glimpse of papers, an engraved money clip, a remote for the fan before the drawer slams shut, making me jump. Eyes on mine, he grabs the edge of the slit and tosses the shimmering fabric over the opposite side, holding it there with his long fingers curling over my hip.

Dress bunched up at my waist, he lays every last part of me bare from the waist down—at eye level with him.

Gaze locked dead center, a whoosh of breath leaves his lungs. With my foot balanced on his thigh, my legs parted and completely open to him, the rush of air skims over all the right places.

His eyes flick to the array of lingerie next to my knives and sheath on the ottoman. "There will be panties covering this pussy when we walk out the door." A growl tears from his throat just before he buries his face between my legs, his determined mouth closing over my clit.

I can't stop the groan. My head falls back and my thighs quiver. The hot rush of blood filling my ears sets my heart racing under the bone-melting onslaught.

Stop him! You'll never survive this!

My self-preservation's voice grows weaker, sounding farther and farther away with every firm swipe of his hot tongue as he devours me.

Burying my shaking fingers in his long, silver-threaded hair, I hold on as I light on fire from the inside out, white-hot sensations almost painful in the voraciousness pummeling me from every direction.

Pulling back, he meets my gaze, his thumb casually stroking back and forth over my clit. With his mouth coated with my arousal, he gives me the single most sinfully satisfied smile I've ever seen. Rolling his lips into his mouth, he sucks every last bit of me from his lips.

"If my every bad decision combined in perfect balance to make a flawless forbidden fruit, it would taste just like you."

His words rumble through me, as his lips suck me back

into his mouth, while his tongue sweeps over me in relentless demand. The orgasm grows swiftly, with a heartbeat of its own, but before it takes hold, he wrenches his mouth away, the pleasure slipping out of reach, leaving me wet, aching, and wanting to punch his teeth down his throat.

I yank his head back with the grip I have on his hair. "What the fuck?"

His eyes flick to my thigh and a smug grin tips his mouth.

I glance down and the blood drains from my face. There, under the gentle glide of his thumb back and forth, he's signed 'Malikov' starting at the inside of my thigh, wrapping around the front dangerously close to where the slit of my dress falls.

A Sharpie marker mocks me from the floor next to his shoe.

"Have you lost your fucking mind?"

"Undoubtedly." He makes quick work of the second shoe before reaching over to the ottoman, where he picks up my sheath and secures the leather strap to my thigh.

My throat thickens with the unexpected gesture. He knows what I am capable of, but he clearly recognizes how my knives have become integral to my feeling safe. Despite every reason why weaponizing me is about the worst idea he can have, he does it anyway.

I refuse to think about what it means. I will not let this one little gesture worm its way inside me. No.

His eyebrows furrow and he shakes his head. "You know what, I don't trust you." He hooks his finger around a pair of panties in the exact same champagne shade as the gown. Holding them open at my feet, he glares up at me in silent command.

Despite being furious with him, I like him like this...

looking up at me. Tunneling my fingers into the underside of his hair, tipping his head back even farther, I hold on.

He never looks away, not for a single second. The unhurried drag of the silk thong stokes the fire he started with his mouth. By the time he reaches the apex of my thighs, I am a panting mess with sweat blooming at the edge of my hairline.

I close my eyes, my chest heaving with the effort of my restraint. He took my virginity and I haven't been touched since. A means to an end, we never had a chance to indulge in the intimacy or foreplay my body was so desperate for. This fleeting taste is excruciating in every way.

My eyes flicker open, locking on my reflection. The woman standing there looks thoroughly fucked despite being brought to the precipice of orgasm only to be denied by the man before her.

Who says the Devil will never kneel? Is there a better disguised evil than feigned acquiescence?

One long finger settles the string between my ass cheeks, deliberately dragging the tip from my pussy, over my asshole, and beyond, eliciting a desperate whimper.

Fingers clenched in his hair, I only just notice how I have tugged him closer, silently begging for what he denied me earlier.

"Mmmm, better." His impossibly deep voice reverberates along my thigh. His featherlight kiss comes next, a momentary warmth from his lips through the silk followed by infinite nothingness.

With one last lingering touch, he stands.

He takes my chin with his forefinger and thumb and tips my face up to his. "Baby steps tonight, goddaughter of mine," he says, smirking down at me. "You don't want to give away all of your secrets."

I stumble as he lets me go, rage making my blood pump furiously through my veins. My heartbeat echoes in my ears, but not loud enough to drown out his parting words.

"We *will* talk about what you said to me about your mother when this is over. You and me? We're going to set a few fucking things straight."

CHAPTER 23

Konstantin

Shadowbrook Lair—the inner sanctum of the Ophidian Society. Home of the Grand Serpent himself. No way this can go wrong. No way at all.

Composed of politicians, billionaires, and some of the most brilliant minds on the planet, there is no limit to their global power, a fact that should give me pause, only it doesn't. No amount of money, power, or intelligence can save anyone who dares risk Nikoletta's life. I'll skin them alive right there on the pristine marble floor.

We arrive in three vehicles. All bulletproof. All full of armed men. Yet none of them relieve the apprehension building inside me.

I scan the surrounding area. In just seconds, Grigori is at my side doing the same. "My gut's screaming at me, boss. And you?"

"Yeah. Stay within twenty feet of her the entire night and don't take your eyes off her for a second."

He nods and slides me a sidelong glance. "Done."

I glimpse her exposed back and the dimples on clear

display just above her mouthwatering ass. "Keep your eyes from the shoulders up or I'll hand them to you."

His lips twitching, a mocking laugh rumbles in his throat. "Is she armed?"

I can't help but glance down at her thigh. "Yes."

"You're sure?"

"I strapped the knives to her myself." Just the thought of her warm skin on the inside of her leg has my cock jerking in my fucking pants.

His hands freeze on the lapels of his tux. "You're going to get us all killed."

"Probably."

He snorts next to me. "Cracking jokes now, boss?"

"Nope." He's getting awfully ballsy, knowing it would be frowned upon to slit his throat in elite company.

"Fucking hell."

"Exactly." From the corner of my eye, I catch Nikoletta shifting her clutch to her left hand, holding it over the slit of her dress, hiding my name marking her as she climbs her first step.

Mine.

In permanent marker now, but fuck if I didn't want it tattooed into every intimate place on her body.

She'll try to scrub it off the minute we get back, her pride driving her to attack her sensitive skin to obliterate my claim. It might fade... but my last name will remain, just as stubborn as I am.

What would she do if she woke up to me looming over her in the middle of the night. Hands gripping her knees, spreading her, my head disappearing between her thighs to trace every single letter with the tip of my tongue?

My lips twitch.

Let the games begin.

Guests draped in designer gowns and tuxedos, women dripping with jewels, make their way up the steps to gather in the grand foyer where they congregate with champagne flutes in their hands and practiced smiles affixed to their mouths.

Everything about the glittering festivities grates on my nerves. As far as I'm concerned, the night already peaked, right about the point I had my face buried between Nikoletta's soft thighs.

We haven't even gotten inside and men are drawn to her. Their gaze sweeping over her from head to toe, lingering way too fucking long on her back, their eyes flaring with interest.

Bastards.

My most trusted men accompany me tonight. I left Dimitri behind with Faith, knowing if anything goes wrong, I can count on him to get her and her twins to safety. Grigori, though, he's always at my side no matter what. He oversees an interesting group of my most intelligent, rather talented killers in Emil, Sasha, Roddick, Isaak, Andrey, Gleb, and Luka.

Maybe they'll be enough keep me from collecting eyeballs because if these guys don't fucking knock it off, I'll stroll out of this motherfucker with my pockets sticky and gratifyingly full, my tux dripping blood, and a satisfied smile on my face.

Roddick stares down the valet, his look clearly dialed to fuck all the way off if you think we're handing you the keys.

Each vehicle has twenty-six hidden compartments loaded with weapons. I'm sure the leader of the Ophidian Society would only employ the best and only after putting everyone through rigorous checks. I'm also sure I don't care.

They aren't my checks, so they don't count. There's always a first time to go rogue.

When it comes to Nikoletta, I trust no one.

I never have.

Every scar I carry proves my intuition right.

In his five short years as a member, Nikolaj has earned tremendous respect in the order. He's the first member to be promoted to Protector as early as on his five-year anniversary.

The way guests greet him, draw him into their conversations, and the cautious whispers they leave in his wake are all a testament to the work he's done to build alliances.

Nikoletta on his arm exposes her in a way that sets my heart racing while steel bands tighten around my lungs until my chest aches. We're walking a tightrope with no net, either way we fall—catastrophic. His move is brilliant if it gives our enemies pause at taking a swipe at her. Taking aim at Nikoletta means declaring war with Nikolaj. At the society itself. This will make sure everyone knows it.

But if it goes wrong—no. It can't. That's it. It cannot go wrong.

By showing she's under his protection, we can narrow down the list of culprits when the time comes... because the time will come. Someone will strike, and there's no guarantee it will come from Maksim, Vlad, or Petrov.

Socially, he's already leagues ahead of where Maksim peaked. Maksim had no choice but to rule with fear, but fear is fluid. Easily transferable to whoever promises the most pain. But when you have true loyalty based on respect, your supporters take the pain to protect you.

He's exactly what happens when you're confident in your abilities but know to leave your ego at the door. Something Maksim and Vlad never have been, nor ever will do.

At the moment, he sticks close to Nikoletta, introducing her to small groups throughout the massive grand foyer. The lingering hot gazes outside had my temper spiking, but now, the brushing of fingers over her shoulder followed by the subtle drag of fingertips down her arm while these men greet her has my blood boiling.

I hear a nasty growl of frustration and look for the threat, only to realize it's coming from me.

Focus, Malikov.

Chest swelling with labored breaths, I clench my fists and force my gaze away.

I sweep the room and guests, desperate to put this snarling energy into something useful. I already know the floor plan thanks to the set of blueprints Nikolaj secured from a talented little hacker friend of his who likes to dabble in seeing what she can get away with.

Now that I stand here in person, I search the exits to see which are clear and which are obstructed by the entertainment and staff. I make note of how heavily guarded the entry points are and which they roped off.

More than half of the exits are blocked, including the one closest to Nikolaj and Nikoletta where they join a group of his friends, including his best friend and Nikoletta's first kiss, Logan Rhodes. Her eyes light up when he hands her a glass of champagne and winks.

This fucker.

She settles into an animated discussion with him, her hand resting on the newel post of one of two sweeping staircases curving on either side of the room leading to a crescent-shaped balcony looking over the foyer. Beyond is a wall of windows with a view overlooking the terrace and gardens sloping down the expanse of the property beyond.

My mind goes back to Nikoletta's journal entry of the couple she watched fucking in a similar setup, discreetly in the open, all but daring the other guests to watch. Taking her up there would be stupid. Not just playing with fire but dousing myself in gasoline and lighting the Zippo myself.

Before I can stop it, the picture of us fills my head. My hand over her mouth, muffling her screams as I pound into her harder. Knowing with every thrust, she'll only get louder, despite everything I do to quiet her, increasing our risk of getting caught.

She'd pierce me with a cutting glare the entire time. If I'm lucky she'd bite the fuck out of my hand and draw blood. Blood I'd gladly drag down the column of her neck and over the rise of her breasts.

I squeeze my eyes shut and pinch the bridge of my nose as though I can grab the image and drag it clean from my skull. Throat dry, I all but vibrate with this irrational need to be inside her now, now, now.

My nineteen-year-old goddaughter is aiming to be my downfall if I don't get a fucking grip on myself. I'm not some horny fucking twenty-year-old for fuck's sake.

My gaze sweeps over Nikoletta for the dozenth time. My jaw clenches a bit more with every glimpse until I swear my teeth will snap with the force.

Men can't take their eyes off *my* woman.

In my head, I expect it. With her shoulders pulled back, the confident tip of her chin, and those eyes of hers glowing like embers of golden fire, she exudes confidence. She not only keeps up with the conversation, but confidently joins in.

Expected or not, I don't have to like it.

She's done her homework. Nikolaj must have given her a crash course earlier on the who's who of the society because she's talking among the masses like they're all old friends.

I force myself to stroll the perimeter when all I want to do is bulldoze my way through, noting the amount of steps between exits and notable areas. My men are all taking turns doing the same, making sure three of them stay tight to Nikoletta and Nikolaj at all times.

Bitterness churns through me as I watch her. Each animated word from her crimson lips she shares with everyone but me searing me in my most vulnerable places. Genuine smiles, easy laughter—she just hands them out to whoever looks her in the eye.

All things she used to give me freely.

How the hell will I convince her my feelings have absolutely nothing to do with her mother? This bond, this goddamn ache left from profound longing, goes so far beyond her childish crush and rivalry I had with her father decades ago.

It's rooted to a place deep inside, as integral to survival as the very blood feeding through my veins.

Nikoletta holds the power. She has me in the palm of her hands. To a degree, she always has, but I saw this connection with her having an expiration date of sorts. Growing up, moving on, and starting a life of her own, distance was all but a foregone conclusion.

It's the way it's supposed to be.

But now this bond between us has twisted into something so wildly different than anything I could have imagined. My future, all the roads not taken so I could stay and protect her, they hover at the fringes of possibility.

Taunting. Teasing.

Each one begins and ends with her.

Grigori is right. This road is fraught with landmines. Nikolaj may be leagues beyond his brother and father, but I'm still the man chosen to nurture, protect, and guide Nikoletta, who crossed every line imaginable. I'm still the man he chose to stand at his side and help while he amasses an army to take on his brother and father. What I've done will destroy the trust he has in me and will make him question everything he thought he knew. He'll peel apart every memory of me with her, looking for a predator who groomed her from childhood.

As he should. I'd be disappointed if he didn't. I would expect no less of a brother who loves her.

What could I possibly do to prove I never once thought of her as anything other than my goddaughter? This tiny human cradled in my hands who had such a huge life waiting for her. The little girl who used to sit perched on the piano while I played for her. The young teenage girl who silently crushed on a boy for six months to the point of absolute lovesick misery until I convinced her to ask him to the Sadie Hawkins dance at their school.

A problem for another day, because first, there'd be nothing to convince Nikolaj of it if I didn't manage to get it through her stubborn ass that she's mine. As much as I'm hers. All the pieces were there. Love, explosive chemistry... all marred by one fucked-up comment from a man who, at one time, was supposed to have been my best friend.

A man who used my worst moment to keep me loyal. We never had a real friendship. I see that now. I owed a debt. It took me far too long to realize he'd never consider it paid.

Keeping her bound to me in my safe house is a hollow victory.

An hour in, and my blood boils watching Nikolaj's friends lean in and greet Nikoletta where she offers them her cheek and collects kisses. I make note of every single one so I can fantasize about carving their faces off their skulls.

Even better if they fuck up and give me the opportunity to bring the fantasy to life. Doesn't have to be tonight... I can be patient.

My phone vibrates in my pocket with an alert unique to my team. I duck into a quiet corner and swipe the screen.

GRIGORI

Unexpected guests. Bar, 7 o'clock. Sasha's gathering intel now.

ME

Looks like I'm drinking tonight.

GRIGORI

Oh fun. Buzzed boss. As if you weren't reckless enough lately.

ME

You're lucky I like you.

GRIGORI

I'm lucky you need me.

ME

That too.

GRIGORI

Don't get dead.

ME

Eyes on Nikoletta. Above the shoulders. Your life for hers. Got it?

GRIGORI

I'll keep your girl safe.

Your girl.

The way those words settle inside me makes every single worry plaguing my mind fade away. There's a way forward. I just have to find it.

The key to these events is looking like any other guest. Smile, wink, leisurely steps so you look like you're mingling, when really you have a destination in your sights. With the jazz band kicking it up a notch, I just look like a man escaping the dance floor as couples shift from polite greetings to more private conversations in each other's arms.

My height exposes me most of the time, but at the moment, allows me to monitor the bar where two serious-looking men scan the room, their heads together as they exchange what looks to be intense words, judging by the shrewd look in their eyes and the serious set of their mouths.

Something about the dark-haired one has my nerves pinging. He's scanning the crowd too fast, with too much interest, searching.

I keep my distance and head to the small bar closest to them, grab a glass of whiskey, and keep to the shadows. The perfect picture of a man who wants to enjoy his drink in peace. I shift bit by bit. It takes about five minutes, but I'm finally in earshot, just in time to see Nikolaj hand Nikoletta off to Logan Rhodes of all fucking people.

With a conspiratorial smile, he spins her onto the dance-floor, her split parting enough that I catch a flash of "ov" on her thigh before he pulls her tight against him, his hand settling on her lower back, his middle finger landing on the one of those fucking back dimples I'm clearly obsessed with.

Possession burns in my gut. For the first time my name is more than just the last name I shared with my father. It's claiming what's mine. It's the guarantee that while she's dancing with him now, dancing is as far as it will go.

Those letters belong to me. They're for my eyes and my eyes only.

She aims her biggest smile of the night thus far right up at him, her eyes light up in a way I haven't seen since... before.

She might as well sink her knife straight into my gut.

Nikolaj catches my attention from where he stands just beyond the band and summons me over with a subtle jerk of his head.

My phone pings in my pocket again, thank fuck, because much more of this and I don't know if I'll resist plucking her straight from his arms and hauling her off caveman style.

So much for listening in on the unannounced guests, but I need to make Nikolaj aware of their presence anyway. Making my way to the other side of the band, I settle in next to him and read the screen.

Sasha: Sandy-blond hair-Jameson Voss, Sentinel in the Order. Distant relative of founder Eleanor Voss. Owns a hedge fund firm in Manhattan. Dark hair-his cousin, Foster Voss. Fired from Stein, Clemmons, and Wright 4 months ago. Gambling and cocaine addictions. Seems to have found a way to stave off the worst of his debts.

I'm sure he did. On the edge. Desperate. Who knows to what level he sank to buy time.

Too much of a risk.

"Something up?" Nikolaj asks, never taking his assessing gaze off the crowd.

I take a sip of my whiskey and keep my eyes on the crowd. On Logan. "Two guys, not on the guest list. Jameson Voss checks out. Foster Voss is a messy fucker."

Nikolaj smiles, keeps his gaze straight ahead, but subtly tips his head. "He doesn't get near my sister."

"Agreed."

He gives his glass a shake, setting the ice rattling. "We don't need him thinking he has a shot with her and we sure as fuck don't want her considering him a prospect."

The hair on the back of my neck prickles. "A prospect. A prospect for what?"

"Marriage."

One word with all the power to peel my eyeballs from Logan's hand caressing Nikoletta's lower back. "What the hell are you talking about?"

He turns to me then, propping a shoulder against the wall. "She didn't tell you?"

"Tell me what?"

He glances around, then leans in, dropping his voice low. "She needs protection. More protection than I can give her. There's one way to get it."

"And she agreed to this?"

"Not at first, but I told her I'd give her time to make the choice. Introduce her to prospects who could keep her safe. But she can't fuck around. There's not a whole hell of a lot I can do to change it, but I can protect her while she chooses."

Every tactical thought disappears from my head. Swiped away by the knowledge that she knew the whole time why we were coming here. Standing on the riser in the single most revealing gown I've ever seen. The flippant smile on her face. The way she practically chirped about going to this party. She knew I'd be watching her pick her forever.

She took glee in the fact.

The blood pounds in my ears. I clench my fists, fighting every single urge pumping through my veins to spin on him.

And now she's dancing with Rhodes. Her first kiss.

Oh, I don't fucking think so.

He claps me on the shoulder a couple times, completely oblivious to my blood pressure spiking to stroke level, and grins. "Won't be long and you'll be walking her down the aisle. What better way to piss my father off, right?"

If he doesn't stop talking, I'll be in the ICU before the night is out.

"Vincent wants to meet in his study for cigars. She's in good hands with Logan but stick close."

She's not in good hands with Logan. There are only two good hands. Mine. "You hate cigars."

"True, but no reason he can't have one while we discuss whatever it is he wants to discuss."

"He wants something?"

"I'm sure of it." Nikolaj grins. "What better way to get ahead than give it to him?"

Any other time, I'd insist on going with him, but there's no way I'm leaving her. "He's the Grand Serpent. What can you possibly do that he can't do for himself?"

"Get my hands dirty." He shrugs and drops his glass onto a tray as a waiter passes by. "Plus, there's one part of New York City he doesn't control. I have a feeling he knows it."

"Be careful."

He slides his hands in his pockets, the absolute picture of calm. "Always."

The minute he's gone, I shoot a message to Grigori.

ME

I need Gleb and Roddick on Nikolaj. He's meeting with St. Clair in the study. They won't be allowed in, but I want them stationed by the door.

GRIGORI

Done.

ME

Have Luka stay close to Jameson and Foster. See what he can hear. Make note of anyone they talk to.

GRIGORI

Want me to stick closer to Nikoletta?

ME

No need.

GRIGORI

What are you going to do?

ME

Rhodes is looking a little tired. Time to cut in.

GRIGORI

Bad idea.

ME

Not as bad as what I really want to do.

GRIGORI

Fuck.

ME

Yup, that's what I really want to do.

GRIGORI

The minute I have to start policing your dick, I quit.

I toss back the rest of my drink and make my way through the masses. Just as I approach, Logan spins Nikoletta away and her back collides with my chest, her back dimples now tucked discreetly between our bodies.

Ahh, right where I want them.

Before he can take her back, I slide my arm around her waist and splay my palm over her stomach. "Mind if I cut in?"

She sucks in a breath, clearly not expecting my words to come out so close to the shell of her ear. She opens her mouth, no doubt to turn me down, but Logan speaks first.

"Not at all. I'll find you in a bit and we'll pick up where we left off."

The fuck he will.

He leans in and kisses her cheek while I picture carving his eyeballs out slowly with my Dremel.

The minute he steps away, I find her hand and give it a

firm tug, spinning her around to face me before dragging her in so close every inch of us from knee to chest is touching. Spreading my palm dangerously low on her back, I cover both of *my* back dimples and clasp Nikoletta's chin, forcing her to look up at me.

Those soft, full breasts rise with her furious breaths. Her sexy molten eyes flash with frustration, knowing she can't do anything here, but promising future violence. A vicious snarl only we can hear escapes her gritted teeth.

Ah, there she is... my formidable little killer.

"Husband hunting, are we?"

CHAPTER

24

Nikoletta

"This is new." I trace my fingertips over the tattoo along the side of Logan Rhodes' head, the bold colors obscured a bit by his short-cropped hair. He barely resembles the man I remember from three years ago.

Then, he was an All-American golden boy with a clean-shaven face, baby-blue eyes, and a smile that could charm the panties off a nun.

But the man holding me now, he's none of those things. His hair is neat, a little longer on top, but slicked off to the side, neat and clean, the way he'd always worn it, but that's where the similarities end.

His baby blues, now ice-cold, narrow a bit more when he looks at you. New creases bracket his mouth, disappearing behind the short beard and mustache dotted with premature gray. He's harder. Edgier. The tattoos are only the beginning of the changes.

He glides his thumb along my cheek, the gesture loaded with a sweet affection that has me leaning into him for a reprieve from the constant tension of being under Konstantin's watchful eye. He smiles down at me, a hint of easy laughter in his voice. "Not quite the clean-cut guy you remember, huh?"

"Oh, I think he's still there. He's just on the inside now. What made you get the ink?" I tip my head to where the butterfly and grenade tattoo disappear under his collar. "A ton of ink, by the looks."

Dancing with Logan is exactly what I need right now. I know the eligible men here are my best option, but they're all leaving me bored, with emptiness gnawing away in the pit of my stomach. The life looming before me with any of them is so stunningly sterile. Every move and countermove for appearances. A life sentenced to empty pretenses.

The victory I thought I'd feel making Konstantin watch me move on without him is elusive and hollow.

"It makes it easier to slide in and out of dangerous places, if you know what I mean. Tattoos used to make people leery. Now, and in this society, not having them has the same effect."

I squeeze him a bit harder and lean my head on his chest. "People leery of you, no way."

"Oh, you'd be surprised. And your brother has me going on a special assignment. Clean-cut won't cut it."

He takes me into his embrace. The way we're dancing is almost improper in its intimacy, but right now, not that I'd ever admit it, I just need a hug and this is as close as I'll get.

How did I live like this for years? Living a glittering, yet anesthetized existence.

"So tell me, Nik, you haven't been settling for mediocre, right?"

Konstantin's name burns on my skin. Fury sweeps through me at the reckless move, a last burst of feeling igniting this insatiable yearning to live boldly.

The handful of kisses, the one time he'd been inside of me, just scratch the surface of the man's capabilities. God help me, I yearn to discover every layer of him. I agonize every moment of what we could be if there was a way through everything dividing us. This hum of energy buzzing between us draws us in despite every deadly reason we should stay away. Every minute, every second, pulsing with the undiscovered euphoria of two damaged pieces who defy all logic to make one perfectly imperfect whole.

If I could just heal the heart he broke. Even if I can, what if he breaks it again? The pain would be insurmountable a second time around.

"I haven't been settling, but then, it looks like I will be now."

"Why do you say that?"

"They're all too polished. Too practiced at saying just the right thing. Their actions are less about what they're actually doing and more about how they look doing it. I'm finding polished men with money and power bore me to tears."

His arms tighten around me for the briefest second. "I told him you'd never find someone who could do you justice here. But the alternative..."

"I know. I know it's the smart thing to do. I just... if I'm going to make this work, I have to bury the woman I've become." My breath hitches. "And I kind of like her. For once, I like her. She's not a product of what others want her to be. She's just... me. I'm losing me to be me—I don't know, it sounds stupid when I say it out loud."

"No, it doesn't." He hooks his finger around a lock of hair brushing my eyebrow and sweeps it away before it can get in my eyes. "Pretend you can have anyone you want. Petrov isn't hovering on the fringes waiting to assuage his pride. Maksim and Vlad, they're never leaving Russia again... and Nikolaj is not preparing to go to war with them for control over New York City. Who's the guy?"

I can't help the way my eyes search for Konstantin. Even though he's the only man who truly ever hurt me, although he's suffocating me, the powerful connection between us draws me to him at every turn.

My secrets bubble discreetly to the tip of my tongue. I step into Logan until my mouth is just a couple inches from his ear and paint my strikingly abstract masterpiece in the barest whisper. "He's unpolished and mysterious. I know everything about him, yet nothing at all. He's ruled by an infectious, inexhaustible passion I can't help but be drawn to until I'm addicted to his chaos."

Konstantin's molten glare carves a path over my skin from where he stands with my brother.

"He's action and reaction incarnate. Every look sets me on fire. I want to kill him almost as much as I madly love him. He doesn't let me get away with any of my rich bitch, princess bullshit."

The cords in his neck flex while barely banked rage rolls off him in agonizing waves as he watches us.

"He doesn't care about appropriateness and decency or some inane protocol as to how I'm supposed to be touched. He doesn't revere me like this goddamned work of art, on display, untouchable, collecting dust and withering in solitude. He wants to break me... and break right along with me. He's pleasure and pain to the point of blissful exhaustion."

His knuckles turn white with the force of his grip on the glass, making me wonder how the crystal manages to not fracture into thousands of razor-sharp shards in his violent hands.

"He's a brutal picture of anger. Bold cutting slashes of red crisscrossing on the canvas. He'll lash at me, leaving a sting that takes my breath away. And when I'm pulsing with agony, he loves it away. When he touches me, he's gold. Shimmering and warm, he soothes every ache."

"Nik," Logan whispers as he pulls back and cups my face, "He's real, isn't he?"

My heart lodges in my throat, choking me. All I can do is stare at him while I harness every bit of my willpower to keep from confirming what Logan just guessed.

"I'm so sorry." Bringing his forehead to mine, he sways with me. For just a moment, it's just my wordless non-confession, but confession all the same. Shared with maybe the only person alive who can understand how impossibly fair it is.

I grip his wrists and squeeze, battling tears, so many fucking tears. "Make me laugh, Logan. If I don't laugh right this minute, I'm going to lose it."

"Did I ever tell you about that time your brother got his dick stuck in his zipper?"

"Oh my God." I let out an unladylike messy snort, my eyes still burning from the unattainable image of Konstantin and me I painted for Logan.

"Yup, broke skin and everything. Had to rub Neosporin into his knob daily. He was late to first period every single day that week…"

With his every horrifying word, my misery slips away and the ground under me solidifies once more with purpose. "Oh, gross."

"Listen, once you've activated the launch sequence, you have to run with it."

"Thank you, Logan. Seriously. I needed this. Now I feel like I can get through another hour… maybe."

He whips me away, spins me, and ends on a dip that has my head spinning and the first real smile of the night spreading across my face. "You'll need another dose of me in an hour, got it."

"Make it a half hour. I like you."

He smiles down at me and winks. "I like you too." Bringing me back into his arms, in a more socially acceptable hold, his eyes trail over my shoulder and he winces. "We're being watched."

I glance over my shoulder and meet Konstantin's thundering gaze. "It's nothing." The lie falls from my lips so easily and I hate it. "He's probably still mad that I called him a boomer."

Logan throws his head back and laughs. "Boomer? Ouch. That would do it. Although, if the last year is any indication, he's only just coming into his prime."

I stumble, but Logan's firm grip keeps me upright. "Why? What happened in the last year?"

My fingers tremble on Logan's shoulder, and my stomach flutters with anticipation. Despite all the reasons I definitely shouldn't care, I want to know how he reacted to my disappearing. I pathetically want him to care.

"He made it his mission to find you and left a lot of bodies in his wake. At least when I go on this little assignment for Nikolaj, I won't be cleaning up the bloodshed."

"He didn't... he doesn't..." Konstantin has never shied away from violence, away from doing what needs to be done, but he never needlessly killed people and certainly not in some uncontrolled slaughter the way Logan makes it sound. "But he wouldn't expose Nikolaj like that. He's too cautious."

He shakes head. "Not in the last year, he wasn't. He was a man possessed. God help anyone who stood in his way."

"Konstantin?"

"Yeah. I don't think Nikolaj was even a blip on his radar in the past year. Konstantin had one goal. Finding you."

I glance over at the man in question, trying to see the man Logan is describing, to find he's reading something on his phone. Something that has him ditching his drink and typing in rapid reply. "He's never been quick to violence. He's methodical, with the patience of a damn saint."

"Not anymore, he's not. When he wasn't searching or killing, when he had no leads or needed rest, he spent most of his time underground. The crypt is the one place we haven't modernized down there. He won't let us touch it."

The crypt, where we kissed for the first time. Where he gave me an orgasm that created a goddamn addiction I can't satiate. Where I finally got to spend the night sleeping in his arms, one torturous time.

"When it comes to you, Nik, Malikov has one setting... scorched Earth," he says before spinning me again.

Damn you, Konstantin. No.

He does not get to coil his way around my heart like this. By being this fucking beast who only exists in fairy tales, tearing the world to the ground to find me. By being the tortured soul suffering in the place where we began.

My back collides with an unyielding, warm body. Konstantin's familiar scent winds around me, tapping at all the fresh bruises left from my conversation with Logan.

His possessive arm locks around my waist, his hand firmly settling over my belly where I'm sure he can feel the fireworks detonating under my skin.

"Mind if I cut in?"

His breath dances over my ear and my skin burns with a rush of blood, followed by goosebumps marching over my skin to the roots of my hair.

Yes, I mind.

My heart can't take this. Not tonight. Not after stupidly ripping myself open in a weak moment.

Logan shakes his head. "Not at all. I'll find you in a bit and we'll pick up where we left off."

When he leans in and kisses my cheek, I want to sink my nails into his forearm and force him to stay with me, but then he'll know. He'll know the man I spoke of was none other than my godfather and the fallout? I couldn't even think about the fallout.

Logan disappears into the crowd right as Konstantin gives my hand a firm tug and spins me in his arms.

His eyebrows are nothing more than heavy slashes over dark, livid eyes. His palm burns where he caresses my back, pulling me in so tight and hard, his hard cock drives into my belly, short-circuiting my every defense.

He clasps my chin, the warmth of his fingertips seeping into my skin, and for just a second my eyes sink closed and I absorb him. I don't have to hate him here. In fact, it's best if I don't. Keep up the appearance of adoring goddaughter with endless affection for her godfather, but not so much so that he thinks he'll ever hold my heart again. And if during the process I pretend for just a minute, just long enough to ease the ache lancing my heart, then so be it.

"Husband hunting, are we?"

The mocking snarl in his words has my eyes shooting open, daggers aiming right at him.

This is the part where everything I do to break free of him earns a lashing from his whip. Where he toys with my splintered heart and shows me all the ways any future without him will be lacking. This is the man I saw in him when he crashed into the commune. The very one who recognized his match as he circled me.

He won't be merciful. He won't hold back.

This is where he makes me bleed.

But I won't bleed alone.

"You want to shop for a husband, I'll let you get away with it... for tonight, but you'll be doing it with my cum leaking out of *my* tight little pussy."

I squeeze my thighs at his words, everything in me from head to toe winding so tight I'm on the verge of snapping. Before I realize what I'm doing, my tongue swipes my bottom lip, drawing his possessive gaze to my mouth.

He leans in, dangerously—indecently close, his every word branding me.

"You'll do it, with my cum drenching *my* supple thighs, keeping those mouthwatering legs glued firmly shut."

CHAPTER

25

Nikoletta

Konstantin's hand locks on mine in a viselike grip as he all but drags me to the stairs. "You can't just go around hauling me off to God knows where. What will people think?"

He skids to a stop and whirls on me. "Now you're worried about what they think? You didn't worry about what they'd think when you dressed in a fucking handkerchief, but this..." He holds up our joined hands and shakes them in my face. "This is what you have a problem with."

I tear my hand from his, quickly glancing around to make sure no one is watching. Using every bit of patience I can muster, I school my features and keep my voice level. "I have a father. He sucks. I don't need another one, so back off."

We stare each other down, neither willing to give in, which always seems to be the way with us now. A server heading in our direction takes one look at Konstantin's face and shifts course.

"Wait! I want one of those." With a wary glance at Konstantin, he stops and offers me a nervous smile and my choice of champagne flutes.

I pick the fullest one and wish I could actually grab one for each hand—*actually,* I snag a second and smile. "Thank you."

Take my hand now, fucker.

"You're welcome—uh, m-miss," he sputters before scurrying away.

Konstantin snatches one of the glasses from my fingertips and tugs me along with him, with less force but no less determination.

I may have gotten my hand free from him once, but the man made sure I wouldn't again with the way he interlaced our fingers this time.

Damn him.

He marches straight up to where Grigori monitors the party from the bottom of the stairs, only coming to a stop when he's looming over him.

Grigori's eyes widen for the briefest moment before he settles into the deceptive look of indifference he's so good at.

"No one goes upstairs. Got it?" Konstantin snaps out, dropping my hand to lean menacingly over Grigori.

Hands folded in front of him, Grigori glances about and leans in. "Boss, this is a bad id—"

"I know what you're going to say. Save it," Konstantin snaps. "No one goes up. Get someone to cover the other staircase."

"Christ." Grigori shoves a hand through his hair in a rare show of frustration and slides his phone from his pocket. "Fine."

With one last quick look around, Grigori uses his body to conceal the fact he's unhooking the velvet rope blocking off the stairs and steps back for us to pass.

"And what the hell do I tell Nikolaj if he comes looking for you guys, *boss*?"

"Tell him we've stepped away to discuss wedding plans."

"Here," Grigori says, shoving what looks to be an untouched drink into Konstantin's one empty hand. "Keep your hands full... of anything but her," he says, sliding a worried look my way before taking in the determined expression, carving hard lines into Konstantin's face.

Konstantin glances back and forth between my extra glass of champagne and the highball glass in his other hand, then downs the champagne in one greedy swallow before shoving the glass back at Grigori and taking my hand once again.

"Jesus. At least try to look like you're just checking out the festivities and not—whatever the hell you're going to do up there."

I can't help but glance at the crowd, constantly checking to see if anyone sees us as he drags me along behind him. The music grows louder with every step. The foyer and curving staircase almost create a funnel effect where the noise rises and collects in the shadows.

The minute we clear the top stair, he circles me, slamming down the drink Grigori gave him on a marble table tucked along the wall. Long fingers wind around my neck, squeezing a gasp from my lips.

Taking this chance here, of all places, is absolute insanity. Being on the Grand Serpent's estate all but guarantees we have cameras on us at all times, in every single corner of this house.

Backing me into the shadows along the wall, pinning me there, he dives his other hand under the slit of my dress, his palm cupping my pussy with a rough squeeze.

Out of control, unpolished, he's at the mercy of his every emotion.

This could easily get us killed. If anyone catches us,

Nikolaj will lose precious standing within the Order he's counting on to help him wage a war—and to protect me.

It's the logical thought coursing through my brain because it's what I'm trained to believe, not because it's how I *actually* feel.

Because when it comes down to it, I don't care.

Everything I've done to break free from the cage led me right here, to dependency. On Konstantin, on my brother, now on the Order, and eventually—some powerful, polished man I'll struggle to remember the name of long after I've married him because I feel nothing. Nothing for him—nothing for the marriage and life trapping me.

But right now, in this moment, I get to feel it all.

My yearning to live in this moment overshadows my deep-seated need to make him pay for hurting me in the worst possible way. His betrayal cost me two people when he stained my mother's memory and turned my hero into a heartless villain.

A delicious hum travels up my throat. The more he believes he's possessing me, the more I'm actually possessing him. Ruling his every emotion. Prompting his every reckless action.

Konstantin's fingers flex, his hot, furious gaze going to my mouth. He bites his bottom lip, one long, thick finger sliding past the scrap of fabric covering the heart of me, plunging impossibly deep.

Biting back the hiss trying to break free, I slump under the onslaught, or maybe my greedy body is trying to impale on him further, chasing pleasure I know only he can give me.

"Tell me, Pcholka. Who did this to you? Who is *my* greedy little pussy soaking for? Rhodes or me?"

He thinks he's so clever. That he has me. But it's going to take more than a finger inside me, more than his demanding palm grinding against my clit to make me submit.

Victory appears in a myriad of ways. Trophies and awards amassed on a shelf. Framed photos of achievements displayed in a shrine to a life smashing goals.

But tonight... in this moment, victory is a man on the edge of reason—fiery, impulsive, reckless, and absolutely out of his mind with jealousy and possessiveness.

It's a man who will burn every rule, every bit of propriety to the ground to take what's his.

Tipping the champagne glass to my lips, I take a long, slow sip, never tearing my eyes from his. Dragging his finger out of me partially, he adds another. Searching for a sign he's gained the upper hand in my expression, his fingers tighten around my neck right before I swallow. A strange fascination crosses over his face as he turns his focus to my throat while the bubbling liquid slides down.

"Rhodes." Logan's last name becomes the only blade within reach in this place of pomp and circumstance.

Konstantin rears back a thunderous glare in his eyes.

Victory is knowing with one word, I can take absolute control.

"That's right, Kostya. *My* pussy is soaking wet for Rhodes." His hand slackens just a fraction and I wrench free from his grip and dart past him. I seek solace leaning against the edge of the balcony, illuminated by the warm glow of hundreds of tiny lights.

My heart thunders in my chest as I stare at his back. Fingers shaking, I grip my champagne flute like a lifeline until I fear I'll snap the crystal with the force.

His wide shoulders rise and fall with deliberate breaths. He lifts his head, his silver-streaked hair brushing the top of his jacket.

Seconds tick by as I wait for his next move, my breathing growing more erratic until I'm lightheaded in my anticipation of what he'll do.

Smooth and purposeful, he carefully turns to face me, his features now blank. Like he's found a new tactic, and he's keeping it all to himself until he's ready to strike. "Did you really think you'd get away with it? That I wouldn't find out what you're up to?"

"I wasn't getting away with anything. Getting away with it means I'm not allowed to do it. I do what I want."

He takes a step toward me, and another, each one prominent, stalking his prey. "So you think you can marry someone else?"

I raise an eyebrow and smirk, wanting nothing more than to prod him into saying it. Just once confessing what he really wants. "Someone else? As opposed to who exactly?"

He touches me as though I'm his. Calls me his. But when it really comes down to it, when it comes to laying it all on the line, including our very lives, can he confess out loud what he ultimately wants?

And can I live with *why* he really wants it?

Toe to toe, he stares me down. The confession is there in the swell of his chest as he drags in a rough lungful of air. The truth in his greedy eyes as they roam over me. The admission in the pinched, flat line of his mouth, with his jaw clenched, trapping the words behind his teeth.

"Turn around."

My mind goes blank at his change of direction. My body responds to his gruff words filled with raw emotion by doing exactly what he says.

"What do you see?"

Resting my forearms on the wrought-iron railing, I take in the party below. The potent scent of gardenias fills my nose from the flower garlands looped through the iron scrolls of the balcony walls.

Dozens of couples glide along the dance floor, their cheeks rosy from the free-flowing alcohol. Surrounding them, people mingle and move, their heads thrown back in laughter. Women lean into one another, hiding conspiratory whispers behind perfectly manicured hands, while their men clap each other on the shoulder and shake hands before moving along to the next conversation, the next connection.

They're a kaleidoscope of colorfully repeating patterns.

Distinct.

And I'm hovering on the fringes of the ever-changing, chaotic image they make.

Distant.

"Them."

The tip of his finger lands on the nape of my neck and my senses blur and refocus, all attuned to the one point. He lazily traces the valley of my spine, setting my skin on fire in his wake.

"And if they look up here, what will they see?"

"Us." I choke out the word as I struggle to fill my lungs with much-needed air.

His hand dips under the edge of my dress, his finger hooking my thong, peeling the thin silk away from where it's nestled between my cheeks. Right where he put it a couple hours before. Just when I think he'll slide his hand between my legs again, he changes direction, leisurely gliding back and forth, toying with the string.

Stepping up next to me, he leans in, his heat and scent curling around me, drugging me until I'm strung-out with wanting. "There's us and there's them, Pcholka." His deep voice rumbles along my neck as we take in the picture the guests make below. His fingers continuously tease me until desire takes on a life of its own, pooling heavily in my belly, my nipples become painful points, and my pussy is slick, swollen, and aching.

My skin grows impossibly hot and damp as my breathing quickens. Elusive pleasure whispers from the distance where Konstantin keeps it under lock and key until he's ready to grace me with the relief it promises.

"There are people who conform to the dangerous worlds they live in. They surrender their moral compass for another. A compass twisted and corrupt with a revised set of rules, keeping them obedient in their new construct."

He crouches down next to me and reaches his hand under my dress. His fingers wrap around the wet silk between my thighs. Knuckles brush over me, leaving me whimpering in their wake.

"And there are people who refuse to submit to worlds predetermined or otherwise. They relentlessly attack their confines until they find a defect in the cage. They get a taste of life beyond their prison and they're instantly addicted."

With a sharp yank, the panties rip, leaving torn fabric draping over his hand. He brings the scrap of silk to his nose and inhales deep. His eyelids sweep shut as he hums in pleasure before slowly opening again as he tucks the underwear in his pocket.

"But it's not just the world beyond the cage they hunger for, it's freeing themselves from the cage itself. They crave the battle and its bloody ends as much as they crave their next hit of freedom beyond."

Turning me to him, his hands curl around my thighs, holding my gown open and exposing me to his ravenous gaze. Countless emotions play over his face. Among them, pure lust that has him sucking in his bottom lip, the tender flesh scraping past his teeth as he lets it go with a gulp and the way he smacks his lips like a man who's slogged through the desert for hours with no water.

He tips his head back then, a hint of surrender in the gesture. "You're the freedom beyond the confines I'm addicted to," he says quietly, his penetrating, dark eyes holding me captive. "*And* you're my cage."

I sway on my feet, blinking down at him, the sting of tears burning in my eyes while heartache sweeps through me, filling my chest with a deep anguish. We'll never escape each other or this battle we've waged between us. Not while we're alive on this earth, and even in death, I know in my heart he'd hunt endlessly for me in whatever lies beyond.

He keeps me on a delicious roller coaster of long climbing hills to searing pleasure and lust, followed by plummets into pure rage, endless loops of fear, happiness, sorrow, and hope, and under it all, an endless current of love.

Pushing to his feet, he lets my dress fall closed, breaking the spell, leaving behind profound loss, wondering if we'd ever have another honest moment like the one that had just slipped away.

He steps up behind me then, his hard chest against my back where he draws a lazy finger along my arm, making me shiver. "If they looked up here right now, do you think they could see me touching you?"

"Yes." I push the word past my tight throat.

"Would it be enough to figure out that I'm a heathen who fucked my spirited little goddaughter in the most profane way possible, condemning me to hell?"

The raw ecstasy on his face as he plunged into me on that altar flashes in my mind. The war raging behind his endless dark eyes as his honor yielded to something far more power-ful. Something bigger than both of us... destiny. "No."

"Do you think I can bury my cock in you again right here without them knowing?"

A tight ball of need bursts to life in my stomach. "No," I croak out.

"No?"

I gulp down another mouthful of champagne. "Kon-stantin—no. They'll see."

"You underestimate me, Pcholka."

A shock of cool air hits my ass when he jerks the back of my dress up to my waist. "Oh. My. God."

"There's an art to fucking in public." The words slither along the back of my shoulder as he nudges my thighs apart. "First, choose your goal." He smooths his knuckle along my cheek and takes a wisp of hair between his fingers, rubbing the strands together before tucking them behind my ear.

My heart skips, then sets to racing out of control behind my ribs.

"Do you want them to see you get utterly destroyed by my cock? Or do you want to get away with it?"

His fingers brush over my clit and I cry out. My vision blurs as the threads of panic take hold in my racing heart and I slam my hand over my mouth. I squeeze my eyes shut as pleasure pulses deep with every sweep of his devilish finger.

Champagne rocks in my glass as I bring it hastily to my lips, as though I can wash away my whimpers. "And if I want both?"

His fingers disappear. But I'm right there chasing after them, sticking my ass out shamelessly.

"My fearless little goddaughter is greedy." His zipper sounds impossibly loud behind me. I can't help but search the crowd below, even though I know it would have been impossible for them to hear. "If we want to live to fuck again—tonight, we get away with it."

Across the way, I spot Roddick standing stoically at the bottom of the opposite staircase, his gaze sweeping the room and then—*Jesus*. My breath lodges in my throat and I reach for Konstantin's hand where it's holding my gown.

I plan to shove him away, but an exquisite warmth burns through me with Roddick's narrowed gaze. The crackle of nerves zing just under my skin, as shocked understanding lights his face. My senses heighten. The music, the laughter, the thundering echo of my heart all grow louder, the lights brighter with flashes of color. A vibrant onslaught advancing from every direction.

He knows. I know he knows. And I don't care. I want him to watch. I ache to be seen. I need to relieve myself of the bone-deep exhaustion I carry every second of every day, hiding my feelings for Konstantin.

The vision of Konstantin's legs widening enters my peripheral vision. Before I can ask what he's doing, he's gripping my thighs, lifting my ass up, making my back arch as I clutch the railing.

"Wet for Rhodes, my ass... your pussy is terrible at hiding your secrets, Pcholka. You're positively dripping." With one thrust, he buries his cock to the hilt.

My eyes lock with Roddick's. My breath lodges in my lungs. His cock stretches me mercilessly until I'm filled with pain. Sweet, forbidden, and addictive, it's a special agony getting everything you want savagely delivered.

I smile and sink my teeth into my lip, my eyelids growing heavy as my walls strain against his invasion.

Roddick's lips part in surprise, his eyes narrow, and the red stain of embarrassment blooms on his cheeks.

But he doesn't look away.

I clench the railing, my knuckles turning white with the force.

A scathing growl tears from his chest as his forehead falls forward into the valley between my shoulder blades. Hot, ragged exhales fan over my spine and his fingertips dig into my thighs as he anchors himself to me. The combination of our labored breaths drowns out the cacophony of sounds from the party below.

"Burying my cock in this weeping, hot cunt is the single most religious experience of my life." His lips linger along the skin between my shoulder blades, his cock slowly sliding out of me. "You are my religion now. And I'm your most devout worshipper."

He punctuates the words by sinking his teeth into my flesh where my neck meets my shoulder as he plunges deep once again. The stem of the champagne glass snaps in my hand, leaving a sharp sting behind as the glass slips from my slack fingers and crashes to the floor at our feet. What's left of the champagne splattering my ankle.

Warmth trails down my finger. I stare blankly at the blood rolling along my finger where the fractured stem sliced me open as threads of bliss flare to life inside me.

"Mmmm, give me that," he says as he curls his hand around my wrist. He brings my finger to his mouth and drags his tongue along the path of blood streaking along my skin.

My lips part in a sharp hiss when he sucks my finger into his mouth. Warm and wet, he gently sucks, lapping over the wound over and over as he rocks his hips in time with the soothing swipes of his tongue.

Abandoning his grip on my thigh, he strokes over my swollen clit. Every sensation combines into one demanding tempo. His hard and heavy cock rocking into me, his hot, wet tongue laving my skin, and the incessant circles he sweeps relentlessly over my clit, until my legs tremble uncontrollably.

Droplets of sweat bead along my hairline until they break free and trail along my skin. No longer able to draw in enough air to fill my starving lungs, I'm clinging to consciousness by a series of sharp pants leaving me dizzy and off-balance.

Just when I think I'll crumble into a heap on the floor, he rams inside me, pinches my clit, and bites down on my finger. My eyes shoot open as a blindingly white explosion tears through me. I'm spasming from head to toe, my pussy greedily squeezing Konstantin's cock.

"Fuck, yes. Choke my cock, Pcholka. Just like that." My finger pops free from between his lips, my arm falling limply to my side as he yanks me onto his cock with a hard grip on my hip.

Grasping the back of my neck with his other hand, he delivers one last thrust, anchors deep, his cock spasming and filling me with his hot release.

Suppressing my every emotion, every reaction, finally takes its toll as hot tears spill over my eyelids, blazing hot trails down my cheeks.

Clinging to the railing, I struggle to calm my racing heart. When Konstantin slides out of me, loneliness rushes in with the stark realization I can't have this. That in my head, I've made it into something it's not. I've pretended he's in love with me and not just obsessed with replacing what he can never truly have.

He doesn't even need to lie to me anymore because I'm all too eager to lie to myself.

In record time he's righted his tux like he didn't just fuck my spirit out of my body while drinking my blood before hundreds of people.

"Now that I've tasted you, I'm hooked," he whispers along the shell of my ear. "I will come for you, Pcholka. Remember that. Marry another, and I'll come. And when I find you, I will fuck you in a pool of his blood right next to his mutilated corpse."

Because if he can't have me, no one else can either.

CHAPTER

26

Konstantin

I keep my eyes on the mirror, endlessly watching Roddick following close behind us, carrying Nikoletta. Deviating from the plan has an itch settling between my shoulder blades, my nerves pinging with every variation of sound and each flash of light as we make our way back toward the city.

Nikolaj left within ten minutes of emerging from St. Clair's office, off to do the man's bidding and climb one more rung on the secret society ladder, no doubt.

Understandable, but it left us down to two vehicles, with no choice but to have Nikoletta either leading in the first or following in the second instead of ensconced safely between the two the way I prefer.

I settled on keeping her in front of me. This way any danger would come from behind and encounter me before it could reach her. But thanks to some dipshit panicking as we approached the construction zone right after passing a vehicle with his four-way flashers on, we now lead. At least until we get through this next section and it opens back up into three lanes again.

Grigori's phone buzzes on the mount between us. Never taking his eyes from the road, he answers with one swipe. "Talk to me."

"I'm pretty sure we're being followed." Roddick's voice holds a hard edge that has my back snapping straight.

"How many?" Grigori bites out as I reach for my gun. Out of the corner of my eye, I catch sight of Sasha in the back seat doing the same.

"One, maybe two. Not sure just yet."

I should have ridden in the same vehicle with her, but I knew, I just knew I wouldn't be able to keep my hands off her. I took enough risks tonight, marching her up to the balcony, doing my best to deliver on the fantasy she scrawled in her journal.

In the single most dangerous place imaginable. And even then, I didn't give her the passionate fuck she lamented on in that damn diary. I toyed with her, then gave her possessive brutality, leaving my bite carved in her delicate skin. I spent the next hour watching with smug satisfaction, knowing my cum dripping from her spent cunt caused every wobble in her step thereafter.

She spent the hour glaring at me, keeping her back to the walls to hide my teeth marks.

The road opens up and Roddick punches the gas as he darts into the third lane. "Fuck. Definitely being followed. Two of them."

The traffic fans out as cars bunched up just moments before get up to cruising speed, making it easier to spot the vehicles in question.

The problem with this particular road is, cars flow a good fifteen miles per hour over the speed limit. We're going twenty over right now. Guardrails run along the right and cement barriers run along the left. Narrow concrete underpasses come out of nowhere in the dead of night and crop up the entire route on our way back into the city.

It's too damn fast, with too many immovable obstacles. A battle on the road risks rolling one of us, maybe both of us, which will surely take out other cars as well.

Then it's a matter of who makes it out of the wreckage quickest and shoots first. I don't like the odds. Not with her life in the balance.

"Get ahead of us, Roddick." I slide the magazine from the grip of my gun and check the bullets, although I know it's fully loaded and ready to go.

"On it." The thread of tension in his voice kicks my heart into a hard and heavy beat, my mind scrambling through all the scenarios.

If they sideswipe Nikoletta—nope. He's got to get ahead of us. I won't even consider the possibility.

If they sideswipe us—we wreck, die, and take innocent people in our vicinity with us, at worst. A gunfight at best. Either way, Nikoletta is miles ahead of us and away from the destruction.

The seconds draw out, my muscles tight, my whole body coiling into a singular focus, ready to strike. Even the most forgettable details around me. The bent corner of the speed limit sign. A missing reflector in a series of evenly spaced reflectors along the top of the guardrail. The exact quantity of stick figure kids in the family bumper sticker on the back window of the Honda we're passing.

Gleb and Sasha sit silently in the back, guns ready in hand. Their eyes narrow as they survey every angle around us.

They're good at their jobs. But for them, it *is* a job. For me, it's my calling. Every time I've intercepted threats to Nikoletta's life, the tiniest of details leading up to the battle carved themselves in my memory.

As though my mind is just waiting in anticipation of my fuckup so I can torture myself with every insignificant detail, looking for where it all went wrong until I drive myself mad or my heart stops beating.

If I lose her—my heart squeezes in my chest—it'll only beat long enough to end it and join her.

"If we can get onto the side streets, we can lose them," Grigori says, his shrewd gaze going to the rearview as Roddick begins to pull up alongside us in the left lane.

"I don't want to lose them."

Grigori does a double take. "Almost half of our team is with Nikolaj. They could easily outnumber us."

"And we'll never know how they found us. No one knew we'd be at the party tonight besides our team and Nikolaj. Someone there outed us. I want to know who and why."

The car ahead of Roddick is taking his dear sweet time passing another vehicle, leaving only a narrow gap. Trying to slip through is a risk. If he doesn't do it just right—well—he better do it just right.

Grigori eases off the gas, opening the space wider. His fingers flex on the wheel. "Maybe this is a distraction and the real target is Nikolaj and they're headed for him as we speak."

The cars Roddick spotted advance on us and slide in tight on our bumpers in a matter of seconds. "Exactly. So let's collect a few of these fuckers and find out. Take the next exit. Get us to Woodlawn."

"The cemetery?" Grigory asks, confusion in his voice.

"Yes. Any attempt on Nikoletta is choosing death. Whoever I don't collect for questioning, I'll deliver straight to the grim reaper's door."

The streak of headlights slashes across the rearview mirror as one of the cars slams Roddick's bumper. Their vehicle lurches forward but stays on the road.

This time.

"Fuck!" Roddick's voice is full of fury.

My skin burns with awareness. The windows are too dark to get a glimpse of her, but somehow, I know she's turned toward me, searching.

She hasn't made a sound in the background, but then she wouldn't. At least not one of panic or fear. I'd bet anything her blood boils back there, just itching to get her hands on whoever made the deadly decision to fuck with us tonight. I should have sent Sasha and Gleb with them. One on each side of her, because what are the chances of the feral little killer I found at the compound staying put when the bullets start to fly?

Fuck.

I check my second gun as I did my first, keeping it in my grip, propping it on my thigh as Roddick gets just ahead of Grigori and leads us off the exit. Four vehicles careening into the otherwise quiet night, in a dense residential section full with cars parked alongside the road, one-way streets, and streetlights on almost every block.

Everything gets quiet other than the sound of revving engines, squealing tires, our angry breaths, and terse communication over the line. Their drivers are cocky little fuckers. Speeding up, swerving to get a reaction, feeding their egos with useless threats they can't really follow through with without drawing attention to all of us.

But what they're really doing is wasting energy they're going to need the minute we enter those gates because we won't be cautious there. After all, everyone there is already dead.

As the gates come into view, Roddick punches the gas again until he's just shy of the turn. Slamming on his brakes at the last possible second, he yanks his wheel, sending them into a sharp, last-minute turn that has the two left tires coming off the ground, throwing off our uninvited guests.

My lungs swell with a sharp intake of air, and then freeze, the breath lodged in my lungs, only breaking free when those tires meet the ground once again and he takes off, putting distance between Nikoletta and our enemies.

The minute we make it through the gates behind him, we're flanked by both cars as they squeeze us and force us toward a copse of trees on the edge of the cemetery.

Tires tear up grass along each side of the narrow lane snaking through the massive burial site. Grigori barely holds the road. The minute we make it over the rise, a granite fountain appears and the car on our left slams on his brakes to avoid taking it head-on, leaving him behind us.

For the moment.

The car on our right swerves away and slams back into us, with a grinding of metal, tearing off the side mirror, sending us off the road where we take out a line of modest stones adorned with American flags.

"There." I point to the towering oak tree alongside the first of several mausoleums.

"On it." Foot slamming the gas pedal, he heads in that direction. Rolling down my window, I prop my elbow and take aim in my sights at the front driver's side tire.

Pop! Pop! Pop!

The explosion of bullets firing pierce the silence. The tire lets out a satisfying pop and shreds just as Grigori swerves out and then back, slamming into them with every bit of force he can. Virtually unable to steer, they head straight into the narrow space between the tree and mausoleum.

Metal screams and crunches as they wedge between the two, the force bringing them to an abrupt, jarring stop. The radiator snaps and hisses, spraying coolant over the hot, mangled engine.

Grigori slams on his brakes so Sasha and Gleb can jump out of the back. Guns drawn, they keep their eyes trained on the wreckage.

"No one gets away. Call Logan for extraction and cleanup. Anyone alive goes to the den. We're getting Nikoletta."

Grigori peels away. The call with Roddick is now disconnected. The tracker on the other vehicle is a reassuring green flash on the screen of his phone.

My heart thunders in my chest and a buzzing fills my ears as we snake through the winding roads, careening around tight corners, getting closer to them with every passing second. "C'mon, c'mon, c'mon."

There's no way Grigori can hear the chanting under my breath between the sound of the engine and squealing of tires, but it doesn't matter. He knows.

"We'll get her. We should see their taillights just over this ridge."

Before I can blink, we're cresting over the incline and my heart lurches into my throat at the sight unfolding before me.

Roddick goes left around a massive tree. The car chasing them goes right. When they converge, the bastards chasing them smash into the passenger rear, sending Roddick into a skid that rips through the grass and dirt so hard it's spraying a good ten feet into the air.

Just as I think they're good and their ass end starts to come around, their tire catches on a rock and the SUV rolls onto its side, skidding until the roof slams against a massive tombstone.

It was too fast. They were going too fucking fast.

Blood pounds in my ears and everything goes eerily still. Grigori swears next to me, but I can't make out the words past the pounding panic in my skull.

She's buckled. If she's buckled, she's fine. She *is* buckled. Roddick would have made sure of it.

If he could control her.

And that fucking temper.

My lungs heave as I search for any signs of movement. Something. Anything.

Our enemies slam on their brakes before the tree line beyond and execute a tight turn back in our direction.

Just as they advance, Roddick kicks out the passenger side window, climbs up onto the door, and pushes himself up to standing. Nikoletta appears next, her face mottled red with rage, her hair slipping from its updo, a blade already in her hand.

My lungs ache in my chest as I search over her skin.

She's fine. Pissed, but fine.

But exposed.

Grigori skids to a stop, and I'm out the door, my gun drawn, aiming right at the gun appearing from the passenger side window of the other car.

Time slows, the smallest action distinct.

"Nikoletta, down!" I yell.

"Stay down!" Roddick barks at her at the same time.

He spins to face the car heading for them.

She doesn't listen to either of us and hoists herself up until she's half-in, half-out of the car.

My heart is literally walking around outside of my chest

once again. For the hundredth time. Maybe the thousandth. I lost count years ago.

Three bullets pop off within a split second of each other.

Roddick's, mine... and theirs.

CHAPTER

27

Nikoletta

My heart pounds in my ears as I blink away the confusion. The roof dips overhead, the lining torn under the gouged metal from where we flipped and slid into the tree. My locked seat belt digs into my hip and breast where I'm left hanging on my side, just a few inches from the door and window now jammed against the ground.

Stars wink in the inky sky over the passenger side windows. Moonlight spills into the cab, giving us just enough light to see.

Already out of his seatbelt, Roddick braces his feet on the driver's side door and yanks on the handle of the passenger side door over him, but it won't budge. "Fuck. Come on," he mutters, crouched over in the tight space as he slams his shoulder repeatedly against the door while yanking the handle.

After three attempts, he flips around and delivers a series of solid kicks, popping the window free from the frame. Just as he's about to hoist himself free, he jabs a finger in my direction. "Stay down inside and stay low."

Hide and do nothing? I don't fucking think so.

Before I can tell him exactly what I think of his demand, he's climbing out the opening.

Fingers trembling, I jab at the button of my seat belt. Just as stubborn as the window Roddick kicked out, it finally releases after the third try.

Konstantin probably had the belts made that way so I would stay put. The thought slices through me. Laughter bubbles up only to turn into a tortured sob at the thought of what could be happening out there to him right now.

Falling the few inches between my body and window, I carefully brace my palms flat on the glass. A series of spider cracks cut across the glass in jagged lines, but the window stays smooth and intact, protecting me from the ground. I push up just enough to reach for the back of the driver's seat and use it to pull myself the rest of the way up.

My body protests every flex of muscle. The ache between my thighs is a relentless reminder of the way Konstantin took me on the balcony. Destroyed me.

Our second time.

My second time.

Now I have to wonder if it will be our last.

The sounds of skidding cars and revving engines tear through the otherwise quiet night. Cold dread pools in my belly.

I know I heard shots before. Distant, but definitely gunshots.

"Where is he? Where's Konstantin?"

Roddick ignores me as he gets to his feet on top of the car and draws his gun.

Pushing to my feet, I slide my knife free and follow, my heel digging into the leather of the seat, giving me a stable foothold.

He's not answering me. Why the hell isn't he answering me?

Grabbing the edge of the door, I pull up and grab ahold of a fistful of his pants. "Answer me, dammit. Where the hell is he?"

"Nikoletta, down!" Konstantin's rough, deep command comes from somewhere in the darkness, just as Roddick yells at me.

Headlights streak across our wrecked SUV and land on Konstantin, where he's marching toward the oncoming car, his gun drawn.

A humming starts in my skull, the scene unfolding slowing down in a series of frames. My lungs ache from the panic that gripped my throat during the crash, of not knowing where Konstantin is, if he's safe, and from the exertion of maneuvering through the mangled SUV.

But now, that pain is bone-deep terror as I watch the car take aim at my Kostya. Heavy dread settles in my stomach. The scream building up inside me is impossible to push past my tight throat.

I thought I had seen him at his most brutal, the night he bought me and Moretti approached him in the street as we were leaving, but no. The promise of retribution on his face then is nothing compared to the pure wrath etched into his every feature right now.

But the formidable, enraged beast before me is mortal, exposed, and fighting nearly impossible odds.

Pop! Pop! Pop!

I whirl on the sound as a bullet glances off the car a mere few inches from my arm.

My eyes meet Konstantin's for a fraction of a second, but I swear everything he feels is right there. Horror seeing how close their bullet came to hitting me, and that look giving way to blinding fury.

A savage roar so raw it sounds as if it's clawing its way out of him, rips from Konstantin's chest. Jaw clenched, hooded, dark eyes never waver from their target. The raw menace in their depths promises vengeance as he squeezes the trigger over and over, still advancing on the car heading straight for him.

He doesn't flinch. He doesn't even blink as he fires relentlessly.

"Do something!" I scream at Roddick as I watch every one of Konstantin's bullets glance off the car. My heart pounds viciously in my chest, vibrating through my veins until my temples pulse with it.

I just got him back. It can't end like this.

The vicious need for payback burns through me, leaving my skin ice-cold. I clutch my knife. A crimson river of our enemy's blood seeping into the dirt is the only outcome I can see in my mind. If they take him from me, they better hope they kill me too, because if they don't, I'll carve every single one of them up slowly, one agonizing piece at a time, keeping them alive and wailing until I reach bone.

Tires squeal and grass rips from the ground as the car veers at the last second.

A whoosh of air explodes from my lungs.

Metal screeches and crunches as they slam into a massive gravestone, ripping it from its foundation. The front end of the car shoots over the mangled rubble, grinding to a stop when the stone catches on the undercarriage.

Blood burning, I secure my other foot and climb the rest of the way out, with zero help from Roddick.

The asshole.

"You don't listen for shit." Roddick bites out the words and shoves me behind him. "Get. Down."

"Fuck you." Avoiding the mangled metal, I slide off the

back, my heels sinking into the damp grass. Dashing from behind the car, I skid to a stop at the sight of Konstantin.

Captivated by the embodiment of living vengeance he makes.

He never slows. There's no doubt. No fear.

He's a warrior avenging the attack a hundredfold.

He fires two more shots, then tosses his gun even as he's sliding another from his back. He doesn't even take the time to grip it with his right hand and instead shoots with his left.

The guy in the passenger seat scrambles for something. When he brings his arms up, Konstantin fires, his bullet piercing the man's hand with stunning accuracy, the gun he grabbed falling to the ground outside the car.

God, look at him...

He's a living, breathing angel of death. Absolutely magnificent with his wild silver-streaked hair tumbling about the sharp angles and harsh lines of his furious face as he tears up the distance with impossibly long strides.

Grigori and Roddick are already moving in on the opposite side of the car, but they're a blur because all I can see—all I want to see—is Konstantin.

He rears back, arm bent, and slams his whole upper arm into the cracked window, sending shards raining over the man who pulled the gun on him. Curling his fingers into the man's dirty blond hair, he drags him through the wreckage of the window, just plucking him out like he's nothing more than a grocery bag he forgot on the front seat.

"Well, aren't you one stupid motherfucker?" he growls at the man before dragging him to the asphalt of the narrow lane. Shoving his face to the ground, he slams his head once, stunning him, before pinning his head with his foot.

The man is six and a half feet tall... it's a big-ass foot.

My chest swells with a demented sort of pride watching

him deliver justice. And jealousy, because I want to be the one to make them scream in pain. They need to pay in the most agonizing way imaginable for threatening me and mine.

Bending down, his face settles into a sinister promise as he digs the barrel of his gun into the man's temple. "You see her?" he asks, jerking his head in my direction.

The man stays silent.

Konstantin takes his time, adding pressure with his foot until the man's one open eye bulges with agony and his jaw pops.

He howls in pain under Konstantin's dress shoe, but it's not enough. It'll never be enough.

"I'll ask you one more time. Do. You. See. Her?"

Sweat breaks out on the man's forehead, but he jerks his head ever so slightly.

"You know who she is?"

He nods yes again as my heart beats in time with the waves of agony on the man's face. A sort of alignment between predator and prey. He rained bullets on my Kostya. I flex my fingers on the handle of my knife. He's going to pay for it.

Konstantin clucks his tongue, draws his gun back, and waits for the man to look at him from his one exposed eye. "You know what else she is?"

I'm his.

I'll never let the words slip from my lips. Not even after seeing him like this. Looming over the fucker who shot at us, the very embodiment of retribution. I can't give him that power and still belong to myself. But finally seeing this side he's always hidden from me, I know it's true. *I've always been his.*

The man finally shakes his head, his dull gray eyes landing on Konstantin's face before darting away.

"Mine." Konstantin smiles then, but it's a bone-chilling smile, the kind you'd see in nightmares. "And I protect what's mine. You..." he says, adding more pressure on the man's jaw until he's groaning in misery. His eyes roll back in his head before coming to focus on Konstantin once again. "Are going to beg me to die long before your heart stops beating."

He's a one-man walking army and as magnificent as he is in battle... he's standing between the life thrust upon me and the one I'm taking for myself.

Enough blood has spilled in my name. By men guarding me, keeping me pristine, perfect, and untouched. Now it will spill by my hand. "Beg *me* to die, Konstantin."

His ruthless gaze snaps to mine and his jaw clenches, biting back his reply.

Raising my knife before me, I turn it over in the moonlight, satisfaction burning through me at the wary look in the man's eye. "He came after me. I'll be the one paying him back for it. For *all* of it."

I'm going to fucking kill her myself.

Popping into the fray like she's watching the fucking opera and not bursting out into the open with bullets flying.

Like one didn't just miss her by fucking inches.

She hovers over the fucker under my shoe, her blade glinting in the moonlight, not a single flicker of understanding on her livid face as to just how close she came to dying tonight.

My head pounds, the adrenaline beginning its retreat, leaving my muscles twitching and my hands shaking. Or maybe that's the fury and the instinct to wrap my fingers around her slim little neck and shake the fuck out of her pulsing through me.

The minute I step back, the man at my feet loses consciousness. "Take them all to the den. Keep them alive. No one touches them. They're mine."

"And mine." Her silky voice drips with cold malice.

If it were any other night, if the target had been anyone

but her, it would be comical to see twin looks of shock on their faces as their gazes snap to hers.

But right now, none of this is funny. It's stupid, reckless, absolute insolence and tonight she will fucking learn to listen.

I crouch, and with one swipe of my arm, she's draped over my shoulder. "We'll be back."

"Put me down, asshole!" She pounds on my back, the hilt of her knife connecting with my kidney, earning her nothing more than a grunt for her effort.

Grigori shakes his head as I turn away. Marching through row after row of the dead, I delve deeper into the darkness, tearing up the cold damp grass as I stomp past endless grave-stones. Most who likely died in old age, but not all, dammit. The young rest here too. Lives snuffed out far too soon. They'd gone to their graves with the barest taste of life on their tongues.

Tonight, she'd almost become one of them.

I smack her ass, putting every bit of force I can muster into my swing, knowing it still won't be enough to make me feel one bit better.

"Shut the fuck up." I bellow the words, the sound a deep combination of every emotion she brings out in me. Rage, helplessness, regret, longing, jealousy, obsession, pride, hurt, and love.

So much love I'm drowning in it. Making stupid fucking mistakes. Mistakes with the highest price tag—her life.

The sudden need to see her face, to reassure myself she's okay, sweeps over me and before I know what I'm doing, I dump her on her feet in front of a tall cross. I raise her arms, settling her hands on each side of the granite. "Don't move."

As I frantically search over her skin, her face softens from furious indignation to quiet understanding. It slices through me, leaving me raw and bleeding because she looks so damn much like she did when she looked up to me, adored me, and loved me. Like when she chose me—out of everyone—she chose me.

I thought I'd felt the worst of the pain from that loss, but I was wrong. So very wrong. Seeing this side of her again—it resurrects possibilities. Possibilities she almost snuffed out with her recklessness.

A new wave of terror sears my gut and I'm suddenly so fucking livid again, I take a step back and clench my fists to keep my hands off her. "What the fuck is wrong with you? Bringing a knife to a gunfight?"

The soft smile slips from her lips and her face slides right back into the fierce little killer I know her to be now. Only she's inexperienced and impulsive and is likely to get dead before she ever reaches her full potential.

She looks me up and down, one eyebrow shooting up. "Oh, and you're bulletproof?"

"Actually, yes, you little shit."

Her eyes narrow to slits with the words 'you little shit' and now it's all I want to call her.

I rip open the top half of my shirt, revealing the Kevlar vest beneath. "All the vital organs are protected."

She aims her knife at the zipper of my pants. "So this organ is expendable then... good to know. Her arm snakes out in a flash. When she draws her hand back, moonlight glints on steel, illuminating my blood streaking the blade.

I wrench open my pants and peel them partway down my hips, staring unblinking at the line she sliced into my skin now welling with blood.

The sting throbs to life, a sharp bite in the skin between my thigh and groin.

Our eyes lock as everything around us goes utterly still. Betrayal hovers on the fringes of love and hunger between us.

Euphoria is our reward, but only after we pay for it in pain and blood.

Before she can even blink, I'm on her. My arms loop around her legs and drag them around my waist.

Scrambling for balance, she clutches the cross tight, but never lets go of the knife.

I go still and take her in, imagining a rendering of her like this on canvas. Her defiant smirk under her intense, unblinking gaze. My snarling, vicious little sacrifice suspended there.

I'd hang her fury in the foyer as a warning to anyone who graces our door.

"You're all doe-eyed adoration one minute and vengeance the next." I graze her proud little chin with my knuckles. "Which of you will destroy me, Pcholka?"

"Vengeance." The word is a growl of warning delivered by her sharp tongue as I tip her up higher. Because of her obscenely high slit, her dress falls around her waist, baring her to me.

A blessing and a curse.

As is always the way with her.

"I hate this dress." The very first touch of my fingers brushing over her clit leaves the breath whooshing from her lungs. Her eyes turn glassy as I begin to tame her in the smallest of increments.

"I hate you." She spits the words at me like a snarling little viper. With a regal tip to her chin, she bucks in my hands, her legs hooking around me and pulling me in.

Her arousal slickens the pad of my thumb. I continue stroking in lazy swipes over her clit. First along the left, then over the top, taking in every single reaction. Looking for the place that will plummet her over the edge. When I brush along the tight little bud on the right, she bucks in my hands, her eyes rolling back and eyelids sliding shut.

Ahhhh, there's the spot.

Now I've got you.

Her hair tumbles around her face in wild waves. She's pale. The blood hasn't completely returned to the skin's surface, except the angry flush of scarlet in her cheeks.

I can work with that.

"The only part of you that hates me is your vicious tongue, but I bet the minute I slide my cock in your mouth and fuck your throat, she'll fall for me too."

Fire burns in her glare, but her hips buck, silently begging me to take her even as she condemns me for it.

Bringing my thumb to my mouth, I suck her arousal from my skin, savoring her taste bursting on my tongue.

"When you learn to fucking do as you're told, I might just have to reward you with my mouth on this tight little pussy and not come up for hours."

She opens her mouth to snarl at me, and I take full advantage. Slanting my mouth over hers, I swallow her barbs. Her spiteful little tongue wars with mine as she strains closer, all mewling whimpers and sharp teeth sinking into my bottom lip.

Warm, wet, and wild, I take until I'm swallowing her moans where they mingle with mine, and we're both a tangle of heaving breaths devouring one another.

Tearing myself from the distraction of her mouth, I take satisfaction in her swollen, wet lips. Resting my hand low on her belly, I swipe her tender flesh with my thumb once again and tease that tight bundle of nerves until her legs tremble.

Finally, the anger in her expression slips away and she surrenders to the pleasure. Her eyes dart around frantically as the release she yearns for hovers so close—I yank my hand away and smack my palm down on her pussy—yet so far away.

Her eyes shoot open and narrow.

"That's for cutting me, you little shit." I tug my achingly hard cock from my pants and drag the head along her hot slit I wrecked earlier, already glistening for me. With zero finesse and giving zero fucks whether I cause her pain after the way she scared the life out of me, I slam inside her wet heat.

Pain is living.

I'll be the man to make sure she's utterly destroyed, while overflowing with life.

Buried to the hilt, I have to wonder how I ever lived without this. How I could *ever* live without this. "You tell me, Pcholka... does this organ feel expendable?"

Her lips break apart in a gasp, her back bows, moonlight illuminating her skin as her head falls back against the stone, stretching out her vulnerable neck before me. Her heart riots out of control, her pulse hammering just under the delicate skin at the base of her throat.

Brushing that vulnerable, sweet spot alongside her clit becomes my absolute favorite thing to do as I watch her soften under the attention. Drawing out of her, the cool air hits my wet cock. A hiss slips from between my teeth.

Gliding my thumb in tandem as I fuck her, she coils tight, her neck flexing as she gulps back a sob.

I slap her pussy again and drive into her. "Can you live without me wrecking you with this cock every chance I get?"

The way she's draped on the cross like a sacrifice is blasphemous. The blatant disrespect to the grave only adds to my mountain of sins, each one shackling to me, ready to drag me to hell.

But it won't be tonight.

I curl over her and sink my teeth into the firm flesh on the inside curve of her breast. "Do you think you can live without me?"

Gliding most of the way out of her, I bury myself to the hilt once again, prompting her choked satisfying cry. She pulses around me, squeezing, drawing me impossibly deep, and my chest swells with a renewed purpose.

Submission.

Victory.

"Would your pussy weep for anyone else's cock the way it does for mine?" My gaze lands on my blood, now smeared along one creamy thigh and my name scrawled across the other.

Both stake my claim, but they're not enough. I want her words.

I grab her chin and turn her defiant face to mine as I thrust harder into her until I reach a maddening pace, only backing off when she gets close to release. I torture myself along with her by tethering my urge to let go and violently take her. "Who do you belong to?"

She yanks her head back and forth, but I don't let her slip from my grip. Leaning in so close her desperate pants flutter over my skin, I growl down at her. "Say it."

"No one." The words drip with stubborn rebellion before she clamps her lips shut.

I rear back and smack her pussy again, the contact splitting the air with the satisfying crack of my palm against her tender flesh. "The fuck you don't. Who. Do. You. Belong. To?"

The answer I want so desperately lingers in her eyes, but she keeps the words trapped in her throat. Admission is surrender, and she's spent a lifetime belonging to everyone except herself.

Any other man would succumb to their wounded pride and force the words from her, but they'd be meaningless.

Could I live with doubt if I forced them from her? Is this how I want either of us to remember the first time she confesses out loud to what we both already know?

Caressing the valley between her breasts, I slow my pace, rocking deep, drawing whimpers of rising pleasure from her throat. Every glide is absolute torture, resisting the high only exploding inside of her can bring.

I want her freely.

I want her to look at me the way she used to.

I want her to ask me who I belong to. Because if she asks, it means the answer matters. It tells me that somewhere, there's a way back. She's been screaming for freedom in a thousand little ways, but no one listened. I didn't listen.

She's been pleading for autonomy. For power.

She already has it... the year I couldn't find her confirmed one thing, if nothing else... she's always had absolute power over me.

My gaze roams over every inch of her, everywhere but her eyes. Seeing what I can't have is too much and we both need relief. Adjusting my grip on her ass, I pull her in tighter and thrust harder, chasing the high. I tease her swollen clit, anxiously waiting as she climbs to her own release, so I can see her so very alive and flying apart around me.

The burn rises in the base of my spine, and I gasp. My balls draw up tight as her walls begin to spasm around me. Despite my determination, I can't resist. I have to look at her.

I need to look into those eyes that haunt me every second as she comes apart.

There's a softness there now. A blissfulness with the wave of release building within her.

This is enough. It has to be enough. I grasp at the sentiment, but I'm not sure I believe it.

"Kostya?" she whispers, and my eyes snap to hers. She traces her finger over my jaw, and my lungs seize on a glimmer of hope. "Who do you belong to?"

Tension I've been carrying for more than a year suddenly drains from my body, magnifying the bone-melting ecstasy of release.

Her walls clamp down on me, milking me, her unfocused eyes locked on mine as every ounce of fear choking me tonight dissipates in this moment as I pour everything into her.

And surrender.

"You."

CHAPTER

29

Nikoletta

We step into the safe house and skid to a stop. Lamplight burns with a soft glow in the living area where Dimitri dances in circles around the living room, humming in tune with the kiddie music coming from the TV. He shed his suit jacket and tie and rolled up his sleeves. Lexi rests on the burp rag over his shoulder as he rubs gentle circles on her back, the ring of her pacifier looped around his index finger. Her eyelids sink shut, then flutter open, before shutting again, each blink getting longer and longer as she drifts off to sleep.

Two guns rest in holsters on either side of his spine, and I can't help but laugh at the picture he makes tall and tattooed, his dress shirt snug over thick, sinewed arms, and a pink butterfly-covered baby blanket tucked under the arm holding up Lexi's little protruding baby butt.

Faith sits on the couch, her knees up, with Alex nestled in against her thighs. A pink flush fills her cheeks, the blush I know she gets from laughing.

Grigori scratches his hand through his hair, wincing at the

picture Dimitri makes. With a resigned sigh, he peels off his jacket and tosses it over a dining room chair.

Konstantin freezes, a blank look on his face as he blinks several times in rapid succession. He opens his mouth, pauses, then closes it. Pinching the bridge of his nose, he heads straight for the whiskey decanter with a resigned shake of his head. Like he's going to need a minute to absorb this new domestic reality.

"Whoa... you guys look like shi—poop," Dimitri says, looking us all up and down. "What happened?"

"Someone at the party outed us. They sent two cars full of boys to do a man's job. Now they're at the den," Konstantin says over his shoulder, grabbing the whiskey decanter.

Faith's gaze narrows and her mouth falls open. After scooping Alex up and tucking him in the crook of her arm, she scurries across the room to get a better look at me. "Oh my God. You look like you were..." She trails off and gulps, whatever she intended to say, dying in her throat.

My stomach clenches with the realization that the last time she saw someone this much of a mess was Regan after Elijah had raped her.

Squeezing her arm, I dredge up the last scraps of energy in me and offer her a smile. "It wasn't what you're thinking. I promise. I'm fine. Pissed off, but fine." I brush my finger along Alex's impossibly soft cheek. So warm and relaxed, blissfully unaware of the chaos going on around him. "Bet you're glad you stayed home now," I murmured.

Konstantin fills two highball glasses and glances at me, his gaze flicking back to the drinks, silently asking if I want one.

His offer takes me by surprise considering I'm not technically old enough to drink, but then, once you cross the lines we have, does it matter? I've ended a life, I'll be ending more, and I'm debating the legality of drinking in my head.

God, I might really be losing it.

But no. No, I don't want one. I want to soak in a tub until I can walk without looking like I've been railed by a savage giant. Then I want to sleep for a week, maybe two. I want to feel normal again.

Whatever normal is.

More than anything, after the way Konstantin touches me, I want to forget. I want to forget what my father said. I want to believe when Konstantin tells me his feelings have nothing to do with my mother, so I can stop sifting through memories. Moments in time, including both of them, searching for a clue in the grainy flashbacks, looking for signs he's only telling me what I want to hear.

What he knows he needs to say to win.

Relegating me to the stupid, gullible girl I told him was dead.

My biggest fear is she's not. I'm terrified she's buried deep inside, so isolated and lonely, she's ready to settle for whatever affection is tossed her way. She's pretending she can't see the glaring truth in front of her so she can live in moments fulfilling fantasies she thought only lived in a teenage girl's journal.

I live in a world where men lie to suit their means. And though I've never known Konstantin to lie to me, is it really possible he's the only man in my life who hasn't?

So I keep searching. Hoping to find some convincing piece of evidence to tell me whether I let him in or let him go.

"Are you okay if I go get cleaned up and get some sleep?"

Faith smiles down at Alex and feathers a kiss over his silky golden-brown hair. "Sure... I'll be fine. Actually, Dimitri brought us cell phones. Yours is charging on your nightstand.

He programmed our numbers already, so if I need you, I'll call."

"Thank you," I say, smiling over Faith's head at the man himself who keeps smiling down at Lexi.

"You're welcome. I figured Faith's got her hands full and sometimes"—his gaze finds Faith and lingers there—"it might not be so easy to go get you, so this should help."

"It will, and I appreciate it." I slide a knowing look at Faith and lean in so only she can hear me. "You have some explaining to do."

"There's nothing to explain. He's nice. We're friends." She says the words, but she's taken a keen interest in Alex's little fingers so she doesn't have to look me in the eye.

"He *is* nice. He's also hot. And I can practically hear your ovaries crying out when you watch him with Lexi."

She peeks over at him with a shy smile, and he winks at her. "We have very different lives."

"You get to choose whatever life you want now. Just be sure you can live with the decision you make." I give her a hug, missing our nights, whispering in our shared room, rocking babies and dreaming big dreams. "Call me if you need me, okay?"

Just turn around and go to bed. Don't look for him.

But my heart won't listen to my head. I meet his eyes and I'm right back in that cemetery. He's curled over me, driving into me, tormenting me, and even in our rush, exploring my body, taking the time to learn how to pleasure me. The picture is distinct, like I can reach out and touch his face again and trace over the stubble on his chin.

The sound of my voice as I asked him who he belongs to is so alive and powerful in my mind. And all I can hear is his answer playing again and again and again.

You.

One word, his complete surrender, brought me the closest I've come to caving. But it was more than the word. It was the agony on his face, as if he feared me slipping away... for good this time.

The same expression on his face right now, right before I turn and walk away.

I force my feet to move until I'm in my room, the door quietly clicking behind me. Slumping against the cool wood, I listen for the faint sounds of them in the living room, but only silence greets me.

I drag off my heels and vow to never wear heels quite that high again. Not with more car chases in my future. Sinking my feet into the plush carpet, I push away from the door, my eyes landing on the Sharpie still lying where Konstantin left it.

He was stealth, I'll give him that.

Blinking down at the marker, I bite my lip. How did he know it was in there? Why was it in there? Along with other personal items that you'd see in someone's room, not their guest room.

The pieces start to come together.

The way he reached in, like he was so familiar with the surrounding space.

How I can't get away from his scent. It's constantly lingering in the air.

It's his room.

I'm sleeping in his fucking room.

Of course I am.

My eyes immediately go to the closet doors and the night-stands. Curiosity has me wanting to rifle through and see what I can find. See how much of himself he keeps here. I round the bed and head for the drawer where my new phone is charging.

Just as I grip the handle, my phone buzzes with a text from Faith.

I'm not a child. What the hell am I doing?

Picking up the phone, I click on the message.

FAITH

He has not stopped staring at the hallway since you left.

ME

Yeah, he's a good bulldog.

FAITH

Stop that. You don't have to do that with me and you know it.

ME

I know. I'm just... I don't know what I am right now.

FAITH

Is it possible not everything is the way you thought it was? Maybe your father was lying.

ME

You didn't see Konstantin's face. What my father said was true.

FAITH

But it doesn't mean it's still true. It doesn't mean it was even true then. Just that it was true at some point.

I type, then stop. That's the problem. Can I handle the truth? What if it gets into my head and ruins everything moving forward? What if I can't believe any compliment, any endearment, any touch... until my own doubts poison us and anything we could have? And that's only after we reveal this to Nikolaj. Which is a massive risk when I can't even be sure I can get past this.

Right now, Nikolaj has a valuable advisor in Konstantin, and he has a plan that's working. He's sacrificed everything he's ever wanted for his own life to take on our father and brother. And he's done it so he can keep me safe. He's the second son. The *illegitimate* second son. He should have been able to do anything, be anyone.

But he knew leaving meant condemning me to this life. A bargaining chip for our father and brother, nothing more. He's spent a lifetime doing everything he could to protect me from the worst of Vlad's advances. As far as he knows, he protected me from all of them. He couldn't live with himself if he walked away.

He's gaining power. There's a real chance he can take on my father and brother and win. He's sacrificed so much already. There's blood on his hands that never would have been there if it weren't for this path he's chosen.

Now I'm supposed to just toss that all to chance, drop the truth in his lap, and hope it doesn't destroy everything.

ME

There is too much at stake.

FAITH

Can you ever be happy if you spend the rest of your life wondering if you were wrong?

With nothing left to say, I head for the bathroom, taking it in with new understanding. The bath sheets make sense now. He's a big guy, and he'd dwarf a regular towel.

Bone-deep exhaustion settles inside me. I stare longingly at the tub that looks untouched and decide against it. Sinking into that warm water would put me right to sleep at this point.

Head hanging under the pounding spray, I watch

Konstantin's blood wash away from my thigh and stain the water swirling down the drain.

The minute he tore open his pants to see what I had done, when I glimpsed the V carving its way down his abdomen to the dark patch of hair, I was a goner. Already erect, I knew what would come next. I knew, and I didn't walk away. I didn't fight.

Because I wanted it. I wanted to be able to see his face this time, the way I had in that church. I wanted to watch his pleasure swallow him whole again.

I wanted to believe it had everything to do with me, with us... not her.

I'm losing myself. Bit by bit, slipping away under his constant assault on my resolve.

I refused to admit I'm his, but I did it with my thighs spread for him, so really, did I even win? Twice in one night, he took what he wanted and I did nothing to stop him.

Because I wanted it too, and apparently more than I wanted to win.

Each time he took me, he kept me from something. First, dancing with Logan. Then when I staked partial claim on the men who came for us.

He'll try to keep me from going to the den... whatever this den is. He'll fuck me, trick me, or lie to me so he doesn't have to share the payback.

So he can be the hero. So he can have the upper hand.

Again.

A growl of pure frustration tears from my throat as I slam my fist against the tile. Every time he wanted me distracted and bending to his will, he came at me with the goddamned godfather rocket and scrambled every bit of good sense I'd gathered in the past year.

And I almost felt bad for cutting him.

Well, now I don't. Now I wish I had cut him deeper.

I grab the loofah, slather it with bodywash, and go to work on his signature on my thigh. Tears leak from my eyes, swept away by the spray as I scour at my skin until it's red and burning.

His name mocks me, only slightly faded from my efforts to scrub him away.

As mad as I am at him for marking me, I also feel the loss of the bold lettering. And I hate myself for secretly loving his unapologetic claim.

Everything he does serves a purpose. Even his name on my thigh. But I'm onto him now. Next time he puts his hands on me, I'll be looking beyond, at whatever he's trying to protect me from.

I wrap myself in a towel and head out to the bedroom. Just as I reach for my pajamas, I catch sight of the closet door.

Don't do it.

I close my eyes, take a deep breath, and turn away. I last all of ten seconds before my hand is turning the handle and flicking on the light.

Three walls of suits hang neatly, mostly black, a couple navy, and a few charcoal suits on the end. Everything is clean, and still, it all smells like him.

I press my face to a crisp white shirt and breathe him in. The fabric is surprisingly soft. Three times with him and still, I don't know what it's like to roam his body with my hands, taste his skin—to feel what it's like to fall asleep skin to skin, wrapped in him.

Reaching out, I hesitate just an inch from the hanger.

He'll never know. This way I can have a bit of him and he'll never know.

Before I can think too much about it, I ditch the towel and

slip into the shirt. It reaches to my knees, but God, this is it. This is what he feels when he wears it. This is what it feels like to be wrapped in him.

This might be the closest I ever come.

I bury my nose in the collar and it's almost as satisfying as burying my nose against his neck. Padding to the bed, I turn the lamp down to its lowest setting and climb between the sheets.

I'm not weak. I'm just exhausted.

I am *not* weak.

I'm not slipping back into the gullible girl I was.

I'm choosing to momentarily lay down my armor... just for now. In the privacy of this room.

Burying my face in the pillow, I let myself drown in his scent.

When I let her in, the endless signs of him no longer haunt me, but instead become a craving I can indulge in.

And I loathe myself for it.

Lying on my side, I peek at my phone one last time. My hand brushes the handle of the drawer as I draw it away.

I resisted opening it before, but really, what harm can it do at this point?

The scrape of the drawer is barely perceptible, and still, I can't help but glance over my shoulder to the door, just to be sure.

God, I'm being stupid.

Sliding it the rest of the way open, I look over what's inside. ChapStick, three pens, a pad of paper, the top sheet grooved with his handwriting from whatever note he'd written last. I brush my fingers over the indentations, then slide it aside and spot a box of condoms.

I clench my fist and immediately want to kick him in the

balls for my sleeping arrangements. Really? He couldn't stick those anywhere else.

Like, I don't know... straight up his ass.

I yank my hand back and the light from the lamp catches on something shiny. Reaching back—because really, can anything be worse than finding the fucking condoms he uses to fuck other women—I tug on the cool metal.

When I open my palm, my stomach plummets to my toes. The air stutters in my lungs and my eyes brim over with tears.

The familiar sacred heart locket my mother wore every minute of every day mocks me for even daring to believe for a single moment he was mine.

It's not like he stuck it away there long ago and forgot about it. The safe house was new in the past year. And in that time, he made the conscious decision to tuck her locket away here where it would be close.

Pain sweeps through my chest, until I gasp. The last bit of him that felt like home to me, cracks under the suffocating doubt churning in my gut. My fingers tremble as I dump the locket back in the drawer and quietly close it.

This is what I get for letting that girl in who so desperately loves him.

The shirt mocks me now, but the pulsing pain keeps from getting up, and instead, I allow myself this one last time to sink into the hurt.

CHAPTER

30

Konstantin

I thought the whiskey would help me sleep after my shower.

And it did, for about an hour.

But then I'd see that bullet in my nightmares. Hear the sound it made as it bounced off the SUV right next to her.

And then the dream would shift. The bullet hit its mark, tearing through her golden dress, lodging in her chest. Blood poured from her mortal wound. The spot slowly trickling down and spreading out, the crimson stain growing by the second, before she collapsed back into the vehicle.

Then the nightmare flipped. The heart-shattering scene slipped away, and I stood in the den. Every man we collected dead, but one.

The one who fired the shot. He's clamped to the chair by his hands and feet, his face nothing more than mutilated flesh and blood. I've taken his eyes, his tongue, his ears, and his nose. His fingers and toes lay scattered on the floor. He's in and out of consciousness. Coming to life the minute the flame of my torch meets his skin, only to lose consciousness again when I cut the scorched skin from his body in small enough patches to deliver the maximum pain and keep him alive for a good long while.

Nothing will ease the pain of knowing she's gone.

I've tortured all of them and it's done nothing to feed this insatiable hunger to destroy everything in my path.

In one final burst of energy, the mutilated man before me slowly smiles. It's a leering grin of pure victory. But it's the laugh that grabs me by the throat and makes my eyes shoot open.

Maksim's laugh.

After dragging my hand down my face, I check the time. It's just after three in the morning and the place is as silent as a tomb. I'm on my feet, putting on a fresh suit, the need to see her churning in my gut.

Making my way into the living area, the sound of the lock disengaging has me stopping, my hand going to my gun.

Grigori slips in, a small paper bag in his hand from the twenty-four-hour pharmacy a few blocks away. His face is grim as he hands me the package and heads for the surveillance room.

I need to have a talk with him, and soon, before this all completely spirals out of control.

Like it hasn't already.

There's still time, though. Still a chance to do this the right way so we don't destabilize everything Nikolaj has built.

One thing at a time, though. Slipping the packet from the bag, I head down the hall to where she sleeps in my bed. With a quick glance down the hall back toward the living area, I turn the handle and slip inside the door. Heading for the chair in the corner, I stop when I see a new set of dried tears leaving streaks down her cheeks.

She cried herself to sleep again.

While I drank, my feral little killer was in here, reduced to tears.

What the hell am I going to do with you, Pcholka?

I ease into the chair, set the packet on the table next to me, and torture myself by watching her. Every rise and fall of her shoulders with the long breaths that come with a deep sleep imprint in my mind. This serene view of her now continually battering away at the one branded in my head from my nightmares.

Her phone buzzes on the nightstand, but she doesn't stir. Narrowing my gaze, I count the dried tear tracks on her skin. Three on her left cheek, two on her right.

What caused them this time?

Didn't I give her what she wanted? I told her the dangerous truth.

I'm hers.

Because she's the only one with the true power to destroy me. She's always been the only one. The only one I let in after the brutal lessons of my childhood.

The only person I let myself love so deeply, every aspect of my life tethered to hers.

A soft sigh breaks from her lips and she flips over. She shoves the comforter to her waist, and flings her arm overhead, her hand coming to rest on her thick waves tumbling over the pillow.

The glow from the lamp hits her just right, illuminating the dark circles of her peaked nipples under my shirt.

Well, well, well.

She *is* mine. I don't need her to say it out loud. I only need to make sure she never forgets it.

A soft click at the door has me reaching for my gun. Light spills in and Faith quietly pads in with a fussing baby in her arms. As quietly as possible, I pull my hand away and set my palm on my thigh, keeping absolutely still.

Fuck.

She rounds the side of the bed and puts a gentle hand to Nikoletta's shoulder. "Hey," she says as she softly shakes Nikoletta's shoulder.

Sneaking in here was bound to bite me in the ass and here we are.

The baby in her arms lets out a wail that has Nikoletta shooting straight up, rubbing at her puffy eyes. "I'm here. I'm up."

"I'm sorry," Faith says as she takes a seat on the edge of the bed. "I tried to call you, but you didn't hear the phone."

"It was a long night. I crashed."

"Yeah, I figured. So, ummmm, I know you said we have to be careful, but what I didn't get to tell you before is we're out of milk in the freezer for Lexi. I thought I could get her back down, but she's not having it."

I tip my head so I can hear them better. Can't Faith just... feed her?

Nikoletta glances at the time. "She misses me. It's okay. I miss her too. I can take her. I'll get her back to you before everyone wakes up."

Heat infuses my entire body... My heart kicks in a hard thump, the beat growing heavy.

She can't mean—she's not—but even as my mind resists the idea, all of a sudden everything I've seen from her—the changes—it all makes sense.

"Okay, she's all changed."

Nikoletta smiles and takes the baby Dimitri danced with earlier in her arms before smiling up at Faith. "Thank you. Just—can you turn the lock for me before you pull it shut?"

"Of course. And you're welcome." Faith turns the lock on

the knob and slips out the door, never once looking in my direction, giving me an inhibited view of Nikoletta.

Her fingers go to the first of the buttons, slipping it from the loop.

Every single inch of my skin buzzes with awareness as my brain tries to keep up with what I'm seeing.

She undoes another button, the curve of her breast coming into view.

She's not about to do what I think she's going to do? This isn't—I—my lungs ache as I force myself to stay quiet.

Slipping the third button free, a megawatt smile lights up her sleepy face as she gazes down at the little girl fussing in her arms. "Shh, shh, shh, it's okay, baby."

A fourth button undone, she pulls back the shirt—my shirt—and brings the little girl to her breast where she quickly latches on, her tiny fist flexing in the air, grasping at Nikoletta's finger.

She transforms before my eyes, the tear tracks fading away with the way she lights up as she feathers her thumb over the cheek of the baby in her arms.

My twisted world tips on its axis, my stomach pitching into a record-breaking free fall.

Her baby.

Nikoletta has a child.

"I know you miss me, baby girl... I miss you too. So much." She drops a kiss on the little girl's forehead and continues to stroke gently over her skin, murmuring to her as she continues to feed from Nikoletta's breast.

Everything I thought I knew plummets into an abyss of confusion while everything I couldn't understand becomes crystal fucking clear.

The fierce little killer we branded her as is actually so much more complicated than a moniker so trite.

She's a mother.

A tormented ache throbs and swells inside me until my joints feel like they'll explode from the force of it. Nikoletta, Faith, how many other women had Elijah forced at that commune? How many of those infants did he produce in his own personal fucking rape den?

The whole year I looked for her, tore through people and places, and the entire time, Elijah victimized her there, got her pregnant, forced her into having his child.

A bellow of pure anguish demands release from my lungs, but I force it down until my throat aches like the fiery flames of hell. Helpless rage tries to sweep me away with the unfairness of all of it, so I focus on Nikoletta, on how the tiny life in her arms lights up her world the way she lit up mine when they put her in my hands.

The way she still does now. Only today, it's new, terrifying, and so far beyond what I ever expected that all I can think about is how to hold on to it.

How will I live with knowing another man made her a mother?

Another man touched her, his child grew inside her.

Unfairness eats through my veins like acid.

He had this intimate part of her I'll never have. Something bonding them in a way that's even more than the bond I share with her. This whole time pride filled me watching her take control and deliver swift justice in the most savage of ways, errantly believing I sparked that part of her soul to life.

But it was never me. Another man who couldn't possibly know every facet of her the way I did, tapped into an untouched sacred part of her and made it his.

He turned her into the most ferocious form of herself.

An unapologetic, fiercely protective mother. Ruled by

animal instinct and absolutely feral in her response to perceived threats.

Which side of the coin do I fall on, friend or foe, if she could keep this from me?

The unrelenting need to know is a wildfire inside me. Before I can change my mind, I reach for the switch on the lamp next to me.

Nikoletta gasps, immediately pulling her daughter tighter, her hand cupping the little girl's head.

"Were you ever going to tell me?"

CHAPTER
31
Nikoletta

I force myself to look him in the eye. This moment was inevitable the minute I swiped that credit card at the pharmacy just days earlier. But I thought I'd have more time than this.

"What are you doing in here?" My shoulders sag under exhaustion and the unceasing weight of secrets.

Mine. His. And the unpredictable future before us.

And maybe it's relief too.

Because pretending Lexi belongs to Faith was slowly killing me. Nursing her in secret. Fighting tears when it ended too soon, and I slipped back into the role of honorary aunt. The resentment burning in my gut the entire time.

The jealousy I constantly shoved down watching Faith get to hold my little girl freely while I slowly withered away under spiteful irrational feelings.

I'm the one who vomited for three months straight, all day every day carrying her. I'm the one who felt her swell and grow inside me. I'm the one who battled through eighteen hours of brutal labor to bring her into this world with nothing more than Faith holding my hand despite having her own baby to care for, just two weeks old.

Every milestone changed me. Endless hiccups and an insatiable craving for cucumbers and salsa, by far the weirdest combination of foods I've ever eaten to this day. The first gentle swell of my hardening belly. Her first kick. And the first time she opened those solemn eyes and looked at me with endless trust.

"Answer the question." His gruff voice cuts through my racing thoughts, an emotion in his tone I can't quite identify.

Focusing on Lexi, I gently turn her in my arms. I push aside Konstantin's shirt, nestling her on my other side, brushing my nipple over her lips until she latches on. "Answer mine first."

"To check on you." His hungry gaze roams my face before trailing along the skin exposed by his open shirt and the swell of my breast showing over Lexi's dark hair. Naked yearning etches his features. Like he's on the outside of some reality he so desperately wants to be a part of.

This is where anyone else would have a niggling of doubt about their decision to keep her secret.

I have none.

The first time I looked into her eyes, I knew I'd suffer whatever I had to for her. I'd force the people I love to endure anything to protect her.

"I wasn't sure we'd be safe." I glance down at my baby girl and think about what the Petrovs do to their women. The choke hold on me is swift, and the spill of tears quickly follows.

Outside these moments, I'm vicious with the need to protect her. People don't have good natures. I don't categorize them by their good deeds, how respected they are, or loved ones waiting for them at home. They're animals at their most basic level. They're a friend, or they're the enemy.

Enemies are a threat. I eliminate threats.

But in moments like these where we're warm and safe, and I'm doing something so natural and simple as feeding her, something only I can do like this, I feel everything.

I feel the deep-seated fear. And the horrible images flood my head before I can stop them.

"It's more than just me now, and if the Petrovs got ahold of us…" I don't have to say it because he knows. My brother's army survives and grows in safe houses and an underground city he built because of the dangers to all of us.

Even if I came back the minute I found out I was pregnant, even if I could tell Nikolaj the whole truth without him putting a bullet between Konstantin's eyes, they lived a good portion of their lives underground hiding out. How long would I have been forced into those tunnels to stay alive? All I could think about was endless days, the walls closing in, no sunlight, and despair. And when it came time to deliver… would we still be underground? Would I be opening some hidden hatch, carrying my little girl down a narrow ladder? The darkness swallowing us the way it had when Grigori brought me down to the crypt. The thought of keeping Lexi down there indefinitely—no.

The alternative comes to life in my nightmares. Where they're tearing her away with sinister laughs as she screams for me.

"We'll never let them get ahold of you."

After seeing him tonight firsthand, there's no one I would trust with my life, or with hers, more. But it's still not enough. If it were just me… but it's not now. I have to think about her first.

We're limited by the same means and share the same enemies. Together we make an irresistible target.

And he was right earlier. I shouldn't have exposed myself while bullets were flying. I made a huge mistake that could have cost my little girl everything. Like playing honorary aunt had skewed my priorities in the heat of the moment and I forgot myself.

I lost my mother far too young, but at least I remember her.

Lexi would have nothing but a few pictures and the surrounding people to tell her who her mother was. She wouldn't remember my scent, the feel of my hair, the sound of my voice talking and singing to her—all things I at least had of my mother.

"You say that, but when Nikolaj finds out, he's going to lose his mind. He won't take this well, and I don't know how to tell him without putting us all at risk. Anger makes people vulnerable. Simple mistakes are deadly. I can't—" My voice wobbles and I swallow against the tears clogging my throat. She's their best weapon against me, and the minute they find out about her, they'll know it. "I won't let anything happen to her. I'll keep her a secret forever if that's what it takes to keep them from getting their hands on her."

"You love her... you're fierce with it."

I stare at him wide-eyed for a couple of seconds before I realize my mouth is hanging open. "Of course I love her. Why wouldn't I?"

He pushes to his feet and paces the floor at the foot of the bed. "Some women can't. When they look at their child, it reminds them of their assault. But not you."

"Assault? What—"

He lets out a growl through gritted teeth, his jaw tight. "I swear, if I could, I'd resurrect that fucker and kill him again for what he did to you." His shoulders hunch with agitation, his clenched fists hanging at his sides.

"Who?"

"Who do you think? Elijah," he snarls, whirling on me.

A burst of laughter slides out of me, startling Lexi. She throws the arm not tucked against me out wide, her eyelids squeezing tight before softening again. "Kostya. You saw what I did to him. Do you really think I would have let him get inside me? Think about it."

"If not Elijah, then who?" He leans toward me with his palms flat on the foot of the bed. "Tell me and he's dead, Pcholka."

Lexi's latch breaks free then. I brush my nipple against her lips one more time and when she doesn't react, I close my shirt and lift her to my shoulder. Smiling, I kiss her soft pink cheek and take a deep breath before I look him straight in the eye. "The only man I've ever been with."

He freezes then, his face freakishly blank, like he doesn't understand a word I'm saying. Or maybe he understands all too well.

"Lexi is your daughter, Kostya."

Before I realize what's happening, he sinks to his knees and drops his head in his hands. My stomach knots with tension and the niggling doubts I buried long ago because they change nothing.

I've never seen him on his knees. Never.

I squeeze my eyes shut, pushing the image away as it slices at my soul.

His harsh breathing fills the room, in and out, in time with the hammering of my heart echoing in my head.

I don't know if he's hurt or he realizes the gravity of what will happen when we tell Nikolaj, but either way, the discussion is not happening until Lexi is out of the room. "Let me put her to bed and we can talk." I reach for him. "I'm sure you want—"

His head snaps up, his hard gaze pinning me to the spot. I can't read him, but something tells me to pull my hand back and get Lexi out. "You probably have a million questions."

When I get to the door, I glance back and he's still on his knees, but it's the cutting look as I passed him that's now burned in my mind.

Careful not to wake Faith, I settle Lexi in the crib next to Alex. They brought in another crib, but we've continued to put them together in one. They'll grow out of it soon, probably in the next few weeks. This special ritual is slipping away, so I'm taking advantage of every moment.

"It's going to be okay, baby girl. No more pretending. You get your mommy back starting now."

Lexi grins just then in her sleep. It's fleeting, a quick twitch of her cheeks. I know it's likely gas, but I don't care. I'm pretending she heard me and she's just as happy to have me back as I am to have her.

CHAPTER

32
Nikoletta

When I get back to my room, Konstantin is off the floor, with his back to me in the corner I'd found him in earlier. Reaching for a packet on the table, he flips the little blister pack between his fingers the way I've seen poker players flip chips during tournaments on TV.

"What was your plan? Marry someone else and let him raise my child without ever telling me a word about her?"

"I would have eventually told you." The packet crinkles with every transition between his fingers as he keeps his back to me. I miss his face already. The way I could read him better than anyone. The way he could read me.

The way we could speak without more than a glance.

"But yes, I would have waited until I was married. Once I found someone who could protect her."

The package snaps to a stop and he goes still. Nerves skitter along my skin and goosebumps bloom on my arm, over my shoulders, along my neck, right into my hair.

"I have just one more question, Pcholka." His even voice

has a strange edge, making the hair stand up on the back of my neck.

When he turns to me, the frigid calm in his eyes sends dread slicing down my spine. I could have handled anything. Yelling. Fighting. Swearing. Insults. Any or all of them would have been preferable to the way he's looking at me right now. An expression more terrifying than any show of anger I've seen from him.

The look he aims at me now is the very look he directed at the guy pinned to the ground under his shoe earlier tonight. The man he promised would beg him to die long before he'd finish causing him pain.

The way he stares me down is a vivid reminder. Everyone falls into one of two categories. A friend or a threat.

When I held my knife to his belly at the commune, even when I sliced him at the cemetery, he'd never been even close to the threat he transformed into before my very eyes in this moment.

"Are you going to give back what you stole from me or do I have to take it?"

I fight the urge to take a step back and stand my ground. "I didn't steal one damn thing from you."

"But didn't you?" Sliding a hand in his pocket, he draws out a Zippo and sparks the flame to life. "You stole an entire pregnancy, childbirth, and the three, maybe four months of my child's life from me. How old *is* my daughter?"

Surely he has to understand why I did it. My God. He spent a lifetime protecting me. He, of all people, should understand better than anyone.

"She's three and a half months old." I work the buttons closed on the shirt, needing to do something with my hands. What I really itch to do is reach for my blade. Maybe both of them.

He holds the flame to the edge of the packet and watches as the plastic curls and blackens, finally lighting with a modest flame. Slowly, methodically, he lays the blistered, twisted remains in the crystal dish and slides the lighter back in his pocket.

"What was that?"

"The morning after pill." He shoots me a piercing, narrowed look over his shoulder. "We don't need it anymore."

"What? Yes, we do! Why the hell would you burn that?"

Oh, he has definitely lost his mind. Twice tonight he fucked me with no protection and—God, I grind my fingertips at my temples and wince. I slept just long enough for my rest to have the same effect as a power nap. Jittery energy courses through me as a chilling calm settles over Konstantin.

The room goes deathly silent as he slides his jacket from his shoulders and tosses it on the chair.

My brain latches on to the math as I try to remember what day it is and how long it's been since my last period. My wildly inconsistent period since it only just came back—if you can call it a full comeback considering the breastfeeding.

He reaches for his cuffs next, slipping the buttons from the holes before rolling the crisp white sleeves up his arm to just below his elbow.

My eyes dart about the room. I choke back hysterical laughter as unease swells inside me to the point it pounds viciously in my ears.

When he finally turns, he slides his hands in his pockets with an eerie calm. "I'll ask you again. Are you going to give back what you stole from me, or do I have to take it?"

Methodical and cold, he tilts his head and I know he won't let me get away with not answering a second time.

But if he thinks he can break me with a tone so freakishly

benign it's terror-inducing, he should sit his ass down and think again.

He didn't teach me to cower. "You're going to have to take it."

A spine-tingling laugh breaks from his lips and I'm hit with the stark realization... I don't know this man standing before me. I have no idea what he'll do or how far he'll go.

"Just the answer I expected."

"I won't make it easy for you."

"Oh, I'm sure you won't. I'm looking forward to the battle, Pcholka." His hand shoots out so fast his watch is barely a flash streaking past my vision before his hands lock in my hair and he yanks my head back. Pain shoots through my scalp.

"I'm looking forward to it very much," he says, marching me backward toward the bed, his other hand going to his belt.

The fingers in my hair flex, easing my pain, but solidifying his grip as he drags my head back impossibly far and looms over me.

"If you hit me with that fucking belt, Konstantin..." My voice dips almost as cold and deadly as his. My throat strains with every word from the angle of my neck as I glare up at him. "I swear on my mother's grave I will cut your fucking heart straight out of your chest and shove it down your throat."

"Invoking your mother, huh?" He sneers the question, a cruel tilt to his lips. "Just remember, you brought her into this, not me."

The minute I open my mouth to reply, he swallows my response with a violent kiss. Sucking the air straight from my lungs, he snarls and bites, keeping my head tipped back so far I'm sure my neck will snap at any minute.

With a brutal yank, the belt flies from his belt loops, his arm rearing back with the force.

My hand is on the knife as the words fill my head once again.

Everyone falls into one of two categories...

I don't think. I strike. My blade slices clean from his abdomen and up over his ribs.

A violent grunt tears from his mouth and he gives me one hard shake. "You think the slice of your blade can possibly do more damage than your betrayal?" He bites my lip and drags it away from my mouth before letting it snap back. "You have no idea what you've done. None!"

He throws me on the bed as though I weigh nothing, knocking the wind out of me. My teeth rattle and the knife rolls out of my hand, his blood smearing on the gray sheets.

Just as I push onto my elbows, he's on me. "Oh no, you don't." He yanks my ankle, leaving me flailing on my back.

Leather hisses through the air and my eyes shoot open wide. "What the fuck are you doing?"

Barely winded, he straddles me. With lightning speed, he cages one wrist, then the other, his movements too fast for me to see much more than loops flipping through the air. Before I know what's happening, he's created snug makeshift cuffs. The leather bites into my skin, a painful promise I will not wiggle my way free.

"I earned every scar on this body protecting you... I guess it's only fitting you leave a few of your own. But tonight, one slice is all you're going to get."

I can scream. I can let out one good fucking scream and someone will come.

But I don't and I don't dare examine why.

Yanking the belt a fraction tighter, he drags my hands over

my head. I crane my neck and catch sight of a metal loop he's dragged from behind the mattress.

The blood-soaked slash of his shirt hovers over my mouth. Crimson leaks from the cut, and a subtle metallic odor tickles my nose. The urge to taste him surges through me. Before I realize what I'm doing, I dive my tongue through the slit of his shirt, landing on the gash over his ribs.

The minute my tongue makes contact, he freezes. He thrusts a merciless hand into my hair and draws me in for more.

I trace my tongue over the damage, lapping over the blood, pain and revenge metallic and warm on my mouth.

When he decides I've had enough, or he has, he settles over me. He has to outweigh me by at least a hundred pounds of pure hard muscle, and although he has me pinned to the bed, he's keeping the bulk of his crushing weight off me.

His eyes flash down to my breasts. The air crackles with curious energy as he dips his index finger into the valley between them.

"Your mother didn't breastfeed either of you."

I stiffen under the quiet words, sounding as though they're coming from another time, another place.

"Fuck you, Konstantin." I buck and thrash under him for bringing her into this. Nothing he's done up to this point was nearly as humiliating as hearing about her from his fucking lips after everything happening between us tonight. "Fuck you for bringing her up right now when you know—"

He grabs my jaw and forces me to look at him. "You don't get to be indignant right now. Not after keeping my child from me," he sneers, tossing my chin as he lets me go.

"I hate you." A sob breaks free before I can stop it and I detest to my core he heard it.

"Well, this time, the feeling's mutual, Pcholka. I hate you

too." His gaze slides away like he can't stand to look at me. Curling his fingers around the lapels of the shirt I'm wearing, he tears the fabric from my breasts, his eyes flaring hot. "But it won't stop me from breeding that tight pussy of yours and putting another baby in you. Only this time, you'll be by my side for all of it. Once my baby begins to grow inside you, you'll never leave my side again."

"No." Could the word have fallen flatter than it did in this moment when my mind resisted everything he promised, but my thighs squeezed tight and I grew impossibly wet with his primal threat?

"Cute, Pcholka," he says with a knowing smirk. "You made the unilateral decisions last time. This time, it's my turn."

He never tears his gaze from my nipples as he peels away his ruined shirt. The angry red line I carved into him sliced through the dark hair smattering over his abs. I itch to run my fingers through the curls. The desire so strong, his confining my hands feels more cruel than anything he's done to me thus far by denying me a way to touch him.

To connect with him and bring him back.

He's doing it to protect himself.

My heart breaks with the realization that I did this. I had to choose between a man who has loved and protected me my entire life, and the defenseless life we made. A life I have to put before everyone, even him.

And now he's closing himself off from me. One piece at a time, he's stealing away our connection so I can't hurt him again.

But in severing our bond, he's embracing the same cold cruelty of men like my father.

I did this.

I did it and I have no idea how to undo it.

"Our little girl looks safe and happy suckling these." Tracing his finger over the inside curves of my breasts, his mouth works as he sucks his lips between his teeth and narrows his eyes. When his lips roll back out, they're wet.

He's the absolute picture of spite, hunger, and resolve. "Oh God, what's that look? What are you going to do?"

"Whatever I want." He leans down, flicks his tongue over my nipple, then traps the stiff peak between his lips and sucks my flesh deep into the warm recesses of his mouth. He's relentless, sucking hard.

When he swallows, I feel the tug so fucking deep, I cry out with the agony of ecstasy even as my skin grows hot with embarrassment.

"Mmmmm," he lets out a sultry hum, his eyelids sinking shut as he savors the taste of my milk.

"Oh fuck," I choke out. "Why do I like that?"

"Because you're not dignified. You're an animal. Just like I am."

My skin bursts into flames. Arousal burns in my belly. When he pinches my nipple and milk spills over the tip, drenching his thumb, a whimper of pure needy anguish tears from me.

"I'm going to spend a lot of time right here, devouring every sweet, warm drop of what our little girl leaves behind."

"Kostya," I whisper as everything inside me screams for more. "Look at me."

He brings his thumb to his lips and sucks the milk from his skin. His eyes narrow to slits as he keeps his focus on my breasts, never even flicking a glance above my neck. "Liars and thieves don't make demands, little girl."

"You should be happy about the lengths I went to in order to protect her."

His jaw tightens, but he stays stubbornly silent.

Another door shut in my face. One more of our connections fracturing before us. A life of longing looms before me. Endless years waiting for any piece of him I can get. Just like my mother did with my father.

Because Konstantin is doing that to us right now. Helpless rage fills me. My brain races, searching for the right words to snap him out of this prison he's locking himself in. "You should thank me for what I've sacrificed for her." I hurl the words like an accusation—anything it takes to get a reaction out of him.

Memories of my mother live inside me. They have a heartbeat and the uncanny ability to bring happiness or endless wells of pain. Days where the light in her eyes dimmed at best and flickered out completely at worst. A childhood spent trying everything to light her up again.

I see Lexi in my mind. She's running, laughing, her dark hair flying behind her. She's picking flowers, and when she brings them to me, her smile slips. Not all the way. Just a little. Because she sees the wistful void, the one she can't fill, eating away at me. Because she's young and hopeful, because life hasn't broken her spirit yet, she tries.

God, how she tries.

Just like I did.

I won't let him send us to that place. I refuse to let us turn into them. "You should be on your knees—"

With a jagged growl, his face contorts. He rises off me, and his punishing fingertips bite into my hip as he flips me onto my stomach, the ring I'm tethered to conveniently swiveling with me.

"You want me on my knees, little girl?" he snarls. "Your wish is my fucking command."

He kneels behind me, the sound of his zipper loud under

the violent jerk of his hand. Gripping my hips, he hauls me to my knees.

The minute I try to push onto my elbows, he dives his hand into my hair, turns my head to the side, and pins me to the mattress. My blood pounds through my system, leaving me lightheaded.

"But you're going to be on your knees with me because I'll never bow down to you again."

In one punishing thrust, he drives into me. I swallow the scream of agony just before a wave of pleasure explodes low in my belly. My eyes sink shut as a shudder ripples through me.

The sound of his labored breathing grows distant as I struggle to keep my eyes open. I'm swollen and soaking, the taste of his blood lingering in my mouth. Intoxicated on every wildly violent thrust, something primal surges to life.

With a roar, he brings his palm down on my ass, the sharp crack splitting the air. Pain explodes over my skin and I suck in a harsh breath. Before I can exhale, his brutal swing slices through the air again, his hand searing my skin like a brand as he lands a vengeful blow on the same spot.

Biting the sheets, I refuse to give him a reaction. Fuck him.

Lungs heaving, he drags his hard, heavy cock out of me completely before plunging back in with a stunningly barbaric shout.

"Do you..." he growls, his hips bottoming out with his thrust.

Pure aggression rolls off him. I drive my hips back, burying him deeper, his rage only fueling mine.

"Have any..." he pants, as he draws completely out of me, leaving me hollow. All of a sudden, with his every dirty word, his violent fucking, I want him to fill me up.

"Idea..." The word is a grunt as he impales me again.

"How exceptional..." He fists the flesh of my ass, spreading me open obscenely to his ravenous gaze.

I told him he'd have to take it, but fuck... I want this. I want him to make sure the whole fucking world knows just who I belong to.

"Her conception was..." His chest heaves as he savagely drags me back on his cock.

I tear my mouth from the sheets, my teeth ripping the cotton with the force. I can't get enough air in my lungs.

"On that altar, where I promised to protect you." The words graze over my ear with his hot breath as he looms over me.

"Your virgin blood drenching my cock," he says before sinking his teeth into the delicate skin of my neck just below my ear. His hair drags along my cheek, teasing me, and I swear to myself I'll get to fist those silver-streaked waves and bury his mouth between my thighs.

"Yeeeesssssss." The word drags out on a low groan as my orgasm painfully throbs, demanding release. Tears stream from my eyes as helpless whimpers tug from my throat.

"You're going to drip with my cum. All day, every day," he promises, dragging biting kisses down my shoulder.

"And when my baby grows inside you, I'm going to keep you dripping with my cum." He pulls me up, yanking me back on his cock by the hand locked in my hair.

On the sheet below me, two dark spots, wet with my milk. I gasp and my pussy spasms with the sight.

"You want to know why?"

"Why?" I choke out.

"Because you're mine, and I can."

He pinches my clit and I fly apart. Gasping and crying, my

inner walls cling to his every hot demand delivered with his punishing hips.

"And you, my feral deceiving little goddaughter, are going to keep me bleeding."

Yes, yes, I am.

"Because you like when my blood stains your skin."

I do. Fuck yes, I do.

"You're a liar, but you're my liar."

His.

"You're a thief, but you're my thief."

Only his.

"I'm going to keep this belly swollen and full so you don't for one minute fucking forget it."

He comes with a ferocious roar, every exhale a growl as he fills me up, pumping his hips, driving his cum deeper.

I collapse the minute he lets go of my hair. I can't even open my eyes when I hear his belt slipping free from the ring. The minute my wrists are free, he's off the bed, wordless in his retreat.

When the door closes, and the only man I've ever loved is gone, leaving me in a cloud of misery and animalistic euphoria, I'm left with one truth.

I've been worried about the wrong war all along.

CHAPTER

33

Konstantin

It's been hours since I left Nikoletta and I'm still vibrating with fury I can't seem to shake.

In the past twenty-four hours, I've had an hour of sleep. Since the moment I found out the little girl at her breast is mine, I've been hard as a fucking rock. Fucking her once wasn't enough. It would never be enough.

But she needed sleep to take care of our little girl.

And I needed... to get away from her. The urge to claim her burned like a wildfire out of control inside me, but the thought of looking into her eyes while I took her had me losing my mind with rage.

She lied.

With her scheming eyes.

With her traitorous mouth.

But there's one part of her that can't lie to me. Not ever.

I gave up any plans of having a family of my own when I made Nikoletta and her safety my entire world. Now that it's not just this indistinct idea I've left in the past—but a living, breathing reality, my reality—there's a raging need to make up for all the time I lost.

All those times I cautioned Maksim about keeping Nikoletta's mother as his lover. Warning him that dividing his loyalties and having children with his wife and his paramour would fracture his empire. The way he would laugh and dismiss my warnings as jealousy because Nikoletta's mother chose him in the end.

Here I am, on the cusp of twisting Nikolaj's empire before it ever gets off the ground. Dismissing my own warnings. Obliterating every bit of advice I've ever given Maksim so I can keep his daughter.

And mine.

I'm going to fill her up again and again and again. When she's pregnant, with one child and another on the way, Nikolaj will have to consider the consequences of starting a war with me.

As for Nikoletta, her husband hunting will be all but impossible with our daughter on her hip and my baby kicking inside her.

My shoulders bunch and restless energy surges through me, the image of her dripping with my cum day in, day out lighting a fire in my gut.

Sleep deprived and wild with the insatiable urge to fuck her raw—the only truth between us—I'm holding on by the tiniest of threads.

So when the front door opens and Nikolaj steps in, my spine stiffens until it may just snap.

"I've got seven men in the den. One is dead. Who's filling me in on what the fuck happened last night?"

He glances at each one of us. Grigori at the island, Dimitri drinking his coffee by the window where he can keep a bird's-eye view on danger that might come from the street below.

Roddick comes out of the surveillance room, shrugging on his suit jacket before sliding in next to me and pouring a mug of coffee. He normally doesn't crash here, but he did last night to help us watch the monitors. And to keep an eye on Nikoletta for me today when I go out.

She's not getting away from me again and I'm going to the one place she wants to go.

The den.

She's going to lose her shit when she finds out I went without her, but too fucking bad.

Fuck with me and find out, little girl.

The den is a privilege. It's reserved for only the most trusted in our inner circle.

Not her.

I turn and lean against the counter, bringing the coffee to my mouth. "Which one's dead?"

"Shaved head. Unfortunate porn mustache."

"Fuck him. He's expendable."

"Is there someone in particular there who's not?"

I picture the dumb fucker I dragged out of the car window and the nightmare where the bullet hits its mark flashes through my mind. "Dirty-blond hair, broken jaw. He's mine."

"What did he do?"

Grigori shoots a nervous look at me. I'm keeping enough from Nikolaj, for now. I'm not keeping this too.

"His bullet missed your sister by inches."

Nikolaj goes deathly still before turning his head, his chin jutted out, leaning toward us. "What was that?"

It's a look I know well. That 'would someone like to explain just how the fuck that happened' look Maksim wore so well.

No need to poke the deadly cub more than necessary.

Grigori and Roddick eye each other.

Dimitri turns his focus to Nikolaj.

Every single man in this place can end a life with their

bare hands in a second. They march into the open with bullets flying without a moment's hesitation. But when Nikolaj's movements become distinct and his voice drops, even our most seasoned man clenches in trepidation.

I can't wait to see the day he rules the Romanoff empire.

As long as I see the day.

Nikoletta steps out of Faith's room just then, with Lexi in her arms, totally unaware of the tension filling the silent room.

When our little girl lets out a wail, Nikoletta brushes her finger over her cheek and quietly reassures her. "Shh, shh, shh, it's okay. Mama's going to feed you, baby girl."

Reassures her and completely detonates a bomb in the silence and sets off a whole new feeling of unease rippling through the room.

No one moves.

I'm not sure anyone even breathes.

The taste of the coffee turns rancid on my tongue as I fight to keep my face impassive when I'm anything but.

Nikoletta glances up, and the smile dies on her lips as she locks eyes with Nikolaj.

Eyes shot open impossibly wide, face leached of all color, Nikolaj stands there.

Dimitri's focus goes back to the view outside, telling me he doesn't understand what just went down. Or the admission is so out of left field, his brain dismisses it before he can really think about it. We'll be having a talk about his lack of awareness. He needs to tighten that shit up.

Roddick now stands stoically against the wall, coffee on the side table next to him, his hands clasped in front of him. From all appearances, he didn't hear a thing. Except the heightened color in his cheeks. It gives him away every single time.

When Nikolaj takes a few careful steps in Nikoletta's direction, his back finally to us, Grigori slides me a suspicious dose of side-eye.

I knew that fucker didn't miss a thing.

That's exactly why he was and always will be my go-to. Unless he forces me to kill him. But when I think about it, he's the closest thing to a friend I've got.

Maybe the closest I ever really had.

I head to the sink and dump my coffee. Leaning against the counter, I watch from a distance, reduced to an outsider in this new reality between them. She might as well plunge the knife into my heart and twist the fucker.

"Lettie," Nikolaj breathes her name as he searches Nikoletta's eyes and glances down at our daughter. "Why didn't you tell me?"

He is seeing my little girl's face more clearly than I ever have.

And for a moment, I hate him for it.

"I wasn't sure I could keep her safe here. I—the more people who know..." She trails off, her gaze never wavering from her brother.

A muscle ticks in his jaw, the only sign that her doubt in his ability to protect her hits him where it hurts.

I'm still reeling from the blow. I kept her alive her entire life, but I'm not good enough to protect our daughter. That's a job best suited for some pompous secret society prick with impeccable breeding, no doubt.

Over. My. Dead. Fucking. Body.

"Who's the father?"

"It's not important," she says with a shake of her head as she smiles down at Lexi who's abandoned her fussing and is now staring up at Nikolaj, quietly studying him.

It's not important. I have to hand it to her, she's good at what she does. Landing another blow and deflecting with three simple words.

Pulsing betrayal slices into me again, but instead of a clean, sharp sting, its course and dull, pulling and tugging, ripping the skin in a jagged gash.

We won't be able to keep Nikolaj in the dark forever. Nor do I want to. But one thing at a time. I need to have my head straight to navigate the fallout. At the moment, I'm about as far from my head being straight as I can get.

My phone buzzes in my jacket pocket, a desperately needed distraction from the bitterness and jealousy choking me.

I swipe the screen and there's Grigori, dragging me from the shit spiral.

GRIGORI

What did you do?

ME

You know what I did. Stop looking at me like that.

GRIGORI

This is my permanent face now. Get used to it. So she's yours?

ME

Fuck. You.

GRIGORI

I'll take that as a yes.

DIMITRI

Looking at him like what? And she's whose? Who's his?

My gaze snaps up to Grigori's, then shifts to Dimitri on the other side of the room whose eyes are glued to his fucking phone.

> ME
>
> Wrong chat, dipshit. You're slipping.

> GRIGORI
>
> That's what happens when I'm doing damage control for your dick.

> DIMITRI
>
> What the hell is happening? I swear I miss all the good stuff.

> GRIGORI
>
> That's what all new mothers say *baby bottle emoji*

> DIMITRI
>
> Fuck you, dude. She had her hands full with the twins. What was I supposed to do?

> GRIGORI
>
> They're not twins.

> ME
>
> Stop. Talking.

> GRIGORI
>
> Make me. He might as well know. Everyone's going to know soon. And you better figure out how to tell Nikolaj in a way that won't get us all dead.

> ME
>
> I'll tell him as soon as she's pregnant again.

Grigori chokes on his coffee.

> GRIGORI
>
> WHAAAAATTTTTTT?

DIMITRI

What do you mean they're not twins? And who's getting pregnant again?

GRIGORI

Nikoletta.

DIMITRI

Wait—so Nikoletta has a baby? Where? So, basically, Konstantin's now, I don't know, kinda like a grandpa?

Grigori snorts and it's the closest I've come to snapping his neck yet.

GRIGORI

Lexi is Konstantin's daughter.

A crack echoes across the room where Dimitri's phone hits the floor. He scrambles to pick it up, and his face goes from flushed to gray in seconds, a particular shade I've only ever seen in the men I'm torturing, during the last moment of peak pain before their body goes into shock and I kill them.

DIMITRI

None of this makes any sense. Konstantin and Faith. And where's Nikoletta's baby. How the fuck—what am I missing?

GRIGORI

Brain cells. The answer is brain cells.

I had to hand it to Grigori, he had natural comedic timing. Someone needs to put this poor kid out of his misery before his head explodes.

ME

Nikoletta is Lexi's mother. I'm Lexi's father.

DIMITRI

But that's not possible.

GRIGORI

Christ, dimwit. What's his motivation to lie? What do you mean it's not possible? They're not blood-related, asshat.

ME

I'm going to need you both to shut the fuck up.

DIMITRI: So wait, you fucked your goddaughter?

I don't respond. Instead, I glance up and wait for him to meet my eyes. When he does, whatever he sees has him taking a step back.

Good.

RODDICK

More than once from the looks. I saw them going at it last night at the party.

ME

Really, really, wrong chat.

GRIGORI

Yes. He fucked his goddaughter. Keep up.

DIMITRI

In the open?

RODDICK

On the balcony. Boss is a badass *fist bump emoji*

DIMITRI

But. But... I don't understand.

RODDICK

He's gonna need a visual aid or two. Or ten.

GRIGORI

Do we need to have the birds and the bees talk again, D?

DIMITRI

Sure, right after you have the protection talk with the boss.

ME

The fuck did you just say?

DIMITRI

Too far? *teeth clench emoji*

GRIGORI

The minute Nikolaj's gone, I need a word.

DIMITRI

The minute he's gone, I need a therapist.

RODDICK

I'm good, boss. Don't need anything. I gotchu.

ME

Oh, we'll be having several words. I plan to do all the talking. With my hands.

GRIGORI

Fair, but let me remind you, I'm the only friend you've got.

DIMITRI

Hey, I'm his friend too.

RODDICK

eyeroll emoji

ME

Jesus Christ.

I silence my phone and slide it back in my pocket. In a matter of minutes two men here will have held my daughter before I have. Before I've counted her fingers and toe. Before I've even gotten a good look at her face, studied her tiny features, while I try to figure out who she looks more like.

I don't know something as simple as the color of her eyes.

I've never seen her smile.

This suffocating loss is a black void closing in on me from every side. In the confines are the whispers of doubts I've carried since my father...

Nope. No. NO.

I can't—I can't do this. "I'm going to the den. I'll catch up with you later."

Grigori slides from his stool. "I'll go with you."

My hands shake as memories I've buried decades ago try

to breathe to life. "No. I want to get a jump on this. The minute I have something, I want you on it. Just wait for word from me. It won't take long."

He lets out a low whistle. "Today is not the day, and you are not the guy."

"No." I glance at Nikoletta and just as I do, she turns to me, the smile on her face not reaching her eyes.

Maybe I should take comfort in the fact her skills in deception aren't one hundred percent, but I don't.

There's no solace in me.

Only hate.

And more fucking hurt than I ever knew possible.

I look away first. "She doesn't leave. Eyes on her at all times."

CHAPTER

34
Nikoletta

"**W**ho's the father?" Nikolaj asks, a thread of demand lacing his deep, commanding voice.

Konstantin's hostile gaze burns over me, never relenting, until I feel like one of those dead bugs, pinned in place, under the microscope, every single nuance studied and picked apart.

Every step I take today is agony in the best way. Not that I'll tell him that. He thinks he punished me last night... and in a way, he did, but more than that, he tapped into something I didn't even know I had inside me.

Something I want.

Something raw and primitive.

A potent, drugging euphoria I can only find with him.

I can't afford to let my guard down in this world. To show weakness.

But when he touches me, when he's brutal with me, I know I can enjoy the way he wields vicious control because to its core, it's in direct response to the power I have over him.

"It's not important." The words come across as calm,

dismissive... resolute, and I know there will be hell to pay when the truth comes to light.

One battle at a time.

It's what I've done to Konstantin's heart that has doubt looming like a bad omen inside me. It's the realization I've fundamentally changed how he feels about me that left me lying awake with a cold, hard ball of dread lodged in my chest.

This is not the mother and father I envisioned for our little girl. I won't let her suffer, trapped on a battlefield between us. She won't be the object of a tug-of-war in some hollow fight, fueled by wounded pride and a sick need for revenge.

"Did you know about this?" The rumbling in Nikolaj's question has my head snapping up to find him and Konstantin in a hostile stare-off that has my heart jumping into my throat.

Konstantin pins me with a hard stare and tilts his head like he's debating just whether or not to throw me under the bus, knowing I'll drag him right under the tires with me if he does. "Just found out myself. Your little sister just seems to be full of surprises."

"You guys have been in this house for two days. How is that possible?"

"Ask the actress. While you guys discuss it," Konstantin says, grabbing his keys, "I'll look into that Emmy for performance of the year." He's out the door before anyone can say a word, his parting words only adding fuel to the fire.

The bastard.

Nikolaj winces and scratches his fingers through his hair. "You pissed him off good."

"He'll get over it." I wish I believed the words, but more

and more I have to wonder. It's the shadows in his eyes, like something died. Something I can never get back.

"Letti, the father needs to take res—"

"Nikolaj... stop." Taking a seat on the couch, I pat the cushion next to me and as discreetly as possible open my dress just wide enough to bring Lexi to my breast. "It's my business. My problem." I peer down at her and watch the rapt fascination on her face as she barely nurses because she can't stop trying to turn her head and stare at her uncle.

He turns to me, but quickly glances away with a pained expression on his face, his mouth pinched with tension. "So it is a problem?"

"Bad choice of words."

"This changes things, Lettie."

"Nothing's changed. She needs the best protection I can get for her." I glance around at the men in the room and desperately wish they were it. Because they're a family of sorts. Powerful, but almost playful in a way at times. Especially Dimitri if last night was any indication. She might be half in love with him already.

Lexi would love growing up wrapping these big men around her little finger. It wouldn't be the cold, strained life we had at my father's estate with his ice queen of a wife and our menacing, twisted brother.

Every man here works for my brother, and by extension Konstantin, but something about them is more. Like an underlying current of friendship. A brotherhood.

The best kind of family, because blood and marriage don't obligate them to stay. Ultimately, they're here because there's nowhere else they'd rather be.

"We slow the process down, then. Once Konstantin fills me in on all the details from last night, I'll dig deeper into your options. She's not just going off with anyone." He reaches out and brushes a tattooed finger over her hair, the gentle smile on his mouth turning serious. His eyes narrow, his dark brows dropping low over his eyes. "He has to be a father to her... as good as he would be to his own. She won't live with some cold fucker hell-bent on payback. She won't have a stepparent like Elena."

"No. She won't." Lexi detaches again and stares at Nikolaj. I sigh, my breasts getting harder by the second as they grow painfully full. My thoughts go to Konstantin for the briefest moment and my skin blazes hot.

Nothing felt the way he did when he—

"You okay?" Nikolaj asks, his inquisitive gaze zeroing in on my face.

"Yup, good." I force the image of Konstantin drinking from my breast out of my mind. As a matter of fact, I'm going to pump after this and march those bags of breastmilk to the freezer just to see his reaction when he finds out my breast pump got more action than him today.

I choke back a laugh, picturing the righteous indignation on his beautiful face. "Okay, Uncle Nik, you ready to hold your niece?"

He nervously glances everywhere but at her. "What? Now?"

Leave it to a tiny little girl to terrify a mafia badass to his toes. "Sure, why not?" He thinks this is bad, wait until she needs one of her uncles to do a tampon run.

"Well, you're feeding her for one and no offense, but I'm going to keep a safe distance from my sister's... you get the idea."

"Oh my God. Big bad Nikolaj Romanoff, mafia mastermind, honorary prince of The Ophidian Order, afraid of a boob." I roll my eyes and prop Lexi up. I'm pretty sure I might have just flashed Nikolaj a glimpse of said offensive boob in the process. Let that be a lesson to him.

"Not any boob, my sister's boob," he says, his voice strained. "Huge difference."

"Well, my boob's got nothing on her fascination with you since she won't stay latched. So come on," I hold her up and laugh as he adjusts his arms three times trying to figure out how to take her.

"Arms just like mine and I'll do the rest. I promise, it'll come naturally after that."

He sits stock-still as I settle Lexi in his arms. When he looks down at her, she kicks her feet and lets out a giggle.

I prop my head on his shoulder and watch him soften under her adoring gaze. Her fist clutches the air, and he instinctually gives her his finger to grasp.

"Look at you. She loves you already."

"Yeah, well, she doesn't know me."

"Oh, I don't know about that. Babies are pretty smart. We're the stupid ones." Warmth fills me as he relaxes into the moment. Peace settles through me, chasing away the fear I have for her as Nikolaj settles into his interaction with her. Even going so far as to turn her so she's cradled between his forearms in front of him.

"You're not stupid. Impulsive, for sure."

I cock my head and laugh. "I guess I can agree with that."

"I thought inadvertently buying my baby sister's virginity was the worst thing I could imagine. Now, I'm just glad her father's not some random fucker who bought your virginity at a cabaret." He coos down at Lexi as if he's been doing it his whole life. "If nothing else, having this little one ensures your reckless streak is behind you."

I stay silent—my lying days behind me. I guess it's a good thing Konstantin isn't random.

"Letti?"

"Yeah?" I ask, grinning down at my little girl who has Nikolaj's finger gripped in one hand and mine in the other while she shifts her focus between the two of us and squeals.

"Did you hear me? Your reckless streak is behind you?"

Okay, so maybe one more lie won't hurt. "Sure, Nikolaj."

An hour later, with Nikolaj finally gone and Lexi asleep in her crib, I pump what looks like it will be an obscene amount of breastmilk. Thirty minutes and eleven ounces later, the goods now sealed in plastic bags, I head for the freezer, keeping an eye out for Konstantin.

The living room is quiet and empty.

The door to the surveillance room is closed and there's no sign of Konstantin anywhere.

Roddick stands at the counter, an almost empty bottle of water in one hand, his phone in the other.

"Where's Konstantin?"

He doesn't bother looking up and I'm pretty sure he's still pissed at me for not listening in the hail of gunfire last night.

Too bad. I know I screwed up. *He* doesn't need to know that.

"He took a walk," he mutters.

I wave my hand between his gaze and the phone in his hand, tempted to smack the cell to the floor. "A walk?"

With an exasperated sigh, he finally meets my eyes. "Yes. A walk."

"Within minutes of Nikolaj getting here, Konstantin decided to go for a walk?"

"Yup." His lips pop with the pronunciation of the *P* poking at the last bit of patience I have at the moment.

"That's the lie you want me to believe?"

Roddick shrugs, the dismissive gesture the last fucking straw. I've spent my morning being calm, reasonable, downright fucking sweet. I'm past my limit and my gut tells me Roddick's hiding something.

My knife is out in a second, the tip pressed into his dress pants right next to his balls. "So let me ask you, Roddick, is he still taking a walk?"

"Shit! What the fuck is wrong with you? You don't aim a knife at a guy's junk unless you mean it."

"Who says I don't?" With a flick of my wrist, the blade slices through fabric, straight down to skin.

"Owwww. Dammit." He leaps back and grabs his junk. "What the hell is wrong with you?"

"Stop fucking playing with me. Where is he?"

He tugs the crotch of his pants up, inspecting the damage. "You drew blood. Goddamn. You're a piece of work, you know that?"

I take a step closer, my knife in hand, ready to go one more time. "Yes, and now you do, too. I'm not in a gown and heels today, Roddick. Do you really want to see what I'm capable of?"

"The den. Satisfied?" He growls, the tone like the one he used last night when he yelled at me. "He's at the fucking den."

Of course he is. After I made it clear those men are mine. Fury comes over me in a hot wave, spiking my temper and annihilating the relief and happiness from no longer having to hide Lexi from the people I love most. From watching Nikolaj move from acceptance to getting to know his niece.

Konstantin will fuck me any way he wants to in order to pay me back, but this... taking this from me, knowing what those men could have cost Lexi? He knows what I'm capable of. He knows I can handle myself, especially in a room full of subdued men.

He only did this to knock me down a peg. He took it because he could. "Take me to him."

The vein in his left temple throbs, his face turning red. "Oh, fuck no."

How many are dead already? Is the guy who shot at me even alive still? If I get there and he's killed them all, so help me... "So you want me to slice your balls off?"

"If I take you to the den, Konstantin puts a bullet in my head. So yeah, living sounds better."

"Okay," I say with a casual shrug. "But I don't see the point of living if taking a leak means dribbling piss out a sad little hole until it runs down your taint, but let's do this."

He scoffs, but his gaze darts down to my blade. "You wouldn't."

Curling my fingers around the hilt of my second blade, I slide it free and dig the tip into the skin over his jugular. A drop of blood rises out of the tiny puncture, slowly growing bigger until it breaks free and trickles down his throat.

"Hear me and hear me good," I say, backing him up a step at a time until he's pressed against the island, his head cocked at a strained angle. "I'll stick your cock and balls in a fucking pickle jar full of formaldehyde and make them the center-piece to this kitchen island so every one of you has to see them day in and day out, reminding you exactly why you shouldn't fuck with me."

"Fuck it. If he wants you to stay put, he needs to put you on a leash. Let's go."

Taking the blade from his throat, I wipe the blood on his pants and slide it back in my sheath, keeping the other just inches from his junk. "I thought you'd see things my way."

CHAPTER

35

Konstantin

The door opens as I'm picking up one of my most vicious serrated blades.

"Miss me?"

The sound of Nikoletta's voice sends my blood racing through my veins. My insatiable hunger for her mixing with the adrenaline coursing through me a dangerous combination in the confines of the soundproof room.

The swift urge to confess to Nikolaj when he asked me if I knew about Lexi had me biting down on my tongue until it bled. Lying to him is against my nature. The weight of my original sin where Nikoletta is concerned already carved away at my reason until I took stupid risks and invited more danger.

For everyone.

Every lie erodes at the foundation of what I'm helping him build and I hate her for putting me in that position, too.

"You want to explain to me what the fuck you didn't understand about my orders to keep an eye on her and not to let her leave the safe house?"

Body parts lay scattered in pools of blood from two hours spent dismantling six of the seven living men, one body part at a time while their screams battered my eardrums to the point of pain.

I turn to them then, flicking the teeth of the blade over my thumb in clear view of the little fucker who almost stole her from me. Every terrified pant from his cracked lips is balm on my haunted soul.

Roddick glares at Nikoletta who stands there with one hand on her hip, in another flirty little sundress, the other clutching her knife, her curious gaze sweeping through the room with zero revulsion. And fuck if I don't love that about her too.

Before—my instinct would have been to protect her from this. Keep her from seeing just how destructive I could be. But now, I want her to see it.

I want the slaughter before her to haunt her nightmares.

I want her to think about what I'm capable of every time I brutally fuck her senseless with the single-minded goal of putting my baby in her.

"Oh, I understood. I also understand that she's eager to slice and dice the shit out of someone, and I'm good with it not being me."

"But if I kill you..."

He slants a look at Nikoletta before jutting his chin at me. "At least I won't be dribbling piss down my taint."

My eyebrows shoot up. "What?"

"It's a long story. I'll give you a full report later. Just... let her fuck some shit up please so we don't have to sleep in shifts with one eye open."

I step up to the fucker bound to my chair and tap the side of my blade on his forehead. His swollen jaw is almost double its size, his face misshapen, a canvas of sickly green from watching the show and deep blue and purple from the bruising.

"If you'll excuse me," I say to him giving him the kind of smile I'd pull out at dinner parties. "This won't take long and then, you and me, we're going to spend some quality time together. You won't be as lucky as these fuckers."

Clasping the edge of the door, I lean down until my face is just inches from Roddick's. "Go."

He shoots a glare at Nikoletta and leaves, closing the door behind him.

"I don't know where you think you get off doing this without me, but you be—"

I curl my fist into the front of her dress and haul her to the center of the room, pinning her against the steel support beam there. "You really think you're up for this, Pcholka? This isn't just some little girl swipe of the blade. The feral little killer I found at that commune better be ready to up her game."

Cheeks flushed, lungs heaving she stares down at my bloodstained hands and licks her plump bottom lip.

Cool steel grazes over my forearm. The light catches the edge of her blade as she drags it over my skin. The flirty little threat has my hard cock twitching behind my zipper.

Her chest swells with a deep breath, and her eyes flare with excitement. And I know... she's greedy for the scent of blood filling the air.

She's hungry to deliver a special brand of Romanoff justice.

"He came for me, and when he did, he came for Lexi." Her lethal tone rumbles with a promise of retribution as her hot glare slides to the man in the chair.

Our daughter's name from her lips cuts me to the core

with her betrayal. Will it fade? If it does, will it take days, weeks, months, years?

How long am I condemned to love the woman before me when all I want to do is hate her?

"This one..." I say as I step up the man secured to the chair. "He's the one who tried to make Lexi an orphan. He's the one who tried to send me to my grave before I even knew I was a father."

A burst of life lights in the man's surprised eyes as he glances between us.

I crouch down in front of him. "I told you she's mine." I inspect the rusted clamps I've grown fond of using to keep my subjects bound. The trick is to get them pinned nice and tight, the disk pressing into their hands and the tops of their feet until the first couple of bones snap. They get real compliant then. Eager to keep still so they don't cause more pain.

"Why clamps?"

The curious wonder in her voice just beyond my shoulder sends chills racing over my skin. Then I feel the heat of her as she steps closer, her skirt brushing my bare arm.

The exasperation she came in with is gone under a rapt fascination very few recognize.

But I do.

It's the killing.

"Because I have about twenty twists of motivation before they go clean through their hand. I have yet to find one who can hold out that long, but I haven't lost hope." I shrug. "Maybe he's the one? What do you think, little girl."

A rumble of pure frustration comes from her at the *little girl* before she scoffs behind me. "The way he whined like a little bitch when his jaw snapped? I doubt it."

The guy jerks his hips in the chair, another burst of life—but we'll take care of that soon enough.

Need courses through me with her so close. I swear I can feel her heart racing next to me and as much as I want to hold on to the hate, I want something else so much more. I reach back, wind my arm around her leg, and tug her up to where she belongs.

Next to me.

Once she's there, I hold his gaze as I wind my hand under her skirt and around her thigh and begin lazily kneading her flesh.

But it's not enough. Nothing is ever enough with her.

She traces the feathers along the set of black wings inked over my entire back where they curl over my shoulder and I realize this is the first time she's seen me this exposed since she spied on me in the pool years ago.

I never wanted her seeing me like this, the heathen stripped down to his blood-spattered tank top undershirt. But with her finger casually exploring me, like I'm hers to do with as she fucking pleases, I'm hellbent on making sure she sees me this way more often.

With my other hand, I lift her skirt with a look of deadly warning for our little friend. "If your eyes drop below her neck, I'll hand the fuckers to you. Got me?"

His eyelids sink shut as he jerks his head in agreement.

Tipping my head back, I glance up at her. "Don't look away from him for a second. If he dares look at what's mine, he pays for it."

Her pretty lips part as she digs her fingers dig hard into my shoulder with her frantic nod.

"If he'd had his way," I say before sinking my teeth into her thigh. "Lexi never would have known the comfort of being tucked to her mother's breast again."

A savage growl rips from her throat as I peel her skirt up

even higher. "Now tell me, Pcholka, how are you going to make him pay for it?"

Her body jerks above me as I land another bite, this one just inches from my faded name on her thigh.

His howl of pain cuts through the sound of our deep, lusty breaths and I can't wait to see her brand of justice.

I swipe my tongue over my teeth marks on her skin and check out her handiwork. "Oh, very nice, my feral little goddaughter." Her knife sticks vertically out of his trapezius muscle between his neck and shoulder. "Tell me, why there?"

"He's too free to move with the clamps. But he'll think about every little shift if it means flexing a muscle with a blade sticking out of it."

"Nice." I pass her the serrated knife I've laid on the floor next to me.

"Our enemy is smart. He made sure every order came through one man." I cup that man's kneecap now, digging my fingers around the edges, adding pressure until his agony-filled shouts fill the air. "This fucker right here."

Looking up at my girl, I find her eyes blazing, an almost deranged edge to her smile. With a savage jerk, his kneecap dislodges, turning his shout to a scream.

Her teeth sink into her bottom lip, her fingers diving into my hair as she watches him suffer.

With another vicious swing, she sends the serrated blade deep into the same muscle on the opposite side.

The pathetic sounds coming from him fade to the background. I tip my head back and study the ferocious mother she's become. "Have you thought about how you'll kill him?"

She slants a hot look down at me. "You're going to let me?"

I cluck my tongue and shake my head. "Does anyone let

you do anything, Pcholka? Or do you just do it, consequences be damned?"

"Kostya, I—"

"You're Lexi's mother. You have a stake in this."

"Is that it? Is that all I am to you now? Lexi's mother?"

"What do you want from me?"

Her wounded look slides away and she lets out a sultry laugh. "That's a loaded question, Kostya. Make sure you're ready for the answer."

"Try me."

She grabs my hair and drags my head back until I'm forced onto my ass and crab-walking backward on my hands. When my back hits the steel beam, she lets me go and drags her flouncy skirt up to her waist, my naked pussy on full display.

I hate her.

I keep telling myself that.

But the more I do, the more I think I just hate how much I still want her.

And right now, while delivering justice to the man who almost made our little girl an orphan, I want to love her.

She hooks her thigh over my shoulder, her pussy just inches from my face.

I suck in a harsh breath and close my eyes, savoring the scent of her arousal.

When she curls her hand around the beam and settles her other thigh over my other shoulder, my cock leaks helplessly in my pants.

And when she's draped over my shoulders, straddling my face, I surrender to my chaotic feelings for her.

My heart takes off until it might just tear out of my body.

Her hot, wet pussy brushes my mouth and pushes me right over the edge of sanity.

I'll hate her again when we walk out that door.

With an angry growl of pure self-loathing, I grip her ass in my hands and bury my mouth in her slick heat. I suck at her clit, nibbling and biting, before dragging my tongue along the length of her slit. Then, I work my way back, and do it all over again.

I need her tighter to me. I need her to suffocate me with her pillowy soft skin and make me forget all the ways she destroyed my heart.

Smoothing my hands over her legs, I guide them around my head and pole crossing her ankles until I'm locked in the prison of her thighs.

My fingertips dig into her as I rock her against my savage mouth. Her harsh breaths turn into deep groans until her spine snaps straight and she comes, her pussy drenching me with her release until it drips down my chin.

This is my cage. My own vile hell.

Where the woman I love is now my fucking enemy.

This is the all-consuming distraction neither of us can afford.

I have to see her like this. I need to see her unfocused sultry stare as she comes down from her release.

Tipping my head back against the beam, I catch sight of the door opening out of the corner of my eye.

Ice cold dread lodges in my stomach. My instincts scream at me for being a fool.

And Nikolaj's shocked face explodes into disbelieving fury.

A split second in real time stretches into several in my head. It's in those drawn out thunderous beats of my heart, I see it in his eyes.

He's questioning every minute I spent with her.

He's wondering how long I've been victimizing his baby sister.

He's asking himself how he got it all so fucking wrong.

He's blaming himself even as he draws his gun with every intention of making me pay.

The crack of a bullet explodes through the air, turning her whimpers of pure bliss to twisted, bitter agony ringing in my ears.

ACKNOWLEDGMENTS

Melissa - To this day, the best decision I ever made was jumping on the Sacrilege project with you. And not because we nailed it and made it wildly successful, but because this friendship is by far and away one of the best things that's ever happened to me. It's rare to have a friend you don't have a complaint about, we're human, we get annoyed, some more than others (ME), but with you, I have not a one. You're my voice of reason, my sounding board, a safe place I can vent every single thought or feeling without judgment. You have an uncanny ability to know just what I need when I need it, even if I don't, and you deliver every single time. This was our year... our year to learn about the kind of friendships we deserve and letting go of the fucking pretenders. I may have been in this industry longer, but man, you've taught me so much more than I think I could ever teach you. I can only hope one day to learn to be as good of a friend to you, and others, as you've been to me. I love you ferociously and have such mad respect for you on every level: as a friend, a savvy businesswoman, and phenomenal author! I live for your sinister laugh in our voice messages... it's the highlight of my day! The occasional background "I'll slice your face off" threat is pretty fucking great too, not gonna lie. And now I will stop with the feelings and making it weird. Until the next time we spoon, LMAO.

Christiana - We both came into this after a hit and run with the massive ego on legs, but fuck, we clawed our way out of the rancid ass trauma cloud, danced around each other a bit, but fuck yes... we totally hung in. Shout to Melissa for making it all happen! Before I even get to how integral you've been to this book and my sanity while making my comeback from simply the worst period of my writing career, you've become so many things to me, but first and foremost, one of my best friends! The thought of going through even one day without hearing your voice is depressing AF. I love our rambles, the nail biting periods where we await the verdict from clients on art/covers, and how you and I understand that constant need to go back and tweak until it's we've nailed it. Fuck Clifton... they don't know. You're totally a restorative! For so many, it's about the client and if they like it, but you and I, it's a whole different beast. They can love it and still we're tearing it up and fixing. Our art is everything to us and we only want to deliver the very best... to the point we're neurotic, but fuck it... I love us! Now, my alpha... my sounding board, my absolute queen of story... WOMAN... this book quite simply would not be here had it not been for you. I one 100% trust you with every messy ass word that comes out of me. It's so damn freeing to know that I can stop agonizing to the point I'm sabotaging myself because there is someone so absolutely smart and honest ready to come in behind me and help me make the story shine. You had every reason to run in the other direction at the idea of reading for someone new... I'll forever be thankful you didn't!

Brooke - Where do I begin my let's be petty together Betty, love bombing little ray of outspoken truth you?? Yeah, I said what I said, LOL. I want to regret what brought us together, but you know what? Fuck that. It sucked. It was the single worst betrayal by someone I should have been able to trust, but joke's on her, if she hadn't been the absolute miserable liar she is, I never would have found the goddamn pot of sisterhood gold. Yeah, I'm getting savage in my acknowledgments and I'm 100% down for it. You had me at our mutual adoration of forbidden, age gaps, and student/teacher, and MM hotness. Buddy reads forever! Here's to more endless voice recordings from the tub while we buddy watch Taylornation, me from my iPad perched on the bathmat of all places, LOL. I live, and I mean LIVE, for our buddy movie nights. Who says 1300 miles has to stop a couple of friends from having movie night together? May we both survive and thrive in the endless sea of beta reads, rants about story, late night anxiety attacks, and proving every doubter wrong about us. Not to get all TS on ya, but I'm having the time of my life fighting dragons with you, ma'am! You're an absolute beast in this business, beating the odds, rising above, keeping it real, and working your ass off on a level I aspire to reaching one day! You're on your own, kid... and you know what, you're all the better for it!

Hey Ashley - See what I did there? LMAO. I'm so freaking happy I decided to give you a shot despite the efforts of one to mislead me about you. Your professionalism in the face of some of the least professional people in this industry is unmatched. It's so damn refreshing to know a unicorn exists in, well, let's just call it what it is, a minefield of sloppy ass bitches out there. I'll forever be grateful and loyal to you for standing up for me as a client in the face of manipulation and ultimatums. Let's keep rising in the face of absolute cuntery. You and me... let's do this shit! Two typo cursed bitches 4ever!

Kimberly - God woman, how long has it been? Eight years? Nine? When I look back, I cannot fucking believe how long we've been doing this. I have absolute mad respect for your knowledge, talent, unwavering dedication to the point you're up all hours of the night with me, a chapter at at time skidding into the finale, right by my side as my ride or die. I wobbled this year. I really, really did. I almost let one unfortunate person and their ongoing heinous behavior squeeze me out of sticking with the single most dedicated professional I've ever worked with. I almost let her steal one more thing from me, something I've had long before her and will have long after. Thank you for standing by my side while I worked through those feelings. Thank you for letting me be messy and still loving me. Thank you even more, for feeling safe enough in our friendship to tell me how unfair it felt to possibly lose me because of someone's bad behavior beyond our control. You've seen me at my best. You've seen me at my absolute worst. You've seen me every point in between and still you're here. You are an absolute crazy AF rockstar who understands me in ways no one else ever will and I'm never letting you go!

ABOUT THE AUTHOR

Beck Knight, the savage and gritty alter ego of a *USA Today* Bestselling author, immerses herself in the dark and twisted psyches of the rich, damaged, and corrupt while bleeding their secrets and twisted desires onto paper with voyeuristic amusement.

She writes every tale of destruction with no rules, no bullshit, and no fucks to give.

Grab one of her books if you're ready to take a walk on the destructive side.

Made in United States
North Haven, CT
18 January 2025

64571328R10238